D1559158

MY SINFUL LOVE

BOOK FOUR IN THE SINFUL MEN SERIES

LAUREN BLAKELY

LAUREN BLAKELY BOOKS

ALSO BY LAUREN BLAKELY

Big Rock Series

Big Rock

Mister O

Well Hung

Full Package

Joy Ride

Hard Wood

Happy Endings Series

Come Again

Shut Up and Kiss Me

Kismet

My Single-Versary

Ballers And Babes

Most Valuable Playboy

Most Likely to Score

A Wild Card Kiss

Two A Day

Plays Well With Others

Rules of Love Series

The Virgin Rule Book

The Virgin Game Plan

The Virgin Replay

The Virgin Scorecard

The Heartbreakers Series

Once Upon a Real Good Time

Once Upon a Sure Thing

Once Upon a Wild Fling

Boyfriend Material

Asking For a Friend

Sex and Other Shiny Objects

One Night Stand-In

Lucky In Love Series

Best Laid Plans

The Feel Good Factor

Nobody Does It Better

Unzipped

Always Satisfied Series

Satisfaction Guaranteed

Instant Gratification

Overnight Service

Never Have I Ever

PS It's Always Been You

Special Delivery

The Sexy Suit Series

Lucky Suit

Birthday Suit

From Paris With Love

Wanderlust

Part-Time Lover

One Love Series

The Sexy One

The Only One

The Hot One

The Knocked Up Plan

Come As You Are

Standalones

Stud Finder

The V Card

The Real Deal

Unbreak My Heart

The Break-Up Album

The Caught Up in Love Series

The Pretending Plot

The Dating Proposal

The Second Chance Plan

The Private Rehearsal

Seductive Nights Series

Night After Night

After This Night

One More Night

A Wildly Seductive Night

ABOUT

A wildly sexy, emotional, and suspenseful romance novel from #1 New York Times Bestselling author Lauren Blakely...

She was my what if girl. The one I longed for. The one I tried to find again after she left for the other side of the world.

Now, years later, fate has swept the only woman I've ever loved back into my life.

With her intensity, her honesty, her passion, Annalise tries to break down my walls, because she's the one who knew me before my family shattered.

When we collide again, it's tender and savage, gentle and rough, and makes me hungry for more of this electric, once-in-a-blue moon kind of connection.

If I want to keep her close, I'll have to serve up the whole truth of where I went and what I did after she left.

But if I do, I risk losing her again, and that's not a fate I'm ready to face. Not when each day brings me closer to finding the people who ripped my family apart and seeing them put behind bars.

Until the day I learn Annalise is holding the final piece of the puzzle to solving the mystery.

MY SINFUL LOVE

By Lauren Blakely

Want to be the first to learn of sales, new releases, preorders and special freebies? Sign up for my VIP mailing list here! You'll also get free books from bestselling authors in a selection curated just for you!

PRO TIP: Add lauren@laurenblakely.com to your contacts before signing up to make sure the emails go to your inbox!

Did you know this book is also available in audio and paperback on all major retailers? Go to my website for links!

This is an emotional, suspenseful series, with high-stakes action and consequences. For content warnings go to my web site.

1

MICHAEL

The letter smelled like her. Like rain.

I ran my thumb over the corner of the paper and closed my eyes briefly. Memories rose to the surface, bringing with them feelings of hope and possibility.

Things that were far too risky when it came to her.

I shut them down, opened my eyes, and stared out the floor-to-ceiling windows of my penthouse on the Strip, trying to focus on the here and now, not the enticing lure of *what-if*. Tonight the lights of Vegas would blink like a carnival unfolding below, from the miniature Eiffel Tower, to the pyramid, to the blazing signs adorning The Cosmopolitan. Neon, glitz, and billboards ten stories high proclaimed the *best night ever*.

But I had to stay fixed on the minute details of the present, not be seduced by the past and how good it was, or of how much I'd longed for a future with her.

I wasn't having the easiest time of that. From my vantage point, twenty stories above the concrete ribbon that beckoned millions of tourists, I brought the letter to my nose for one final inhale.

The scent of falling rain.

Try as I might to fight it, a reel of sensory images rushed back from years ago, like the *snap, snap, snap* of old film. How many times had I kissed Annalise in the rain? Brushed her wild red hair off her cheeks and touched her soft skin? Listened to her laugh?

Countless. Just like the times my mind had lingered on her over the last eighteen years, including that heart-breaking day in Marseilles, which had damn near slaughtered all my hopes in the world.

Carefully, I folded up the letter, slid it back into the tiny envelope postmarked from France, and stuffed it into my wallet next to a crinkled, faded, threadbare note from my father that I carried with me always. Her letter had arrived a couple of weeks ago, and I'd read it a thousand times already. I could read it a thousand more, but it wouldn't change my answer—the same one I'd emailed back to her.

Yes.

It was always yes with her.

Dear Michael,

I hope this note finds you well. I will be in Las Vegas for business in a few weeks. I would love to see you again. Would you like to have a coffee with me? Come to think of it, do you drink coffee now? If memory serves, you were never fond of it. Perhaps tea, or water, or martinis at midday? Any, all, or some would be lovely.

My information is below so you can respond. I would have emailed, but a letter seemed more fitting. And, truth be told, easier to ignore, should that be your preference.

Though I will be wishing to see your name pop up in my email soon.

xoxo

Annalise

As if I stood a chance of *not* emailing her. As if there were any universe, parallel, perpendicular, or otherwise, where I wouldn't take her up on her offer for coffee, tea, liquor, or a few minutes in a café.

Any, all, or some.

I turned away from the midday view of the city I loved and headed to the stereo system above my flat-screen, piping music through my home. This Sunday afternoon, following a long, hard run and an even longer workout at the gym, I'd cued up my favorite playlist as I got ready to see her, methodically picking songs I'd discovered in the last few years, rather than the music I'd shared with her when we were younger.

Not that I didn't still love my late '90s tunes. I just knew I'd be a goner if I let myself trip that far back in time.

I turned off the fading guitar riff, and silence descended on my home.

I grabbed my keys and my phone from the entryway table, locked the door, and headed down the hall, wishing my pulse wasn't already competing in a race.

The ride down the elevator was both interminable and not long enough. Anticipation curled through me as I left my high-rise building, crossed the big intersection, and headed toward Las Vegas Boulevard. The air had cooled—September had rolled into my hometown. This brief walk in the crisp air would surely quell the nerves that bounced in my chest.

I didn't want to feel them. Nor did I want to experience this wild sense of hope rattling in me like a marble sliding down a chute. Dragging a hand through my hair, I tried to focus on anything but her.

Later this afternoon I had a meeting with a client, then this evening I'd review some new contracts for work. Sometime this week I'd meet with the detective working my father's case, touching base with him before I left for a trip. I also needed to check in with the private investigator.

My phone bleated from my back pocket, and I grabbed it quickly. My friend Mindy's name flashed across the screen. "Hey there," I said, while winding my way through the throngs of visitors on the sidewalk.

"Whatcha wearing?" she singsonged. "Wait. Don't tell me. You went for your favorite jeans and a lucky T-shirt."

I laughed. "I assure you I don't have a lucky T-shirt."

"Well, you should. I would get on that right away."

"Duly noted. I'll order up one lucky T-shirt after this meeting."

"*Meeting.* You make it sound so businesslike."

"How should I make it sound?"

"Like you've been counting down the hours for this since you received the *letter,*" she said, making the note sound ominous. An information Hoover, Mindy had a way of wheedling details out of me ever since we'd graduated from professional colleagues to good friends over the summer when we'd paired up on a moonlighting project.

"Speaking of counting down the hours, I'll see you early evening still?" I asked, sidestepping her far too accurate assessment of how I'd measured the time since Annalise's missive had arrived.

"Yup. I'll be there at five. I fully expect you to tell me every dirty detail."

"There won't be any dirty details."

She scoffed. "Oh, I bet there will, and I plan on extracting them all."

"Goodbye, Mindy," I said.

The thought of seeing Annalise Delacroix had pretty much played on a loop in my mind since I'd flipped through the mail on my desk a couple of weeks ago, the lavender envelope sliding from the top of the pile into my palm, the past thundering into the present. I had a shoebox full of her letters from years ago. I hadn't looked at them in ages though. I couldn't bring myself to chuck them, but I also wasn't interested in inflicting the kind of self-torture that reading them would bring.

I threaded through the crowds outside the Bellagio as sprays of water from the fountains arced in their daytime ballet, shoes clicking against the stone pathway that curved around the man-made lake and took me inside the hotel lobby, with its marble floors, glass sculptures, and grand archways.

As I cut a path toward the casino floor, I tried to pretend I was here for business. Meeting a potential client. Seeing an old friend. But the way my heart tried to torpedo out of my skin, I was going to need some much better tricks.

When I reached the hostess stand at the upscale Petrossian Bar, I simply resigned myself to the storm brewing inside. Besides, how else was I supposed to feel right before I was about to see—as my brother Ryan had so aptly called her—my what-if girl?

"Like this," I muttered to myself. Like a case of what-if bombs had exploded inside my chest.

"May I help you?"

The even-toned, sweet-sounding voice jarred me because it was so normal. How could anyone feel fine in this moment? I felt the opposite of fine. I felt a mixed-up, jumbled mess of emotions that boiled down to two warring ones—a fervent wish that this *meeting* would not be a repeat of the one at the airport in Marseilles, and the hope that all my ex-girlfriends were incorrect in their diagnosis of my heart trouble.

I was *not* hung up on her. No matter what they had said to the contrary.

The hostess in her trim gray suit cocked her head, waiting for an answer.

"I'm looking for . . . someone," I said, my voice gravelly, as if words were new to me.

"Would you like to have a look around and see if . . ." She trailed off, letting me fill in the blank.

"Yeah. I'll take a look."

The pianist in the bar tapped out an old Cole Porter song. I turned the corner, scanning the lounge-style seating for a tall, willowy woman.

Briefly, I wondered if I'd recognize her. I'd first known her when we were teenagers, then I saw her again at age twenty-four in Marseilles. That was ten years ago, and surely I didn't look the same. I had crinkles at the corners of my blue eyes, and my hair, inexplicably, had darkened. My sister, Shannon, joked that it was turning black, like my heart.

I was also sturdier than I had been before. My shoulders were broader, my arms more defined. At twenty-four, I'd been in the Army, working in intelligence; now, I was a twice-daily fixture at the gym and had the bigger muscles to show for it.

But whether Annalise Delacroix had dyed her hair or shaved it all off, I was pretty confident I'd find her easily without having seen a photo of her recently. I hadn't stalked her on social media, but I *had* researched the most important detail before I'd emailed her back.

I'd found the obituary.

The one that gave me permission to have a cup of coffee. I shuddered. I still didn't like coffee. But coffee was the only path to her. Follow the road map, turn this corner, and see the first woman I'd ever loved. It had taken me forever to fall out of love with her, but I was there. I was absolutely there. That's what I told myself.

My eyes roamed over the crowd at the upscale establishment until I spotted auburn hair swept high in a twist, long elegant fingers, and the cut of her jawline. Her black top had sloped down one shoulder, revealing soft flesh, and her right collarbone was exposed.

My heart thundered, and my blood roared.

Trying desperately to tamp down the riot inside me, I inhaled, exhaled, then walked the final feet to reach her. Her back was to me. When I arrived at the sofa where she was seated, she turned fully, and her green eyes lit up.

Gorgeous green eyes, like gems.

Carved cheekbones.

Lips so red and lush.

She held a cup of espresso and had just brought it to her lips.

That lucky fucking mug.

She finished the gulp and laughed lightly. "Some habits never change."

Truer words . . .

2

ANNALISE

I hadn't been to Las Vegas since I was a foreign exchange student during my junior year of high school, living with a host family and perfecting my English on American soil.

Odd, in some ways, that my job hadn't brought me back to this town even once in all these years—but perhaps that wasn't so strange, considering business was plentiful in Europe. For now, for a few days at least, business was here, and so was the man I'd fallen madly in love with as that young foreign exchange student.

He was more handsome than ever.

Imagine that.

The prettiest boy in America was now the sexiest man I'd laid eyes on in a long, long time. But lusty admiration wasn't all I felt as I drank in the sight of Michael Sloan. A myriad of emotions I wasn't prepared for swam through me—regret, loneliness, wistfulness, topped with excitement.

I zeroed in on that one, shoving all the others aside.

Setting down the cup, I stood and dusted a barely-there kiss on his right cheek. His five-o'clock shadow stubble—

even though it was only one o'clock on a Sunday—scratched me in a whiskery, sandpaper way. As he then pressed a kiss to my left cheek, the slightest whoosh of air escaped his lips.

Lips I'd known well. Lips I had spent years wanting to touch again.

"Cheek kisses. You haven't forgotten how the French do it." I sounded breathless, even to my own ears. And I no longer sounded French since I spoke now without an accent. That had been a purposeful decision long ago.

"How could I forget? And you haven't forgotten your American accent." He said it lightly, as if he was talking only about the kisses, but there was so much more I hadn't forgotten. Was it that way for him too?

"It's stayed with me. You look . . ." I let my voice trail off as a lump rose in my throat, and that storm of emotions stirred up again, churning inside. It wasn't his looks that had knocked the wind out of me. Though, seriously, there was nothing whatsoever to complain about in that regard, as I surveyed him in his black pants and crisp gray shirt, taking in his trim waist, strong shoulders, and tall frame. Nor was it his dark black hair, his cool blue eyes, or the cut of his jaw.

The tumult was courtesy of the past, hurtling itself headfirst into my present. I hadn't expected to be walloped by the mere sight of him. I swallowed harshly, trying to dislodge a hitch, wanting to feel some semblance of cool and calm. My shoulders rose and fell, and I tried desperately to breathe in such a way that didn't require me to relearn how to take in oxygen. I dug my black stilettos into the plush carpet, seeking purchase as I attempted to reconnect with my ability to form words.

"You look good," I said, the understatement of the year. Wait. Make that a lifetime.

"And you look . . . lovely."

Lovely.

That was *so* him.

He'd never been one for *hot, smoking, gorgeous, babe,* or any of those sayings of the moment. There was something in him that spiraled deeper and leaned on words that had more heft. Like *lovely.*

I should have scripted this rendezvous. Wrote out talking points. But now I didn't know which direction in the conversational path to turn, so I went for the obvious.

"We finally made it to the Bellagio," I said, gesturing to the crowds clicking by outside the bar. God, this was hard. How do you just have a drink with someone you once thought you'd marry? Someone who was your everything? I'd been his rock; he'd been my hope.

"We finally did," he echoed.

It had only taken eighteen years, an ocean, countless letters, two broken hearts, and a lengthy online search for him, which had taken time and research, since he'd changed his name and was absent from social media.

But here we were. The Bellagio was the symbol of all our promises. Young, foolish, and wildly in love, we'd always said we'd come here for a drink someday.

A promise to reunite. One of many promises we'd made.

Some kept.

Some impossible to keep.

"Join me. *S'il vous plaît.*" I patted the back of the sofa as I sat down again.

"*Merci.*" He took a seat next to me, and at last I felt like I could breathe. My warring emotions settled, and now I was simply in the company of this man. Someone I'd been thinking about more and more lately.

"So," I said.

"So . . ." He rubbed his palms against his thighs.

"How are you?" I asked, stepping into the shallow end. "Are you well?"

"Good, good," he answered quickly. "And you?"

"Great. Everything is great," I said, as chipper as I could be, even though I'd hardly use *great* to describe the tundra that my heart had become during the last two years. "I'm glad you made it," I said, in an effort to keep going, lest any silence turn this reunion more awkward.

"And I'm glad you asked me to meet you," he said, as if he was waiting for me to tell him *why* I'd wanted to meet. I didn't, though, because when he looked at me like that, the breath fled my lungs. His eyes were soulful—they seemed to reveal a depth forged by years of heartache and tragedy.

I parted my lips to speak, but I wasn't even sure what to say next. Did I go for lightness? For more catching-up chitchat? Or plunge straight into the heart of why I'd wanted to see him? I was so accustomed to charging into situations fearlessly, to chasing after what I wanted, but all those skills escaped me in this moment, and I was a tea bag steeping in a pot of awkward.

Fortunately, the waitress arrived and asked Michael if he wanted anything. "Club soda," he said, and when the woman left, I tilted my head.

"So, you still detest coffee?" I asked, because that was a far easier conversation entrée than all the other things we could talk about.

"Evidently, I still do."

"I never understood that about you," I said, shaking my head in disbelief. Funny that we'd gotten on so well when we were younger—except about this. Our one bone of contention had been over my passionate love of the deliciously addictive substance, and his disdain of it.

"It vexed you, I know."

"I tried to get you to like coffee. I even tried to make espresso for you."

"You were relentless," he said, and the corners of his lips quirked up. That smile, that lopsided grin I'd loved . . . Okay, this was better. This was a slow and steady slide back into the familiar.

"Remember when I hunted all over Vegas trying to find something like what they'd serve in a café in Paris?" I asked, reminiscing, slipping back into the time we were together years ago.

Like it was yesterday, he picked up the conversational baton. "You even used your babysitting money to buy an old espresso machine at a garage sale," he said, and the memory of my determination and his resistance made me laugh. "Remember that?"

"I do! It was a Saturday morning. I scoured the papers for garage sales, and hunted all around the neighborhood until I located the only one I could afford."

"Found one for ten dollars."

I held up an index finger. "Ten dollars and twenty-five cents."

"Ah, well. The quarter made all the difference," he said, as the waitress brought his drink and he thanked her.

"I took it back to Becky and Sanders's home that afternoon, and I thought I'd win you over. That if you had a proper coffee, made like we do back home, you'd be converted." It was only coffee, but it was a thread that connected us to the distant past, when our lives were so much simpler. It was a far easier topic than the present, and certainly less painful than the words said the last time we saw each other, on that heartbreaking day in Marseilles after he'd sent a letter that had torn me to pieces.

"Alas, I was inconvertible." He took a swallow of the club soda. "So, what brings you to town?"

"Work."

He frowned and glanced from side to side, like he was sweeping the bar for trouble. "There's a war in Vegas I'm not aware of?"

I laughed and shook my head. "I'm not a photojournalist any longer. Now I shoot fashion—lingerie and boudoir. I'm here doing the high-end catalog for Veronica's," I said, naming the famous lingerie chain with which I'd nabbed a plum gig. "Some of the shoots are at The Cosmopolitan and around town. We did the Venetian canals earlier today. Caesars Palace is tomorrow."

"So this is you now," he said, waving a hand at me. "Shooting barely dressed women in silk and lace instead of racing across the desert in a Humvee?"

I nodded. "From shrapnel to strapless."

"What happened to make you switch?" The question was direct.

So was my answer. "Death happened."

So did heartbreak and unfinished love.

He nodded in agreement, his expression turning somber. He cleared his throat. "I'm sorry to hear about Julien."

My throat hitched, but only briefly. I'd cried enough to end California's drought. "Thank you."

More quickly than I'd expected—and I was eminently grateful not to linger on talk of Julien with this man—Michael led us out of that conversation, returning to safer ground. "Do you enjoy fashion more?"

I glanced up at the ceiling, considering. That was a tough question. I'd loved the adrenaline rush of photojournalism, the thrill of chasing a story that didn't want to be found, the chance to capture an image that would show my nation the truth of what was happening in the world, whether during my time in the Middle East, or covering breaking news across Europe for a French news agency. But the job became too risky and the costs too high, so I'd pivoted.

I had no regrets.

I met his eyes to answer. "Yes. I like fashion better now. I love what I do."

We chatted more as I told him tales of the models and their over-the-top requests at shoots—from the imperious blonde who required celery sticks chilled to a crisp sixty-five degrees, to the willowy brunette who would only drink artesian water—and how it compared to the bare-bones style of hunting images in my combat boots, cargo pants, and photographer's vest, in one of the most dangerous areas of the world.

"What about you, Michael? You're not fronting a band. I didn't see your guitar in any of your company photos," I said, nudging his arm gently. His strong, toned arm. So firm. I was going to need a reason to nudge him again.

He shrugged. "That was high school. I was just messing around in the garage with friends. I don't play much anymore."

"What happened to going to Seattle and becoming the next rock star?" I asked, then my stomach dropped. "*Merde. I'm sorry*," I said, heat flaming across my cheeks. How could I have been so foolish? I knew the answer. I lowered my chin, embarrassed.

His hand touched mine. My breath caught the instant he made contact. "It's okay. It was just a teenage dream."

Just a teenage dream. We'd had so many. They'd felt so real at the time.

"We had a lot of those," I said softly.

"We did." He looked away. His jaw was set hard, but when he returned his gaze to me, he simply said, "I barely think about all those crazy dreams. I like my life now. I like running the security business. That's why I'll work on a Sunday. Speaking of work, how long are you in town?"

"A few days," I said, and my voice rose higher, as it did when I was nervous. Because the first thing I'd thought when I landed this assignment was—*Michael*. Like a big, blaring sign. A flashing light at the end of a road. I had to see him, find him, connect with him. "I'm glad you're happy now . . . Michael Sloan." I paused, his new last name rolling around strangely on my tongue. "I'm trying to get used to it. *Sloan.*"

"Took me a while too."

"When did you change it?"

His eyes darkened. I'd touched a nerve. "Ten years ago," he said, his tone gruff.

The journalist in me didn't want to back down. "After I saw you in Marseilles?" I asked, nerves tightening my throat as I mentioned that day. That wonderful, horrible day.

He stared up at the ceiling, his brow knit together. "I suppose that'd be about right. But that wasn't the reason," he added.

"Why, then?" I pressed. "It made it harder to find you. I had to ask Becky."

He heaved a sigh. "Made it easier for me to live."

That made all the sense in the world. "I understand," I said, then reached for my cup. My fingers felt slippery. I gripped the ceramic more tightly as I took a sip.

He rubbed a hand across his jawline, silence sneaking between us, but not for long. He was direct once more. "Tell me. Why did you look me up?"

"Because I was coming to town," I said, stating the simplest answer first, avoiding the tougher topic.

He stared at me, his blue eyes hooked into mine, telling me he didn't buy it.

"Because I was seeing Sanders and Becky," I said, mentioning my host family from when I was an exchange student.

"Did you see them?"

"I'm going to. Tomorrow."

"So, then this," he said, pointing from me to him. "This is . . .?"

I looked at his mouth, blinked my eyes back up to his, and dropped my voice even more. We were surrounded by noise—the clink of silverware, the slip of ice cubes against glass, and the chatter of nearby patrons ordering smoked salmon and vodka samplers. I spoke the truest words. "This is because I wanted to."

3

MICHAEL

There were things I wanted as well. More time with her. More talking. Mostly, I didn't want for this to end. She was like sugary sand crystals in my hand, slipping through. I wanted to clutch my fists closed and hold them tight for just a few more moments. A few more days.

So I went for it. "What are you doing tonight?"

* * *

The dealer slapped a card down on the table.

"Wait. I want to write this down." Mindy shook her head in amusement as she reached for the card. "I want to record this moment. You, asking me for dating advice."

I narrowed my eyes. "I know how to date," I grumbled.

She held up a finger. "Correction. You know how to date women you just met. You don't know how to date the woman you were in—"

"Do I see if she wants to meet for a drink?" I asked, cutting her off because I didn't want the reminder. I knew how I felt.

As Mindy checked out her cards at the poker table at the Luxe, her favorite gambling spot, she said, "Yes, you want to have a drink with her, because you definitely need some lubricant."

I laughed. Mindy didn't mince words and that was one of the reasons I enjoyed our friendship. "Noted. Use liquor for lube. Any other advice?"

She slid some chips to the center of the green felt, staying in. "Yes. You used to like music? Went to concerts together, right?"

"We did. Lots of local and indie bands. That was one of our things."

She shrugged, as if to say *duh*. "There you go. Brent said there's some new band at his nightclub tonight. A hot, young indie-rock band. Take her to that. It'll be like old times."

"Is that what I want? Old times?"

"Yes. That's what you want," she said as she set down her cards, winning the hand with a trio of sixes.

"Nice," I said, with a low whistle of admiration.

She dragged a handful of chips closer. "So what was it like? Seeing her?"

That was the question of the day, one I'd been pondering since leaving the Petrossian Bar a few hours ago.

How could I even begin to describe seeing Annalise? It was like resistance meets infatuation. The whole time, I'd reined in my desire to kiss her, touch her, taste her lips. Because, well, that would be wholly inappropriate, and I had no clue if she wanted it. A wild, delirious thought popped into my brain. Had she looked me up for the same reason I'd tried to find her ten years ago?

Ah, hell. No. I couldn't go there. Couldn't linger on the biggest heartbreak of my life. On the absolutely epic shellacking I'd walked right into, like a fool who thought the past could be resurrected. The past was best left buried. Tonight would just be . . . fun.

"It was awkward, but easy at the same time," I said, after much consideration. "If that makes sense."

Mindy nodded thoughtfully, her blue eyes serious. "Yeah, it does."

"We sort of slid right back into conversation about work and past memories. It was good, even though I still feel like there are a million things I want to ask her."

Mindy patted my arm. "I know. But perhaps it's best to save 'Do you ever think about me?' for another time."

"Good point."

"Keep it light and fun," she advised, then tipped her chin to my phone. "And maybe let her know the plan for tonight."

I texted Annalise the details, lingering to appreciate the ease of communicating now with the woman I'd once had the hardest time in the world staying in touch with. So much had changed over the years. Even things like . . . text messaging. We hadn't had this luxury when we were younger.

When Mindy finished the round ahead, she thanked the dealer, collected her winnings, and walked away from the table. She was a measured player, always knowing when to stop. We wandered through the casino, then down the hall toward the restrooms, stopping outside the ladies' room where it was quiet so we could catch up on other matters.

"Did you see the report from Morris?" she asked, mentioning the private detective I'd hired. Mindy had worked with the guy, so when I was looking for a solid recommendation, I'd taken hers.

"Yeah. Not much there. The guy goes to the grocery store, and to buy sheet music at the piano shop. Doesn't even take his girls to school. I swear I don't get it. How can he be the head of a street gang?" I dragged a hand through my hair in frustration. I'd hired the detective to gather some intel on Luke Carlton, the mild-mannered local piano teacher by day, leader of the notorious street gang the Royal Sinners by night. The cops were trying to gather enough evidence to bring him in, and I wanted to do everything I could to help take down the fucker I was sure had played a role in plotting my father's death.

"But that's how it's always been," Mindy said. "This guy has supposedly been running the Royal Sinners for years, so he damn well knows how to be inconspicuous."

"That's the trouble," I said, as my phone buzzed.

Annalise: A concert! Sounds great. I will be there.

I promptly forgot about Luke and zoned in on those last four words. She would be there.

My Annalise.

4

ANNALISE

I peered in the mirror, considering the skinny jeans and boots I wore, as the phone trilled in my ear.

"It's two in the morning," Noelle grumbled when she picked up, sleep thick in her voice.

"I know," I said, checking out the side view. *Not bad.* "But you instructed me to call you the second I had a report."

My older sister groaned, then I heard sheets rustle, and I assumed Noelle was dragging herself out of her tiny bed in her tiny flat in the Fifteenth arrondissement. "Fine. Report."

"I'm seeing him again. Tonight," I said, a grin tugging at my lips.

"You've already seen him once?"

"Yes. This afternoon."

"And you didn't think to give me a report then?"

"I wanted to wait until I knew for certain that there would be another time. He just texted me the details a few minutes ago."

"*Mon petit papillon,*" Noelle said in a playful huff, using the nickname she'd bestowed on me many moons ago. It reminded me of what Michael used to call me. Not a butterfly, but he had given me an affectionate little name, and I hadn't thought about it in ages. I thought about it now, though, and how much I'd liked it. "Tell me more about tonight."

I gave her the details of our coffee conversation, because it was Noelle who had encouraged me to see him in the first place. *Time to move on*, mon petit papillon. *No more crying in the croissants*, she'd said a few months ago.

I wasn't crying in the croissants—or my pillow— anymore, thank you very much. I hadn't for many months. Still, was I truly ready? And ready for what?

To love again, Noelle had said, and I had scoffed and shaken my head. But Noelle had suggested simply starting with a date.

Fine, a date seemed reasonable, if I could call it that. And there was really only one man on my mind when I considered who I'd want that date to be with, and it seemed kismet once I learned I'd be flying to Las Vegas for work. Finding Michael had been no easy task, but persistence had paid off, and I'd tracked him down, then sent the letter to his office.

I was nervous, sure, but he'd also always made me feel safe. And for my first time out with a man in two years, that was comforting. But, after all, we were high school sweethearts.

Falling for Michael Sloan—back when he was Michael Paige-Prince—had been the easiest thing in the world when I was sixteen and living far, far away from home. He ran the radio station at our school and played guitar in a band with some friends in the afternoons. He was laid-back, easygoing, and quick with a joke. I was the arty French girl who liked the same indie music and who took pictures of him and the other guys playing their instruments in the garage. We were teens in love, bonding over music and style, American jargon, and kisses that lasted well past midnight. Endless kisses, the kind that made me feel like my skin was humming.

"Call me when you're done with the concert," Noelle said from the other end of the line.

"So you do like my report at any time of day," I teased.

"I'm a glutton for punishment when it comes to you. Just make sure it's a good report."

"What would make for a good report?"

"You know precisely what would make for a good report."

Yes. Yes, I did. Was it so wrong to hope he'd kiss me tonight? The flutter in my chest said a kiss would only be right; the spate of nerves flying across my skin told me the opposite.

I inched closer to the mirror, pursing my lips, studying them, wondering what it would feel like . . . It had been so long since I'd felt anything. I ran my index finger over my top lip, both wanting something desperately from Michael and terrified of how I'd feel if anything happened.

Anything at all.

A few hours later, I entered the dark, pulsing nightclub and found him at the far end of the steel bar, his eyes on me the whole time as I walked toward him.

I wanted to photograph him. I imagined raising the lens to my eye so I could capture the cut of his jaw, the determination in his gaze, and the tiniest twinkle of a grin tugging at the corner of his lips.

Framing him in my mind's eye, I snapped the shot. Michael, in dark jeans and an untucked navy-blue button-down. There—I'd have it later to linger on.

"You look handsome in your navy shirt," I said when I

reached him. I lifted my hand as if to run a finger across the collar or down the row of buttons. Then I scolded myself and dropped my hand to my side. That was muscle memory, an echo of the past.

I had no more permission to touch his clothes than I did to kiss him.

His eyes raked over me, as if he too was recording all the details. "And you look as stunning in dark green as you did in black."

Stunning.

He'd never failed to compliment me when we were younger, and he excelled at the pursuit as an adult too. "Even in this dark club, you can tell the color of my top? And that it's different from earlier? I'm so impressed, Mr. Sloan. I never knew your color-matching skills were so top-notch."

He shrugged casually. "Impressive, I know. I've been working on it for some time. Can I get you a drink?"

"A drink sounds fantastic," I said, and he gestured to the bar, then placed his hand on the small of my back to guide me through the press of people waiting to get service. A spark zipped through me from the possessive touch. The hum of music surrounded us, the low thump of the night-club, though the band hadn't started yet.

At the bar Michael raised a finger, and the bartender at the far end nodded, indicating he'd be on his way.

"That was quick. Do they know you?" I asked.

"No. Brent just has really good bartenders. They're fast with all the customers. Which is one of the reasons this place does so well."

"I'm glad to hear that. And he's married to Shannon now?"

Michael nodded. "They *eloped* this summer. Translation: got back together and went to a twenty-four-hour chapel to tie the knot."

I laughed. "Perfect for them. And congratulations to the happy couple. How is your sister doing?"

Michael made an arc with his hand over his belly.

A morsel of glee spread through me. "How exciting! When is she due?"

"About six months I believe. She just told us," he said as the bartender arrived, a young man with a goatee who asked what he could get for us.

Michael turned to me, letting me go first. "Champagne," I said to the man behind the bar.

"Make that two," Michael added.

"I wouldn't have pegged you as a champagne fan," I mused as the bartender set to work.

He arched a brow. "Why not? Do I seem like I have a dislike for drinks that are delicious?"

I shook my head. "No. I'd just have figured beer or scotch or something strong and manly."

He held up a hand. "Wait. Now I'm not manly? Because I ordered champagne?"

I laughed, shaking my head. "This is coming out all wrong. You're very manly. And champagne is very good. I'm glad we didn't have to sneak around to find some. Do you remember the time on New Year's Eve when we tried to figure out how to steal some from Becky and Sanders's collection?"

"Never found that damn champagne," he said, but the sparkle in his eyes as they latched onto mine told me he remembered the *other* way we'd rung in that New Year—a long, lingering kiss at midnight that didn't stop at the lips. It went on and on, and led to hands under shirts and below belts, to low, muffled groans, heated sighs, and our names falling off each other's lips.

The memory moved through me, heating me up. Or maybe it was just being near him now that did that.

"And now we don't have to track it down like thieves," he said.

"And now it turns out champagne is good for you. Did you know that?"

"I read that recently. What's the story there?"

I tapped the side of my temple. "Supposedly, it helps improve memory."

"Ah," he said, holding my gaze meaningfully, his tone turning serious. "But I don't seem to have any problem at all where that's concerned when it comes to you."

And just like that, I was speechless.

5

MICHAEL

My pulse hammered, and I hoped she couldn't tell how goddamn hard it was to stand this close to her, to be so near to her, and not talk about the things I most wanted to know. The *why*.

Why she was here?

What did she want?

Did she ever think of me?

And how the hell was she doing, after everything that had happened to her?

But I couldn't go there. Not yet. I couldn't handle that kind of conversation. It would remind me too much of why I had loved her like crazy. Because I'd talked to her about all those sorts of things once. Real things. Life and death and love and hope and dreams.

If we dared tread on that territory, I'd be lost.

But I also couldn't help but reveal that I'd never forgotten for a second what we'd shared.

She leaned against the bar, and I stood facing her. Annalise's green eyes seemed to know me intimately still. Her voice was the sound I'd longed to hear on those nights when I needed it most, and her lips were the ones I'd craved all the days we were apart. Now she was so close I could grab the hem of her shirt, tug her to me, and kiss her. I could run my hands along her arms and thread my fingers into her hair. I wondered if my thoughts were written on my face, or if my wishes were clear in my eyes.

I had to clench my fists to remember Mindy's advice.

Don't ask her if she ever thinks about you.

"So, where do you live now in the city?" she asked, and I startled, her words knocking me back to the present.

"Hmm?"

"Where do you live?" Her lips curved up, soft and naughty.

"Why do you ask? Are you planning to surprise me later?"

The question tossed me back in time to the day I met the willowy redhead from Paris. She'd just arrived at my dad's best friend's home to stay with them for the year. My first thought had been that I had to see more of her.

Want me to show you around town? I'd asked her the day we'd met in Becky's kitchen.

I would love that.

Is there anything you want to see in Las Vegas?

Surprise me, she'd said, with a curve of her lips, the hint of a smile.

I will, I'd said, and that had been the beginning of the love affair of my life.

I blinked back to the present as she leaned in closer to me at the bar. "Would you like that?"

I knit my brows together, trying to stay rooted in the present instead of tripping back and forth between then and now like a time traveler caught in a slip. "Would I like what?"

"For me to surprise you?"

God, yes. So much. Surprise me. Come over. Knock on my door, dim the light, and kiss me like it's the thing you've been dreaming about all day.

Before I could answer, the bartender returned with our champagne. I thanked him then raised my glass, clinking it with hers. "To . . ." I began, but I didn't finish.

6

ANNALISE

A flicker of sadness passed through his blue eyes as I lifted the glass. In that bare second, everything that had unfurled between eighteen years ago and today jabbed at me, like sharp little needles prickling my skin. My fingers itched to run through his hair, to offer a reassuring touch, something that showed I understood what was unsaid. I resisted the impulse, not knowing how it would be taken, and afraid, too, of how it would feel. Good or bad.

"To the present," I said since that was what I most wanted.

"To the present," he repeated.

As he took a long swallow of his drink, I studied him. By nature I was an observer, and I cataloged the details— his lips on the glass, full, curved, and kissable; his Adam's apple bobbing in his throat as he drank; his strong, sturdy fingers on the stemware. Then, the bend of his wrist, the cuffs of his sleeves rolled up twice, revealing his forearms.

Muscular and corded.

Why were forearms so delicious? But I knew the

answer. They spelled strength and power, and the ability for a man to anchor himself over a woman as he took her.

I slid my eyes away from him, trying to chase off my own dirty thoughts.

He set his glass down on the counter. "You said work brought you to town, that you're shooting the catalog all over the city. Are you enjoying it?"

"Immensely," I said with a nod. "The models are beautiful, the locations are playful, and the lingerie is, as you say, *to die for.*"

His eyes flashed with mischief as he made a noise of approval. "Big fan of lingerie myself."

"That so? Something you want to tell me?" I asked, coyness coloring my tone as we bantered, so much that it filled me with an effervescence that rivaled the champagne's effect.

"Very funny." He dropped his voice to a whisper. "I meant . . . on women."

That buzzing intensified. This was chemistry. This was the electricity in the air before a storm. I was wrong about him being a safe choice for my first time out in years.

Now that I was centimeters rather than an ocean away, I was intensely aware of how *not-safe* he was.

I threw caution to the wind. "Anything in particular when it comes to lingerie? Baby dolls? Corsets? Garters? Hip-huggers? Bikinis? Cheektinis? Stockings? Bikini briefs? Boy-cut shorts? Thongs?" I asked with the speed of a freight train, rattling off anything and everything silky that hugged a woman's bare flesh.

His lips quirked up as he took a drink. "That one," he said dryly, tapping the air with his index finger.

"Which one, Michael?"

He made a rolling gesture with his hand. "All of them.

Every. Single. One." Then he scratched his chin. "Question though. What on earth is a cheektini?"

I lowered my arm to my hip, shifted my pose, and drew a line mid-cheek across the denim of my jeans. "They go right here."

Heat flashed in his gaze as he stared at my ass. "Right there, you say?"

"Yes." I traced the line once more across my rear. "The panties cut across, so your cheeks hang out."

His eyes stayed on me the whole time, darkening. I hadn't expected the intensity of his stare. Nor had I expected the rush it sent through me. It had been so long since I'd felt like this. "Yes. And the one I'm wearing right now is red with lace trim."

I shocked myself when I said that. I hadn't expected to be so bold. But it felt easy and right and so damn good.

Perhaps I'd surprised him too, because he licked his lips, then groaned softly as he uttered, *"Red."*

Like it had six syllables. Like it was the sexiest word in the world.

Before the conversation could turn naughtier, the music shifted, and the lead singer tapped the microphone, said hello, and launched into the first song.

"More champagne and then we go stage dive?"

"Absolutely. Let's start a mosh pit."

We did neither, but a few minutes later, we were watching the band, listening to the music, and drinking another round. Someone bumped into me, and I moved closer to Michael. Before I knew it, we were shoulder-to-shoulder, hip-to-hip, swaying to the music.

By the time the band finished, we'd polished off another glass or two. The buzz was headier, and so was the intoxication from the music, the low lights, the energy, and this whole night that felt like a cocoon of possibility.

I wiped a hand over my brow. The club was hot.

"Let's step outside," he said, "where it's cooler."

I nodded, and once again, his hand was on my back. He guided me to the tall glass doors that spilled onto a terrace attached to the club. As he opened the door, he reached for my hand, holding it as we walked to a bench and sat down. Groups of club-goers were scattered at nearby tables.

He traced my palm lightly with the pad of his thumb, and my heart sped up. That barest touch was bursting with heat. Electricity flared between us. We could power the lights at this club, the billboards down the street. I barely understood how it was possible to *be* like this with someone I hadn't seen since that unexpected and heart-breaking day when we were both twenty-four. I'd been going one way in life; he'd been heading in another. Seeing him then had been as close as I'd ever come to the fire of temptation. I hadn't given in.

Now, we were both thirty-four, and my heart stuttered just from being near him. This torch might have flickered to a soft, ashen glow in years past, but it could turn fiery and bright in an instant. "I'm glad you were free tonight," I said. "I'm glad you asked me to the show. I've had an amazing time. Most of all, I'm glad you said yes. I've been thinking of you."

"You have?" His voice sounded stretched full of hope, like he was holding all the world in that two-word question.

Like my answer had more power than I would have ever suspected.

7

MICHAEL

This was what I'd wanted, but knowing she'd been thinking of me barely scratched the surface of my curiosity.

My voice was low, rough. "What do you think about?"

"How you are," she said, her gaze locked on mine. "What you're doing. What your life is like now."

I licked my lips. "And that's why you wanted to see me?"

"Yes."

My skin was hot. My bones vibrated. *Want* sounded damn good to me. After feeling like she'd slipped through my fingers in Marseilles—my head had understood, but my heart had rebelled when she'd walked away from me—I liked being wanted by her.

"So, were you wondering if I'd gone gray? Or bald maybe?" I teased, running my hand through my thick hair. Now that she'd revealed a modicum of truth about tonight, I could return to this zone, where the terrain wasn't rocky and fraught with so many jagged ridges.

She laughed with her mouth wide open, her white teeth

straight and gleaming. How I'd adored that smile of hers, the way she quirked up the corner of her lips when something was particularly funny. "I see you've held on to it all," she said.

"And yours is even redder." I gestured to her long, lush locks. Then I figured, *Fuck it.* She'd said the words I most wanted to hear—that she was thinking of me. I touched the end of a wave of her hair. It had been auburn before—now it was almost a dark cherry red, and so soft.

I let go.

"So is that what you wanted? To check out my hair color? Maybe to see if I grew wider?" I asked, patting my flat stomach.

"Looks like you've maintained your boyish figure," she said.

Perhaps that was all tonight was. A check-in with the past. I was worn so thin with wanting something, *anything* from her, but I had to remind myself this was only one night, only drinks. I was the one who was investing this moment with too much importance. Hunting for a deep, meaningful reason—one like *Michael, I had to tell you I never stopped loving you*—was pointless.

I scoffed. She wasn't here to say that, even if she had been thinking of me. Thinking was nothing. She was here for the class-reunion effect. To say hello, to check me out, and to breeze back out of town when she was done shooting skinny models in skimpy clothes. I needed to get the fuck over her. More importantly, I needed to get out of my own head, and stop thinking that a letter that smelled like rain meant Annalise Delacroix wanted to curl up on my lap and tell me she hadn't forgotten me either.

We'd been torn apart by time and distance, not by hurt or anger or falling out of love. No one had cheated. No one had said unforgivable words. No invectives were lobbed, and no terrible secret had come between us. Our biggest foe when we were younger was miles. Thousands and thousands of uncrossable miles. We'd tried to fight it with letters, a seemingly endless stream of them. But after a few years of letters and phone calls, we were in college and too far away from each other. It wasn't going to happen. It wasn't meant to be. I didn't have enough money to fly to see her, nor did she have the funds or her family's permission to return to see her beau. The flames turned to flickers, then to low embers in the ash.

But the fire burned again tonight.

I couldn't resist. "And you look as beautiful as I remember."

Music from inside the club seeped out to the terrace. She lowered her forehead and whispered "Thanks" at the same time a lock of hair slid over her eyes. My opportunity. I slipped my index finger under those strands and brushed them off her forehead.

She raised her lashes and looked up at me. "So . . ."

I ran my finger along the side of her temple. My pulse thundered under my skin. "Ask me what else I haven't forgotten."

Her green eyes shone with a hint of something, a flash of desire. She tilted her head curiously, taking the bait. "What else haven't you forgotten?"

All the world around me slowed and stilled to this moment. The music seemed to emanate from another dimension. The waitress walking past us operated in a parallel universe. I threaded my fingers into her soft hair, letting it fall like silk over my skin.

One more taste and I could stop longing for her. Stop lingering. I could finally put to rest the arguments my ex-girlfriends had waged over the years, insisting I was hung up on someone else. I was going to take the one thing that had strung me up all these years and get it out of my system. One kiss and I could say goodbye to my first love.

"How you like to be kissed," I said, my fingers curling around her head. She gasped quietly, arching her back.

Her voice was soft as the question ghosted across her lips. "How?"

"Like this."

Gently at first, I pressed my lips to hers. My heart stopped, and my blood stilled, as if it simply had to make sense of this new input before it could reengage. *Kissing Annalise again.* It was as if a new map were being written, a new route sketched out. So this was what it was like to kiss her once more.

Sublime.

My heart ticked again, catching up as I swept my tongue over her lower lip. She murmured. Soft, like a purr. That sound was new from her. She'd always been quiet.

And she'd once liked lingering kisses that were like melting chocolate, like the rising sun. Our kisses had been easy and carefree. They'd turned me on, riled me up, and made me want so much more of her. They were tongues and lips and mouths and heat.

But now, there were teeth.

Hers.

She pressed her teeth against my lower lip and drew it into her mouth like she was trying to suck on it, and with that, whatever wisp of apprehension she'd seemed to feel moments ago must have evaporated. My thoughts spun out of control, slipping into darker, more urgent territory. I moved my hand from her hair, held her face, and angled my mouth over hers, resuming control of the kiss and devouring her lips.

I drew the corner of her mouth into mine and nipped her. Her murmurs intensified. Louder. Hotter.

She'd never been like this before, but now she demanded more. Her own hungry lips slanted over mine, saying *Mark me.*

"Oh God," she gasped, her eyes squeezed closed.

I broke the kiss, whispering, "You okay?"

She nodded against me. "Yes. *So* okay."

"Good." I quickly moved my mouth to her jawline, kissing a trail there as I traveled along her skin. Each press brought out a tiny little growl from Annalise, a sexy sigh, a needy gasp. It made me want to rip off her clothes, push her against the wall, and see how rough she liked it. I bent my head to her collarbone and grazed the exposed flesh with my teeth. Her hands shot up, roping through my hair as she moaned. Annalise was under some kind of spell, her body moving and flowing against mine. She clutched my skull tighter, her nails digging in as I kissed her shoulder then returned to her mouth. That gorgeous red mouth. The lips I'd been obsessed with. The ones I'd memorized.

The lips I'd missed for so many years.

Like a persistent, aching hole in my chest, the missing had defined me. Propelled me. Given me a focus when I'd needed one. Now, the missing disintegrated and turned into a white-hot desire to have her. To have all of her, as I never had before. Now. Tonight. No more goddamn waiting. I pressed my forehead to hers and ran my thumb over her mouth. "It's different now."

She nodded. "Yes. But so good," she said, breathless.

"Not good. It's better."

"It is," she said, her eyes wild.

"Think everyone's watching?"

She shook her head against me. "It's Vegas. No one cares."

"Do you care?" I whispered as I traced her lips, the sweetness of her breath on my fingertips.

"That you're kissing me like crazy on the terrace of a nightclub in a hotel?"

"Yes." I dragged my thumb along her teeth.

"No. I don't care where we are," she said, darting out the tip of her tongue to meet my thumb. Then she bit down.

My mouth twitched in a knowing grin. "No, you don't care at all," I said, then crushed my lips to hers, wrapping my arms around her shoulders and kissing her with everything I had. Greedy kisses that promised red swollen lips tomorrow.

This kiss was dizzying. It was a rush of blood to the head, then everywhere else. When we were younger, we'd held back because we were sixteen and foolish romantics. We'd done plenty below the waist with hands, but hadn't come close to going all the way. Tonight, we seemed to be charging in that direction. Good. I was no fool anymore, and I was hardly romantic. I had the distinct impression life had hardened her too.

And that tonight she wanted hardness from me.

The sound of clinking glasses echoed from many feet away. The noise jarred me, and I pulled away from her briefly. I swept her hair away from her face, then bent my head to her ear. "Where are you staying?"

"Across the street. The Cosmopolitan," she said, her voice like a torch song.

"Do you want to leave? With me?"

Her lips parted, and I felt her soft breath on my neck. I pulled back to look into her green eyes. In them, I saw a lust that matched mine, but a fear too.

"Yes," she said, but a second later, she shook her head. Then she nodded and said, "No."

Opposites. Okay, maybe she didn't want the same thing.

She sighed. "I mean . . ."

I pressed my finger to her lips. No way was I pushing her into this. I wanted Annalise with a fierceness I hadn't felt in ages, but she was either in all the way or not at all. "It's okay. It's good to see you."

"Is that it? You're just leaving?" she asked, her voice angry.

I pretended to look around. "Did I say I was leaving? Did I get up to go? I'm still here."

"I'm sorry. This is just . . ."

"You don't have to explain anything."

"I know. But I don't want you to think I don't want to."

"Do you want to?"

"Yes, but it's been a . . ." She didn't finish her thought, and I didn't push. Changing gears, she said, "It's late. I'm shooting tomorrow. Do you want to come by?"

"Visit you at a lingerie shoot?"

"You always used to come by my shoots."

"You shot bands. The soccer team. The pep rallies," I said, reminding her of her days as a yearbook photographer.

"And now I shoot beautiful women. Do you like beautiful women?"

My lips twitched, and I eyed her from head to toe. "Very much."

"Come by," she said, her fingers darting out quickly to touch my cheek for a moment. "I want to see you again before I go."

I swallowed dryly, but didn't ask when she was leaving. I'd rather linger on the feeling of her hand on my face instead.

"Give me the time and place."

She told me where, then added, "Tomorrow at one. You can see the end of the shoot, and maybe we can . . ."

Her words went unfinished.

Whatever she meant, I wasn't in the business of filling in her thoughts. All I knew was one taste wasn't nearly enough to forget her.

8

ANNALISE

The elevator was too loud, too bright, too full of people.

As the couple in the far corner waxed on about their dinner of small plates and the fratty guys by the number keypad debated how many more shots they could plow through, I asked myself how long I could wait.

I'd been on ice, cryogenically frozen in a state of suspended animation for two years. My body was still working, going through the motions, one foot in front of the other.

But inside? Beneath my skin?

All those parts had been dormant.

Turned off.

Now, I was turned all the way on. I was like one of those blow-up balloons in an old cartoon, shooting through the air, ready to pop. I was sure everyone in the elevator saw the desire written all over my skin. But as the car shot up past the tenth, eleventh, and twelfth floors, they remained in their own worlds.

I wanted my own world now. I wanted to live in the bubble of lust.

The elevator stopped on the fourteenth floor, and the couple exited. Only the guys were left, and the tall one in the crew once again stabbed the silver button for the penthouse. "They'll be here soon. C'mon."

Hookers?

I almost breathed it aloud.

Instead, I covered my mouth with my hand, my fingers touching my greedy lips. But that was stupid. Because that only made me want to touch myself more. I couldn't help it. I dragged my index finger once across my top lip.

Like a match to a flame, it reignited me. My God, those kisses. My lips were bruised from Michael's mouth. He'd imprinted himself on me, and I felt him everywhere—on my skin, inside my organs, and deep in the dark, protected corners of my heart.

And yes, most exquisitely, between my legs.

If I'd stayed a moment longer at the club, I would've grabbed his hand and dragged him to the restroom. Even the return to my hotel had felt terribly long, a new and cruel sort of torture as I'd walked with a wet, needy ache between my thighs.

For so long, I hadn't let myself feel a thing. Now, I was nothing but nerve endings rubbed raw, cells crying out for relief.

The elevator dinged at the seventeenth floor. I practically vaulted out of the open doors and down the hall in a mad dash for my room. I reached it, fumbled for my key card from the back pocket of my jeans, slid open the door, and stepped inside.

My room was dark and cool, and the lights from the Strip winked through the windows. The door shut behind me with a heavy groan.

My breath was hot and fast, my hands even faster. I

dropped my purse to the floor, unbuttoned my jeans, and dipped my hand into my panties.

I groaned, my fingertips slipping through my wetness.

This was what happened when you banished sex, what happened when you extradited it from your life, your heart, your bed. When you told yourself you weren't ready, that you're better off without it. I hadn't wanted anyone to touch me, and I hadn't even touched myself in a long time.

I couldn't stop now. I was a rocket, flying to the atmosphere, hell-bent on a jet-fueled trip to the stars. The floodgates were unleashed, and I stroked myself, riding my own hand urgently as a flash of images sparked before my closed eyes. Michael's kisses. Michael's lips. His voice in my ear. His teeth. He hadn't kissed me like that before. Like he wanted to consume me. Bite me. Fuck me hard.

"*Michael.*"

I moaned his name, feeling its familiarity yet utter newness on my tongue as my fingers flew faster. There, standing against my hotel room door, breath tumbling rapidly from my lungs, sex on my brain, I made myself come for the first time in two years.

My orgasm slammed into me, fast and sharp as a hot knife. Seizing my body. Lighting me up. Racing across every inch of my skin. It was everywhere, rapid and furious, pulsing, and over far too soon. I was left panting, and not nearly sated enough.

His name fell from my lips once more.

I didn't feel cold tonight.

I was burning up.

My body was alive again, and I feared I would become addicted to this feeling before my heart was ready.

9

MICHAEL

The dog's legs flew, like a flip-book at high speed, as I cruised down the trail.

No one ever beat the dog. Not even Colin, and he'd recently finished the Badass Triathlon. But today I was a few footfalls behind Johnny Cash, and my brothers Colin and Ryan were eating my dust.

Pent-up lust could do that to a man. Desire could drive me to finish faster, push harder, focus more intensely.

With sweat slicking down my chest and my heart pounding, I ran as the sun peeked over the hills at Red Rock Canyon. My thoughts cycled between the bare-bones one-foot-in-front-of-the-other adrenaline and sheer, unrepentant want.

Last night was intense, sure. But it was only physical. It had to be that way. My ex-girlfriends had simply been wrong. As I whipped around a switchback, the black-and-white border collie in my crosshairs, I felt more confident than ever that my past relationship woes were never about Annalise. I wasn't a player. I didn't have a string of three-and-out dates trailing behind me. I'd had plenty of serious girlfriends over the years. I hadn't settled down with any of them because I simply hadn't met the right woman.

Not because I was hung up on *her*.

That was so not the case.

As the dust churned up beneath my sneakers, my mind flashed back to Katrina's comments a year ago. I'd been with her for ten months, but taking things to a serious level had never crossed my mind.

When she'd ended it, she'd simply shaken her head in frustration and said, "You're in love with the past."

I'd scoffed, doubtful. "What does that mean?"

"Ask yourself. I'm done trying to figure you out."

"There's nothing to figure out. What you see is what you get."

"Well, what I'm getting isn't enough. You're stuck some-place else, Michael."

My quads burned from the fast pace on the dusty trail. *Stuck*. Ha. I was fine. Work and family were all I needed. Besides, I had too much going on. Business was booming, and the investigation into my father's death had gotten its first big break in ages last month when the police had arrested the getaway driver.

I was stuck on absolutely nothing.

Seeing Annalise had proved that, hadn't it? I wanted her, but I wasn't caught up in her. I'd be a stone-cold idiot to be hung up on someone who'd moved on more than a decade ago.

That kiss had proved it, I reasoned, as I neared the trailhead.

That was enough to get her out of my system.

Except I couldn't stop thinking about that kiss.

That intoxicating kiss.

That fucking kiss, which had ignited all my fantasies last night. She'd felt like fire in my arms, and just as hard to contain. But I'd craved the danger, the risk of touching her. Of what it might do to me to have her.

It would either free me or wreck me.

Those thoughts powered me the final feet to the end of the trail, where I caught up quickly to Ryan's four-legged best friend. Johnny Cash panted hard, tongue lolling from his snout. My heart beat furiously as I pressed the spigot on the water fountain. "Here, boy," I called, giving the dog first dibs on the water as Colin's relentless pace bounded closer.

"You bastard. You on the juice now?" he shouted as he caught up.

"No. Ryan is. That's the only way he can manage to finish within a minute of us," I said, panting.

Colin laughed as I took a drink of the water, then stepped away from the fountain for Colin to get his shot. When Ryan arrived, wiping his palm across his brow, I adopted a look of feigned disgust. "I see your almost-married life is slowing you down," I said, teasing my brother, who'd recently gotten engaged.

"Nothing slows me down. Not ever," Ryan said. "I let you win."

"You wish."

I wandered over to the wooden fence that edged the lot, parking my foot on a post to stretch. Colin and Ryan joined me, and Johnny Cash trotted behind, slumping in a furry black-and-white heap at Ryan's feet.

"Listen. We've got some things to figure out," I said, diving into a conversation I'd told my brothers we needed to have on our run today. "I was thinking we need to take care of Marcus when shit starts going down. Probably even sooner."

Colin nodded, shoving a hand through his dark hair. "Definitely. I've been talking to him about what to expect.

He's already working on transferring to another college out of state," he said, breathing hard as he stretched his quads after our five-mile run. "That way he has a real reason to get out of town without his dad knowing he's been giving key details to the detectives. He's looking to go to school in Florida."

"Smart kid. And that's where we come in," I said. "We need to pay for his school and his new place, and make sure he's got around-the-clock security for a while, even if he's clear on the other side of the country."

"Absolutely," Ryan quickly agreed.

"No question about it." Colin nodded.

I pointed at Colin. "You see him the most. You let him know we've got his back on this, all right? He's our brother, and we'll take care of him. Without him, we might not have a chance at taking down the other men who killed our father. I want them all behind bars. Every last one of them."

With the revelation that our half-brother Marcus's father, Luke, was the leader of the notorious street gang the Royal Sinners, the cops were working to devise the best way to dismantle the gang and connect Luke to our father's murder. I reasoned that any sort of sting operation to take down the group's head, who'd successfully operated as the clandestine leader for more than two decades, would put Marcus square in the face of danger.

One man—the gunman, Jerry Stefano—was already in prison and had been for eighteen years. So was our mother, who'd plotted the murder. Now, Kenny Nelson, the getaway driver who had been arrested a few weeks ago, was likely on his way to the big house, but I wouldn't rest until TJ Nelson, the alleged mastermind of the gunman's hits, joined him there, along with the head of the gang. Apparently, Luke had been pulling the strings all along, hiding behind his harmless piano-teacher persona as he operated a gang of thieves, thugs, and murderers. I had hired the private detective, with Mindy's help, to conduct my own recon, do my part to push things along.

"I've got to hit the road. Lots to do in the office," I said, then turned to Ryan. "I'm taking the afternoon off."

Ryan stopped in his tracks. "Whoa. You never take off. You prepping for your New York trip?"

I was slated to meet with some clients in Manhattan at the end of the week. "Nope. Just a meeting locally."

"With who?" Ryan asked, and the question was perfectly reasonable because Ryan and I ran Sloan Protection Resources together.

I didn't answer. I didn't like lying, but I didn't want to get into the details. I reached for the door handle of my car, trying to ignore the question.

"Wait." Ryan's hand came down on my shoulder. "You're seeing *her*."

I spun around. "What?"

Ryan wagged his finger and grinned like he'd caught me red-handed. "Yep. I knew it. You told me she wrote to you, and I fucking *knew* you were going to see her."

I shrugged, trying to make light of it. "Big deal. So I saw her."

"And now you're playing hooky to see her again," Ryan teased, wiggling his eyebrows.

I waved him off. "Not playing hooky. I'll be working late tonight."

"Or working late on Annalise," Ryan called out as I shut the door.

I flipped him the bird, and my brothers laughed. There wasn't much that got past them. They knew how over the moon I'd been for Annalise back in high school. Hell, they knew *her*. Everyone knew her—my grandparents, my sister, even my father.

My father had thought she was perfect for me.

I flashed back to the note in my wallet. The one I kept with me at all times. My father's last written words to me were about Annalise. As I peeled away from the hills and drove back to my home on the Strip, I replayed the thirty-six hours before my father had been killed. The breakfast with him the day before was a blur; the next morning with Annalise at the airport as I said goodbye was a smudge in my memory too.

The one starkly clear event had happened after midnight.

A snapshot blazed before my eyes. I swallowed hard, jammed the brakes, and pulled over to the side of the road.

The image was too powerful to drive through.

I'd been in my bed, trying to sleep. I'd bolted upright, remembering I'd left something in the car that day. I'd barely been sleeping anyway. I got out of bed, padded to the front door, and unlocked it. My father's car was in the driveway. He'd been driving the limo that night, taking some teens to the prom, and after returning the limo to work, he drove his own car home.

I headed for the car door then nearly tripped.

On my father.

My veins ran cold with fear, then denial, then a soul-ripping agony as I fell to my knees, grabbing, clutching, holding the lifeless body in the driveway. Soaked in blood. Heart no longer beating. Wallet open, ID and photos spilled everywhere along with, I'd learn later, a note my father had likely written to me earlier that day.

The black of night cloaked me as I held my father, and I began to know the true meaning of the word *horror*.

Pressing two fingers against the bridge of my nose, I let

the memory recede, like a wave rolling out to sea. It would crash into me again, but for now, that image sent me back to the investigation. To the role my mother's lover had played in the murder.

The question remained—did Luke want Thomas Paige dead because he was in love with Thomas's wife? Or was there some other motive at stake?

10

BECKY

"Coffee or tea? Tea, right?"

The words seemed to float past me, indistinct, indecipherable. I hunched over the menu, studying it intently. Eggs, chia seed pudding—whatever that was—oats. My focus was singular—avoid the topic of my husband.

That wouldn't be easy. For so many reasons.

But surely, perusing all of the food options here—so many avocado toast customizations at this hip breakfast café—would keep me busy for some time.

"Tea with sugar, right?" Annalise said it louder, jarring me.

I startled, then looked up. The waitress was here. I hadn't even noticed her arrival.

"Sorry, dear. Tea is fine," I said to the waitress, fiddling with the edge of the menu.

Annalise added, "Some sugar for the tea, please. And a coffee for me. Black."

The waitress nodded and swiveled on her heels.

"Do you know what you want to eat?" Annalise asked

when the woman was gone, and I shook my head. Now, if I could just stare at this menu the whole time.

Except I wanted to catch up with the young woman who was the closest I'd ever come to having a daughter. I hadn't seen her since she lived with my husband and me all those years ago, but we'd kept in touch from afar over the years.

But I hardly knew how I would maintain a blank face once she surely started asking me about Sanders. How he was. What he was up to.

There was a reason I never played cards—terrible bluffer.

"Can't decide." Absently I ran my finger across the fork on the table. Perhaps I could delay ordering until the last minute, then I could simply focus on Annalise. Ask her about her job, keep her focused on that, and then deflect any and all questions about Sanders and Thomas and the past that had been dredged into the present.

"Maybe the special, then? I saw it on the chalkboard. Eggs and chives with homemade sourdough bread," she offered.

"Sure, fine," I said, since I had to choose something.

After the waitress swung by again, Annalise ordered, then, straight shooter that she was, began with the obvious. "So, Sanders couldn't make it today?"

No, I wanted to shout. *He couldn't come. He's busy. And no, I can't tell you what he's busy with, but it's eating me alive.* Instead, I plastered on a smile and did what I'd learned to do the last few months. "He's busy with some things." I waved a hand airily, like Sanders's goings-on were all so ordinary lately. When they were anything but. "Appointments . . . you know." Then I patted her hand. "Enough about me, love. I'm a boring old woman. Tell me all about you. Your life, what you've been up to. I want to hear everything."

I did my best to listen intently, only occasionally sneaking a peek at my phone, as we caught up on the highlights of the last eighteen years. There were highs and lows —awards she'd won in journalism, meeting her husband then losing him to an early and not unexpected death. I also took my turn, sharing what my boys were up to—their families, their jobs, their lives.

"And Sanders?" Her question was gentle, but firm. She wanted to know how he was. Which was understandable.

"Great," I said, but something hitched in my voice.

"Is everything okay?" Annalise reached out a hand, resting it on top of mine.

"Yes," I said quickly. My answer was both a lie and the truth.

"Are you sure?" I said nothing. "Becky," she said in a soft voice. "Do you want to talk about it?"

My eyes squeezed closed, pained. I had to keep it together. Had to keep it inside. But, my God, carrying *this* —all these details—was a terrible burden. When I opened my eyes, I wiped a finger under my lashes, erasing the threat of tears. "I'm sorry. I'm not usually like this."

"Is it Sanders?"

I sighed heavily, admitting the barest truth. "I'm trying to keep it all together. I really am."

"Are you guys okay? Is he sick? Is that the appointment?"

"Oh, no. He's fit as can be. Well, he has that bad back. But he's all good otherwise. It's just . . ."

"You're not separating, are you? Divorcing?" she asked. Even when she was younger, she'd never been one to tiptoe around a tough situation. And I wanted to talk. Oh, how I wanted to tell her—tell someone—everything.

Instead, I shook my head. "I wouldn't let him out of my grasp. Same for him," I said, adding a light laugh. "It's just been a tense few months."

She offered a soft smile. "I'm here if you want to talk. Or if you just want me to listen. After all, I'm leaving soon. Your secrets would be tucked safely away in my luggage on the return trip home," she said playfully.

The clawing desire rose up inside me to tell her how our lives had changed irrevocably since that day my husband was caught speeding.

"Ever since the investigation . . ." I began, but then I trailed off. "I shouldn't say anything. I can't say anything."

She squeezed my hand. "I understand."

But did she? Did anyone? Would anyone understand when they knew? When the truth came out.

She reached for the sugar, poured some into her coffee, and shifted gears. "So . . . is the big cruise still happening after Sanders retires?"

"I hope so." The cruise was our goal. If we made it there, we'd be in the clear. Blessedly in the clear. "Fingers crossed it doesn't get put off."

Every night I made that wish, for a thousand reasons.

And for one big reason.

11

ANNALISE

Something was off.

But I had no idea what.

I could speculate though.

As we talked more about little things, the wheels in my head started to turn, and I wondered what would defer Sanders's retirement, and why was Becky so tense from the investigation. What on earth would they have to be worried about from an inquiry into an incident that had occurred eighteen years ago? Sanders was Thomas's best friend back then. They'd worked together.

The wheels picked up speed. Did Sanders know something? Was he talking to the cops?

My heart squeezed.

Oh.

The appointment.

Was it regarding the case? Did Sanders have something to hide? Did Becky? As the possibilities took shape, I cycled back eighteen years ago to a night when I'd slipped into the house late, lips bee-stung and bruised, hair a wild tumble, heart racing from being with Michael. Becky had been reading, waiting up for me, and we'd talked briefly in the living room.

"So, young Michael Paige-Prince. You sure do like him. Is it serious?"

I had nodded with a grin I couldn't contain. "How do you say it? I am crazy for him."

"Yes. And I can see why. He's smart, kind, a handsome young man."

"He is," I had echoed, feeling dreamy, the way I'd always felt when I thought of the boy I was falling in love with.

Becky had smiled. "He gets his good looks from his father."

At age sixteen, I'd barely registered the comment.

Now, years later, I lingered on the remark. *He gets his good looks from his father.* Surely that was nothing, right? There had been no secret affair between Becky and Thomas, no long-simmering desire? It was just a comment, wasn't it?

I quieted my skeptical side, telling myself that Becky's remarks from years ago couldn't possibly have anything to do with her odd behavior today.

As I said my goodbye at the end of the meal and slid into the back seat of the Uber waiting to whisk me to my shoot, I replayed last night.

The bar, the kiss, Michael's hands. His mouth, his teeth, his tongue.

I'd see him this afternoon. The first man I'd ever loved, back when I hardly knew what that butterfly feeling was in my chest—flutters, wings, and all.

First love was like that. Enchanting and light, stitched from an endless thread of hopes and dreams. It made you feel invincible and hungry for more all at once. I'd wanted to be with Michael so much when I returned to France. I'd tried so hard to fight the distance through letters. We'd attempted to stay together through the end of high school and into college.

But just like proximity breeds closeness, distance kills it. Too many days apart, weeks alone, and years gone by. Eventually, our love became unsustainable. Stretched too far, it collapsed under the weight.

We drifted apart after the first year of college. Even then, I'd clung to the distant possibility that someday, somehow we'd meet again. Hope powered me even in the years when we no longer were in touch. Then all I had were memories. The fondest ones to be sure, but I'd had to move on. He'd moved on too.

I graduated from The American University in Paris, fully fluent in English. The first thing I did was reach out to him. I sent him a letter, saying hello, letting him know I was as free as I could be. An adult, able to make all my own choices. But it was returned to me—no forwarding address. That seemed a sign, that perhaps we were only meant to have been young lovers, high school sweethearts. Besides, I knew he'd gone into the Army, that he owed years to his country, and that was that. I moved forward, hunted for jobs across Europe, and eventually landed the gig of my dreams as a photojournalist. There I met Julien, a rival photographer who I fell in love with and married. I knew my time with him would be short-lived—he had a lethal arrhythmia, a genetic condition that meant he could die of cardiac arrest at any moment. The odds were not in our favor. They never had been. We were married eight years when Julien died in exactly the way doctors predicted he would, and in the two years since, I'd mostly been consumed with work and the simple daily acts that had guided me out of my grief. That's also when I made the change in my career to fashion photography. My heart had been too heavy for the weight of current affairs.

My life had taken a different course. I'd had to march onward, and I did. But with so much once between us, perhaps it was no surprise that the first man I'd ever loved would be the one to rekindle all that was dormant in my body. Last night had ignited something inside me.

The car veered right onto the Strip, and the bright light of the sun pounded down from the sky. Las Vegas in daytime was exposed. Nothing hidden. Every trick, every mirror, every trap was starkly visible in the daylight.

As the car pulled into the portico at Caesars, I glanced at my watch. A few more hours until Michael arrived. My stomach swooped, remembering last night, fast-forwarding to what might happen this afternoon.

Julien had wanted me to move on. My sister wanted me to move on. I didn't think I'd ever *want* to love again. It was too risky, too dangerous. What if I let myself, then lost again? I shuddered at the thought. Once was hard enough to find the man you love gone from this world.

But a moment, a snapshot of not feeling so goddamn empty and lonely? I'd experienced that last night. I'd held it in the palm of my hands, felt it deep in my chest.

That.

I wanted that.

12

THOMAS

Eighteen years ago

"You want to do this?" I scooped some pepper steak from the buffet onto my plate, eyeing my eldest son.

"I do," Michael said with a crisp nod, a fierce certainty in his stare. My son had my eyes—cool and ice blue. Some people thought that meant I didn't care. Hardly. I cared too much at times. About everything. About my wife and how distant she'd become the last several months. About my children and how they were growing up so damn fast. About my present job and the one that I wanted to do, the one that would make it possible for me to do more for my kids.

Right now though—as my sixteen-year-old spooned lo mein from the silver vat at our favorite cheap Chinese restaurant, the one that boasted all-you-can-eat for four twenty-nine a person—I cared about Michael. The kid was a chip off the old block. He'd fallen madly in love at such a young age. Hell, I knew what that was like.

I'd been like my son, crazy for the girl in high school. Of course, I'd gone and married her a few years later, and we'd had our first kid when we were both only twenty and just scraping by at crummy jobs. No college, no nothing. That was why I was heading to night school after dinner with my son, to shore up my associate's degree in accounting. A practical skill, and one that would surely help me get the job I wanted.

If I scored the new gig, that would spell opportunity for my kids. "All right, let's find a way to get you to Paris next year."

"Dad, you think I'm crazy, don't you?" Michael asked when we sat down at an orange booth with cracked vinyl seats.

"For being in love?" I raised an eyebrow.

"For wanting to be with someone who's going to be really far away."

I shrugged happily. "Nah, love is good. Chase it. Embrace it. You're focused and driven in other areas of life, and now you're that way about her."

I'd do everything I could to help Michael follow the girl. I'd help him go to college abroad if I could pull it off. Help him see her more. A love like that, you didn't throw away. Especially with Annalise. She was a special girl; she'd do right by my boy. It was a long shot, a Hail Mary pass, but maybe Michael could nab a scholarship at a university in Europe, find some study abroad program for Americans, and learn the French language.

But even if he landed financial aid, we'd need greenbacks for airfare and lots of other expenses. Ergo, I needed a new job. Needed it badly. Being a limo driver only got you so far. Sure, it was a step up from driving cabs, but I'd have to reach higher.

"How would we ever be able to pay for it?" Michael asked as he picked up his fork and dug into the steak.

I rubbed the back of my neck, a knot of tension setting up camp. But it dissipated, because I had a plan. A damn fine plan. Fingers crossed. "There's a promotion opening up at work. Think I'm going to apply for it."

"You are?"

"Can you see me being a desk jockey? Instead of a driver?" I asked with a wry smile.

"Sure. Why not? You already have to wear a suit and tie."

I wanted that job. Wanted it desperately. Wanted the bigger salary to help fund my kids' dreams. They were my everything.

* * *

That night at class, I focused on how to apply my newfound math skills to the job application, and when I returned home, I told my wife about an upcoming work party.

"We should go. I think it'll help as I try to get a new position. Get to know the people in the other departments," I said as I took off my jacket and tossed it on a hook.

She glanced up from her sewing machine, her green eyes eager for once. Lately, her eyes had been different—either weary or glassy. Now they were simply *hers*. I was happy to see that look in them. She'd been so far away and I hoped she'd come back—to us.

"Will there be piano again?" she asked, her tone strangely breathless at the mention of the instrument.

Her comment surprised me. Didn't think of her as a piano fan. "I think so. You mean like at that other party?"

I'd taken her to a holiday party last year, and she'd been transfixed by the Christmas tunes some local musician had tapped out on the piano. Absolutely enchanted. Maybe that's what she needed to come back to us.

"Yes. That one, Thomas."

I smiled, squeezing her shoulder. "Pretty sure there will be piano."

"I'll go," she said, and she seemed happy.

That was a relief.

At least she wasn't giving me a hard time about money. She used to do that a lot. Too much. Always nagging me about our finances. She wanted me to make more, wanted to have more.

Hell, so did I.

Who didn't?

Lately, though, that pressure from her had lessened, and I was glad of it.

Glad, too, that something so simple would make her smile. We hadn't had the easiest time all these years, but maybe, just maybe, things were changing.

A man could hope.

13

MICHAEL

The pools at Caesars Palace were lush with palm trees and rich with stately Roman architecture and statuary. The Venus pool was the most exclusive of all—it was topless, though today all breasts were covered.

Barely.

A half dozen beautiful women lounged by the Venus pool at Caesars, which was closed for a few hours for the shoot.

The scene was such a stark contrast to my morning. After my run with my brothers, I'd met with Curtis, who operated a gentlemen's club that my company provided security for. Curtis wanted to beef up our services, given the increased gang activity across town. That was something I had been hearing from many clients these days. Caution was the new watchword as the Royal Sinners and their crimes made businesses wary. After my meeting with Curtis, I'd finished a walk-through of a bank that had hired more protection in light of some recent robberies.

I was liking the way the afternoon was shaping up much better.

I'd told the intern guarding the pool area that I was here to see Annalise. She checked the list, found my name, and waved me in. I picked a potted palm tree to stand by on the terrace, out of the way of the models and the photographic entourage.

There was plenty to stare at, but my eyes were fixed on the redhead behind the camera, as I watched her work. Such a familiar image—Annalise viewing the world through her lens, snap, snap, snapping. Strong arms raising her camera, hands working the shutter, her eye capturing the women in repose. She wore jeans and a black tank top, her red hair swept high on her head.

After several minutes she stopped shooting, and they took a break. Annalise scanned the pool area, and when her eyes landed on me, they lit up. My heart slammed against my chest at her reaction. She weaved through the lounge chairs, around the edge of the pool, and came to stand face-to-face with me. Then, her lips pressed to my ear, she whispered, "You're here."

She sounded amazed that I'd made it.

"Did you think I wouldn't show?" I asked, regarding her curiously.

She shrugged as a small smile of admission crept across her lips. "Maybe."

"Hey," I said softly. "Why would you think I wouldn't show?"

She shook her head. "It's not that. It's just . . ." Her voice trailed off as she raised her chin, meeting my eyes. Her gaze went soft, almost vulnerable. "It's just that . . . you never know."

I nodded my understanding. Yeah, I got that. You never knew if someone would show up or if something would derail them, or if a fate would change in the blink of an eye.

She grabbed her camera bag from a nearby table under a big yellow umbrella. I followed her. "Thanks for inviting me," I said, looking at her over the tops of my shades. "Was it a good shoot?"

She raised her face, and wispy little tendrils of red waves moved with her. "It was. These women are terrific. They love the camera, and the camera loves them. It makes my job easy, having such talent to work with."

I smiled at her comment. It would be easy for her to say something catty, to toss a quippy one-liner about a difficult model. Instead, she'd done the opposite—praised them, not for their beauty, but for their ability.

"I doubt your job is easy," I said. "You've always been good at what you do. Yours is a natural talent as well. You have the eye."

"All I do is point, shoot, click," she said with a wink, then lifted her camera and snapped a candid of me without even looking in the lens.

"Hey now," I teased, covering my face with crossed arms, pretending I was a star avoiding the shutter.

"Too late. I've got you here. For all of posterity," she said, tapping the camera. Her gaze drifted to the back of the Nikon. "You look good."

I rolled my eyes.

"I mean it. Come see," she said, gesturing for me to come closer.

I waved her off. "I don't need to see myself."

"Oh, stop being so modest. You are beautiful, Michael Sloan. You were always one of my favorite subjects," she said in her straightforward way, so open and direct. My heart pounded faster, my skin heating up from her compliments. It was hard to keep my feelings for her in a neat, organized box when she said things like that.

"Thank you," I said softly, as I moved in closer to her,

my arm bumping her shoulder. Her breath hitched slightly as we looked at the image together. I resisted touching her, even though all my instincts told me to. Instead, I studied myself on the screen of the camera, and I looked like the guy I'd always been. And yet, as I saw myself through her eyes, through *her* lens, I seemed . . . happier.

Maybe I looked more complete because I'd been caught staring at her.

"See," she said, nudging me with her elbow. "Your eyes are so expressive. Your cheekbones are perfection. And your lips are . . ."

I picked up where she'd stopped. "My lips are what?"

She met my eyes. "*Red,*" she whispered, saying it in the same tone I'd uttered the word last night. Her cheeks flushed pink.

Ah, hell. I was going to have the hardest time not losing myself in her. I needed to put an end to all these sweet nothings, or I'd be completely ruined. But no way could I tell her to stop. I liked her compliments too much.

"By the way, I enjoyed watching you work," I said, side-stepping to a safer topic.

"You did?" she asked as she returned to her camera bag and zipped up a compartment.

"You sort of radiate energy, but it's focused. It's almost like an athletic event when you take pictures."

Her lips curved up. "Sometimes it feels that way."

"You perform like that. At the top of your game. You with your camera, seeing the world in ways other people don't."

She stilled her movements and cocked her head, looking curious. "Is that how it seems?"

"It does. Both watching you work and seeing what you saw. I always enjoyed looking at your photos after the concerts we went to. Seeing the pictures afterward was like opening up a whole new view of something I'd already experienced," I said, taking off my shades and tucking them on the collar of my shirt. "What's your favorite thing to photograph?"

"Surprises," she answered quickly, as she zipped another compartment.

"What do you mean?"

"Something that's out of place. Something you don't expect to see. A pink sock fluttering on a bush and making you wonder why a pink sock is there. A dog with a goofy expression that makes him appear almost human. The moment before a kiss when the woman is surprised."

"Do you photograph kisses often?"

She shook her head. "Not often enough. I'd like to though. I'd like to do a photographic book of kisses."

"Would you put yourself in it?"

She shrugged. "Maybe. Depends if I looked like I wanted the kiss desperately."

Oh, that was too easy. I stepped closer, swiped my thumb across her chin, and held her face. A tiny gasp came from her throat, and her lips parted.

"Yeah, like that," I said, my voice rumbling as I held her gaze. The look in her green eyes was hazy, full of want. "That's the image you want to capture."

"Maybe I don't just want the *before*," she whispered, with a touch of her accent reappearing. She was more French when she was aroused, I was learning. I brushed the barest of kisses on her lips, a small, gentle kiss that made my skin sizzle. "I want the *after* too."

Before. After. In between. I wanted it all with her. One simple kiss and I was on a slingshot into wild longing.

"I want it too," I said, my voice low and hungry.

She pulled back and blinked, as if refocusing. "You keep distracting me from packing up," she said, her voice soft and playful. "And I need to, so I can steal you away from here for a few moments."

I swept my arm out grandly toward her camera bag. "By all means, pack up, then."

She tucked the remaining items in pouches and pockets, keeping her eyes on me. "Thank you for what you said about my pictures. About how you see something in a new way from them. That means a lot to me. Sometimes I go back through old photographs and see new details. Some slant of light, or a new angle. Something that wasn't there before."

"Will you look at them all later? Hunting for details?"

She nodded, meeting my eyes. "I will. Including that one of you."

The temperature inside me rose. "What will you search for in that one?" I asked, and when she looked at me like that, her gaze intense and knowing, the breath fled from my lungs, and I felt . . . disarmed. She was so direct. And yeah, she'd been like that when I knew her before, but it was magnified now, amplified by age and worldliness, as if all her inherent confidence had been strengthened and sculpted over time.

"Maybe I'll remember how it feels to have you in front of me."

My head felt dizzy. My blood rushed hot. "How does it feel?"

"Like a favorite memory is real once more. And real is very, very good."

14

ANNALISE

I didn't want another ghost. I wanted the solidness of Michael. The warm skin. The beating heart. He was flesh and blood, and here with me. That fueled me, made me want to answer this persistent hum in my bones asking for nourishment, asking for all I'd been deprived of.

Contact. Connection. A thread binding me to another human being.

But asking for all of that was too much, too soon.

Instead, I gestured to the edge of the pool area as I hiked my bag on my shoulder. "Walk with me?"

"Where are we headed? Are you hungry?"

"Starving." I patted my stomach as we walked. "You know I always have a good appetite."

A smile spread slowly on his face, and he nodded. "Your French metabolism," he said.

"So they say." I was trim, but I didn't deprive myself. My secret was simple—I put one foot in front of the other and burned it off.

"Still walk everywhere?"

I nodded and then held up a finger as we reached the

doorway leading into the hotel. "Wait. That's not true. I took an Uber today," I said, like it was a confession.

He arched an eyebrow. "Naughty girl."

"I know. But in my defense, I was several miles away. I went to breakfast with Becky."

"Yeah? How was that?"

I scrunched my brow. "A little odd, to tell you the truth. I'll tell you about it at lunch. If you want to get lunch? I have about an hour."

He nodded. "Sure. I know some great spots here at Caesars."

I set my hand on his arm, wrapping it around his bicep. Oh, that was nice. He was so toned, so strong. "I actually thought we'd be done by now. That I'd have you arrive at the end of the shoot and then . . ."

"And then what?"

I shrugged happily. "And then . . ." I let my voice trail off once more, leaving possibilities lingering in the air. The truth was I'd been hoping for more of last night. For a repeat performance, and then some. I wanted to touch him, to smash into him, to feel him grind against me, and to wrap my legs around him. Call me greedy, call me needy —I'd own up to all of that. But when the director had told me a little while ago that the shoot would last well into the afternoon, and maybe the evening, I wasn't so sure I'd get the time I wanted with Michael. I'd have to settle for lunch. I gestured right at the next corner, indicating the hallway that led to the business suites in the hotel.

"Where are we headed, Annalise?"

"I left my purse in our suite—the one we all use for the day. It's kind of cool. Like a dressing room, because the models get ready there."

"So it's full of bikinis?"

"Yes. It is."

"Will you model some for me?"

"Would you like me to?" I volleyed back, as the sparks zipped between us. The flirting—this heady, decadent flirting—was fantastic. I wanted to inhale it, let it fill my body like oxygen after too long without air.

"I believe that was established twice—a few minutes ago, as well as on the terrace last night."

"Last night was interesting," I said softly as we reached the door.

He tilted his head. "Yeah? What made it interesting for you?"

"Seeing you, of course."

"Was that all?" he asked.

I knew he was fishing. But I wanted him to catch me at the end of his line. I needed him to reel me in.

I leaned in close, my head bending to his neck, my breath traveling across his skin. He smelled so damn good, clean and masculine, his aftershave hinting at the scent of the forest. "Touching you."

His hands shot out, gripping my upper arms. Tightly. "You like touching me?" he asked, his voice low and gravelly.

Like? I fucking loved it. I wanted my hands all over him. Wanted to explore him.

"So much."

He exhaled hard. "One hour, you say?"

My lips pressed against his neck, then I whispered softly, "Sixty whole minutes. Minus ten now, from the time we spent on the pool deck." I said it like an invitation.

"Let's get out of the hallway, then."

I nodded, reached for my key, and opened the door.

15

MICHAEL

Bright lights assaulted me. Fluorescents shone starkly from the ceiling, revealing one wall lined with makeup counters, four mirrors with exposed light bulbs framing each. I reached for the switch to dim the light to a normal illumination so I could be alone with Annalise without my retinas frying, when the wispy blonde model from the shoot waved a hand.

Ah fuck. That was a buzzkill. So much for the privacy of this room. My shoulders sagged. It was like being in college again, roommates crawling out of every nook and cranny, right when I'd been hoping to have my hands all over Annalise. My fingers itched to touch her.

"Hi, Annalise," the blonde said, stretching her arms over her head, pushing them into a gray sweatshirt. She poked her head through the hole.

Annalise cleared her throat. "Hey, Candy. What are you up to?"

"Just going to do some yoga during our break."

"Great plan. Good use of time. I just need to grab my purse." Annalise gestured to a beige couch littered with purses, bags, and jackets. "Then you can do your downward dog to your heart's content."

Candy waved a hand. "I'm meeting my yoga guru in his room. He travels with me."

"Oh," Annalise said, seeming to rein in a smirk that tugged at the corner of her lips. "That's smart. To have him travel with you."

"Thanks! I better go. I only have a few minutes to clear my mind of dangerous toxins," she said, then seemed to float to the door.

She left, and the door clicked shut with a satisfying *thunk*.

"A traveling yoga guru?" I asked dryly.

"Don't you have one? I mean, really. How else could you travel?"

I held up my hands. "Can't imagine how I've managed without one," I said, then glanced around the room.

"It's a good thing she had to leave to see him, though, don't you think?" she said.

"It's a great thing. Think anyone else will pop in?"

"It's possible." Annalise gave an indifferent shrug. "But that's what chain locks are for."

She dropped her camera bag to the carpeted floor and slid the lock into place. In a second I was behind her, dragging my nose along her exposed shoulder. "I like touching you too. So fucking much."

"I like you touching me," she whispered, facing the door, her fingers frozen on the lock.

I dragged my hands along her sides, traveling over the fabric of her tank top, along her waist, up her ribs to her breasts, then back down. With her hair pinned up, her neck was bare and inviting. I dipped my head to the soft, sweet flesh, inhaling her. She trembled, shudders racking her whole body. I kissed a path along her neck, up to her ear, then nipped her earlobe.

"Michael," she said, all low and needy.

"Yes?"

She twisted to face me, looping her arms around my neck. "Last night was . . . intense."

"Yeah?"

She nodded, then nibbled on her lip.

A part of me knew there was so much to say. Words about time and distance and longing. Questions about her heart and her head. Practical matters too, like how long she was in town. Would I see her again after today? And had she missed me over the years with the same kind of intensity I'd missed her?

My brain fought back, reminding me I was being ridiculous. This was just fiery lust, and it had been reignited so furiously it blazed white-hot.

"How intense?" I asked, brushing the backs of my fingers along her cheek. "We only kissed last night."

"Kissing can drive you crazy, though, don't you think?"

"I made you crazy last night?" I toyed with her, wanting to hear the admission from her, the breathless, gasping *yes*.

"*Wild.* I was wild," she said, then reached for my hands and led me to the row of mirrors with the lights. She hopped up on the counter, perching on the edge, and beckoned me closer. With my thigh, I nudged open her legs and wedged myself between them. Ah, my favorite place to be. The place I wanted to get to know so much better. Ideally when we were both naked, but this was at least a good start.

She roped her arms around my neck and raised her eyes to mine. Hers were a confession. A dirty one. "Last night wasn't just the two of us kissing. When I returned to my room, there was more."

"Tell me," I said, threading a hand in her hair, letting the silk flames fall against my fingers. "I want to picture it exactly."

"Standing up. Against the door. Fast, intense."

I breathed out hard, electric heat sparking through me. "Did I make you come? Like I did all those other times?" I asked, reminding her that I was the first man to bring her to orgasm. My fingertips stroked the denim on her thighs, traveling a path I'd loved when I was younger. She'd loved it too—falling apart in the back of the car, my hands under her skirt. Her body had been such a discovery to me. Learning how she liked to be touched, how she moved, how she felt, so silky hot in my hands. How she sounded when she had her first orgasm. She'd learned all those things too. We were explorers together, mapping the terrain of our bodies.

"Yes," she said on a breathy pant. "I moaned your name. The way you liked it."

Desire surged in me, climbing up my spine, spreading over my skin. I'd loved the way she said my name when she came.

I cupped her cheeks in my hands, holding her face firmly, and sealed my mouth to hers, kissing her hard and rough, the way she liked it now, because she wasn't the same girl I'd made out with after midnight in the back seat. She was a woman, and I was a man. I needed it harder, rougher, hungrier too. I drew her bottom lip between mine, sucking and nibbling as she writhed closer, wrapping her legs around me.

One hand snaked down her tank, brushing the top of a perfect breast, and I moaned deeply into her mouth then resumed the kiss, a commanding kiss that would leave her lips bruised. She arched her back, seeking more closeness.

Traveling from her breasts to her stomach to her jeans,

I flicked open the top button. A clock sounded in my head, awareness that time was ticking, that someone could knock at any moment. The lock was in place, but even so, I wasn't going to fuck her right now. That would happen when I could spread her out on a bed, worship her beautiful body, and kiss every inch of her skin. It would happen, too, when she was ready.

My blood heated as I imagined how intense it would be to have her.

There wasn't time now for all that I wanted, but there were more than enough minutes to make her come. I unzipped and pulled down her jeans, and she gripped my shoulders, her breath coming out in a hungry moan. Sliding my hand over the fabric of her panties, my fingertips traced what I suspected was a perfect auburn landing strip waiting for me beneath the lace. I dropped lower, touching the wet panel of her panties.

"And evidently you're a bit turned on now too," I said, the understatement of the year.

"Just a tiny bit," she said, as her mouth fell open. Her head rolled back. Legs widened. There was so much want in her eyes. So much need. Wedged between her legs, my cock throbbing and pressed hard against her thigh, I slid my fingers inside her panties, brushing wet, swollen lips.

Fuck.

Hot and velvet and so damn wet.

"I can take care of this for you."

"Please." Her voice was feathery, a soft, gasping cry.

I wasn't sure who needed this more—me or her. I desperately wanted to make her lose control, to surrender. Hell, she seemed to crave it like air. Her heady moans, her breathy gasps told me she was a woman consumed. I could smell her need, could feel it radiating off of her. She was a tuning fork, vibrating at the highest frequency of desire.

I ran my fingers through her slick heat until I was coated in her.

"So good," she whispered, as I traced circles over her clit.

I brought my fingers to my lips and sucked off her taste. Her green eyes widened, watching me. "How do I taste?" she asked breathlessly.

"Decadent," I answered in a growl.

"Give me some," she demanded.

And that was entirely new. This was not the Annalise I knew before. She'd never demanded to share. I was thrilled at this dirtier side of her.

"Such a greedy lover," I teased, as I rubbed my fingers over her lips. Instantly, she drew me into her mouth, taking my fingers all the way in, sucking off her taste as if she were sucking my cock. My dick twitched, hardening to nearly uncomfortable levels in my pants. But I'd take this kind of torture. I'd fucking endure it for hours, just to witness the sight of her mad desire. She twirled her tongue around me, as if simulating how she'd take me in her mouth. She'd never done that. I'd never felt her lush lips on me.

She looked so good like that. So hot and greedy, her cheeks hollowed out as her lips gripped my fingers tight. *More.* I wanted to see more of this.

Taking my fingers from her mouth, I dipped them across her slick folds again, then returned them to her lips. I fucked her mouth with my fingers as I brought my other hand between her legs. As I stroked her, I learned her pace quickly—she liked it fast and hard—and I rubbed her clit like that, in perfect, speedy circles.

She moved her hips against my hand, writhing into me. Then, with her tongue, she pushed my fingers out of her mouth, freeing herself to moan broken words of bliss in her French accent.

Oh God.

So good.

Yes. More. That. Fuck me.

God, there was so much I wanted to say. So many words that threatened to escape. Words like *dreamed about you*, *wanted you for so long*, and more, so much more. Words I wouldn't let myself say, because those were only the hormones talking, right?

"Did you fuck yourself like this last night? Thinking of me?" I asked, my voice rough as I plunged my fingers inside her slick heat.

"Yes."

"Thinking of how much you want me?"

She nodded as she lifted her chin, asking for a kiss.

I dipped my head, crushing my lips to hers, tasting her as I fucked her pussy with my fingers. With my free hand, I gripped the back of her head, holding her tight against my mouth.

But then, in a flash, everything shifted.

She grabbed my hand between her legs and gripped my wrist. She circled her hips, jerking her body, rising against me, and holding me in place. I'd become her goddamn vibrator as she rocked into my hand in frantic jerks, desperately racing to come.

"Do it," I growled, urging her on. "Do it till you get there."

She fucked my hand with reckless, untamed need, clenching tight around my fingers until she moaned into my mouth, her lips falling away from mine. She cried out, gasping "*I'm coming*" in French.

That was the girl I'd known. She'd always come in French. Her words always returned to her native language when she soared off the cliff into orgasm. Hell, her sexy, breathy moans right now were rich with her accent that she only had in moments like these.

I lowered my mouth, kissing her neck, dragging my teeth across the tender skin, biting her. I needed to mark this woman who'd haunted me. For years, she'd been the yardstick, the dream, the what-if fantasy. The trouble was, making her come, watching her lose all control for me, did nothing to abate that pent-up desire for her. The opposite had happened. It stoked the flames. I wanted her more than ever. Wanted to slide inside her, wanted to feel her snug and tight around me, wanted to know what it was like to make love to—*no*. Not that. To *fuck* this woman.

She shuddered, her shoulders shaking. It occurred to me that my fingers were still inside her. Gently, I removed them.

She looked up at me from hooded, sated eyes. "I think I treated your hand like a dildo," she said, a sweet little smirk on her gorgeous face.

"You did. But I'm perfectly okay with you treating my hand, cock, or mouth as a sex toy anytime you want," I said, and she laughed. I leaned in, moving my lips to her ear. "Because I want you with every part of me. I want to fuck you in every way," I told her. "To have you in any way I can."

She wrapped her hands around my neck. "I want that too. I want it desperately."

"So what do you want to do about that?"

I waited for her answer, watching her expression change from one of euphoria to something else entirely, something that looked a lot like uncertainty.

My heart cratered.

16

ANNALISE

As soon as *I want it desperately* tumbled from my lips, I caught myself.

A strange sensation washed over me. I'd just come with another person for the first time in two years. I should feel ecstatic, but instead a seed of doubt pushed and shoved against my skin, because it was the first time I'd been with someone new in more than a decade, and this wasn't just someone. It was Michael. I was ready to love again, but I wasn't ready to lose again.

I was scared.

I shouldn't be.

I really shouldn't.

But as I brushed my messy hair from my face with fingers that had clutched Michael like a lifeline, fear turned my blood sluggish. I pressed my lips together, holding in this feeling, sucking it down. Maybe I could just ride it out.

Like he could sense my panic, Michael tucked his fingers under my chin and raised my face. "Hey. Are you okay?"

His voice was warm, full of concern, and his eyes searched my expression. It was then that I realized why I'd thought he was a safe choice. Because in this moment, he was. We'd always talked; we'd been as open as a couple could be. I said softly, "I just can't believe I'm here, and you're here, and we're here. It's a lot to take in."

"I know," he said carefully. "And I don't want to push you into anything."

My eyes widened. "No. God, no. You didn't push me. I wanted all of it. I wanted you. I just need some time to catch up."

He smiled. "We can slow down, Annalise. I just want you to feel good. In every way. Your heart, and your body." He ran his hand down my arm. My gaze followed the path of his fingertips, and I registered what he'd done. He'd gone from pleasuring me to comforting me. He could do both, just as I could talk freely to him about this pendulum swing of emotions.

I took a long, deep breath, met his gaze, and made a choice. To live in the present and not worry about the future.

"Thank you," I said, my voice strong again. I wrapped my arms around his neck. "For that. All of it. Every part."

A smile tugged at his mouth. He looked at his watch. "We need to feed you and get you back to work. I would love to see you again, if you want," he said.

"I want that."

"But I don't even know how long you're in town."

I winced. "Not long. I leave tomorrow for New York."

His smile spread. "Me too."

The words rang in my ears like a song.

And suddenly, I knew I wanted to live in the present with him for a little bit longer.

* * *

The Thai restaurant served us lickety-split. With my fork I twirled the noodles and took a bite of my pad Thai. I hummed as I ate. Maybe I was still high from that orgasm, or maybe it was from the knowledge that we'd have more time to spend together in New York. Quite possibly I might be feeling this way because we'd talked about what was happening, and I'd moved through it for now.

"The pad Thai . . . it's that good?"

"Maybe it is," I said, after I finished chewing.

"Or are you grinning about something else?"

I leaned across the table as he worked his way through his shrimp dish. "You," I said with a naughty grin. "Your tongue."

A smile spread slowly across his handsome face, as he licked his lips. "You looking forward to getting to know that part of me?"

I nodded and took another bite, moaning around the food. "Mmm. I bet you're spectacular at that."

"What makes you say that?"

"The way you kiss me."

His eyes darkened. "You have no idea how badly I want to show you other ways to kiss you." He dropped his voice lower. "I want to kiss you until your taste is all over my lips."

I dropped my fork. My entire body went up in flames. He reached across the table, picked up the utensil, and handed it to me.

"Thank you," I murmured, and I wasn't sure if I was thanking him for the fork, or the orgasm, or the promise of more.

Somehow I managed to take another bite of my noodles, but I couldn't rein in my grin as I ate.

He laughed, wiped his napkin across his mouth, and took a drink of his water. "I like seeing you . . . happy. You deserve to be happy."

Happy was one way to put it. *Unlocked* worked too. That first kiss had turned the key on a closed door in me. I'd shut off the woman who'd loved sex and intimacy and closeness.

But as soon as I'd let myself go there last night, with my own fingers, I'd become a woman unleashed. It was as if that single orgasm against my hotel room door had uncorked me. And I wanted more.

And I wanted more with Michael. He'd been my first taste of love, and the connection we'd shared years ago had been so deep and strong. Even though loving again was too dangerous, surely I was still allowed to experience passion and erotic joy. Especially with someone who'd once been the center of my world.

We'd waited for each other when we were younger, but now we'd matured into adults who could have sex without labels. As teens we'd been wildly idealistic; as grown men and women who'd seen the world, we had the freedom to have unfettered sex. He would be the balm to my wounded soul, the warmth to my cold heart. Maybe then I could finally live again, and stop feeling like I was walking around the earth half alive, with a frozen heart encased in my icicle ribs.

"I am happy. I'm looking forward to New York. It's everything we couldn't do before," I answered him.

"Being young made some things too difficult," he said, his tone both serious and nostalgic.

"Now we can be naughty adults. In taxis, on airplanes, in restaurants," I said, as my dirty dreams spilled forth.

"You want all that? You sure?"

"Yes," I said emphatically, waving my hand behind me as if to gesture to the room where we'd been. "Please don't let my momentary freeze before scare you off."

He held up his hands. "I assure you, I'm not scared off."

"And I assure you that I desperately want all of you," I said, choosing total directness right now. The truth was I'd mostly had bedroom sex, and while it had been good, I wanted hot, dirty, thrilling sex. Sex with abandon. The kind he seemed to be able to give me.

The waitress appeared to refill our water, breaking up the flirty, dirty moment. That was fine, because I also had something serious to discuss with him. "I wanted to tell you about Sanders and Becky," I said.

Michael nodded, an intense look in his cool blue eyes. "Talk to me. What happened?"

"Becky seemed off. Like something was really bothering her," I began, and I shared the details, including the fact that Sanders had missed the breakfast because of an appointment. I hadn't intended to tell Michael at first, but I'd lingered on the exchange with Becky, and the fact that my old friend had said, *Ever since the investigation.* And the more I reflected on the conversation, the more it seemed necessary for him to know. "She seemed nervous, but sad too."

Michael nodded, his expression focused, his jaw set. "Sad in what way?"

"She wouldn't elaborate. I have no idea what's going on, but something is on her mind. And I don't want to sound the alarms, but I wanted you to know."

"I don't know why she'd be like that. But I'll try to find out if it means anything."

I reached across the table for his hand and clasped mine over it. He let out a breath, seeming to relax the slightest bit. I rewound to all the times we'd talked about his loss. He'd shared everything with me—all his hurt, all his pain. He'd cried once or twice on the phone with me, and I'd comforted him from afar as best I could as he told me the horror of what happened to his family the night after I left town.

The story was shocking to me, especially since I'd seen Thomas Paige less than thirty-six hours before he was killed. Michael and I had had breakfast with him at a little diner, eating eggs and toast as we talked about our plans. He was such a good man, so committed to doing everything he could for his son, and by extension for me. I'd thanked him, hugged him, and even told him I looked forward to the day he'd become my father-in-law. I'd believed it then—at the time, I was so certain I'd marry Michael.

"How is everything going with the reopened investigation?" I asked, threading my fingers more tightly through his, wanting to be his anchor if he needed me, like I'd been before.

"They arrested one guy, the getaway driver. And they're looking for the mastermind, TJ Nelson. He was the guy who brokered Stefano's hits. Apparently, he's wanted for several murders over the years, including this one."

I shuddered, imagining the trail of carnage the man had left behind. "Do they think your father's death was connected to others? I thought with your mother in prison, and the gunman's confession, that they knew the motive." How much more clear could it be? Dora had her husband killed for the life insurance money so she could run off with her lover.

"Yeah, I don't think that's changed. But the shooter had accomplices, and now it turns out the guy she was involved with is the head of the entire Royal Sinners gang."

My jaw fell open, and my eyes widened. I knew of the gang from all of our talks after the murder. I grabbed my water, taking a drink, processing this newest twist. "She was involved with the head of a street gang?"

"Turns out she was buying drugs from them and running her own ring. That's part of what the cops have uncovered now. She was selling drugs to a long list of people, including the two guys they think assisted in the killing. The shooter was her supplier, and the guy she was cheating on my dad with—well, turns out Luke wasn't just some local piano teacher. He's, like, the 'deep undercover, appears innocent on the outside, but is really the leader of a street gang' teacher."

Shock coursed through me, spreading from my chest all the way to my fingertips, a cold, liquid sensation under my skin. "Are they arresting him too?"

Michael rubbed a hand across the back of his neck. "That's the thing. They *know* he's head of the gang, but they have to have specific evidence to link him to a specific crime, so that's what they're looking for. Since all the other players were part of the Royal Sinners, they're trying to figure out if somehow that means my dad's murder was related to the drug trade the gang is part of. The guy who supposedly masterminded the hit, TJ, was involved in a lot of the gang's other crimes."

I shook my head, taking it all in. I remembered details that had emerged during the trial—the lover, the affair, the life insurance. Michael had told me everything. It was crazy now that the crime might have had deeper roots. "Do you think they can find TJ?"

"I sure hope so. I want nothing more than to see all those fuckers behind bars. Forever," he said, his voice a low seethe, his eyes sharp as knives. "I will never forget."

His hand tightened beneath mine into a stony fist. I

rubbed my palm over it, wishing I could comfort him. As I touched him, a memory flickered before me. A party. His mother saying something about a piano.

"Do you think she met her lover at a party? Your mom mentioned something once about a party with a piano."

"You remember those kinds of details?"

I nodded. "I have a ridiculously good memory. I remember her making a dress. I asked her what it was for, and she told me."

"A party with a piano?" he asked, raising an eyebrow.

I nodded, then told him bits and pieces from a brief conversation I'd had with his mother in passing one afternoon. "I don't know if that's helpful though."

His expression seemed grateful. "It's all helpful. Every detail matters."

We finished lunch, and he walked me back to the shoot a few minutes early.

"I can't wait to spend some time together in New York," I said, cupping his cheek. His eyes blazed, and his breathing intensified from that simple touch. For a moment I felt powerful, eliciting that reaction in this strong, stoic man. I stood on tiptoes and pressed a soft kiss to his lips.

"I'm counting down the hours." He'd said he had a dinner with a client that night, so the flight would be the next time I saw him.

Then, because I was feeling frisky, and because things had been one-sided so far, I pressed a hand to his flat belly through his shirt. "Don't think I'm selfish—I'm not," I said, whispering in his ear. "I want to taste you. I want you in my mouth. I want to feel you in my throat."

He swayed closer, a sexy sigh escaping his lips. "You're killing me," he growled.

I wiggled an eyebrow, turned on my heel, and left with a spring in my step, knowing that tomorrow I'd be coming again.

17

MICHAEL

My grandmother kept everything. Which meant it took me nearly an hour to find the box of photos from when I was sixteen. If my hunch was right, my mom had met Luke that year. I grabbed a shoebox from the top shelf in the garage, cluttered with tools, old toys, and clothes headed for donation.

"Found it?"

"I think so," I said, tucking the box under my arm as I climbed down the ladder to join Victoria Paige, the woman who'd raised us after my mother went to prison.

"Let's go inside and paw through it," she said, gesturing to the door into the house. I had come straight here after lunch with Annalise.

We parked ourselves on stools at the kitchen counter, and I took the top off the shoebox.

"What exactly do you think you'll find?" my grand-mother asked as she grabbed a thick handful of curled-up photos from nearly two decades ago.

I shook my head. "I'm honestly not sure, Nana. But I

want to look to see if any of the photos give me a clue about that guy. Anything at all. I know he had to have been involved in Dad's murder somehow. It can't be a coincidence that my mother was trying to run away with that man."

She nodded resolutely. If anyone understood the drive to leave no stone unturned, it was Victoria. I had lost a father; she had lost a son. That loss tethered us more tightly than a grandmother and a grandson should be. Now we were driven by the same need—the one for justice.

What if it was in our grasp? What if there was a clue in the family photos? Annalise had said photos sometimes held surprises, that when she looked at them again, she'd find things she hadn't noticed the first time. Maybe it was wishful thinking, but hell, if there was a speck of evidence under my nose, I wanted to find it. I wanted to know if there were *any* photos that would tell me about my mother's relationship with Luke Carlton, and how it had played a part in my father's death. After all, Shannon had told me that on her last visit to Hawthorne, our mother had said that Luke being married now to someone else proved something—it proved he lied, she'd said to Shan. At the time, it seemed like the ramblings of a woman losing her hold on sanity.

But turning it over, was that some veiled clue she was sharing that he'd lied about other things? Well, I figured he'd lied about every damn thing.

Except, for our mother to finally admit that—it made me damn curious if she was dropping crumbs for us to follow, something she'd started doing recently with Ryan. Crumbs that had led us to some of the accomplices.

And so I followed them too.

I flipped through picture after picture from that fateful

year, from posed school photos, to shots of Ryan playing hockey, to pictures of Shannon dancing.

"Let me have that one," Victoria said, grabbing a photo of my sister on stage, leaping high. "I need to frame that and give it to her."

I smiled and draped an arm around my grandmother, squeezing her shoulder. "She'll love it."

My sister didn't dance after she tore her ACL in college. She'd become a world-class choreographer instead.

My grandmother and I thumbed through more pictures. Shots of dance recitals, pictures of sunsets, images of family barbecues, including one of my dad flipping burgers with my grandfather, then one with me standing at my father's side, the two of us laughing together.

A lump rose in my throat, and my fingers lingered on the photo of my dad and grandfather.

"I remember that day," I whispered.

My grandmother's eyes shined with wistfulness. "You do? Tell me," she said, resting her chin in her hand.

I shook my head, surprised at the clarity of the memory. "It was just an average Sunday in the fall. October, I think. All of us were there hanging out at your house. I think Ryan and Colin were watching college football, and Shannon was playing with the dog you had then. Dad was grilling with Grandpa. Nothing special. They were placing bets on whose barbecue sauce was better, and at some point, the stakes were so crazy, we were all cracking up."

Victoria smiled widely, her eyes misty. "I can see it all now," she said, then tapped the photo. "Why don't I have this one framed too?"

I scoffed and tipped my head to the walls around us. They were thick with framed family photos. "Can't frame everything."

"But I can try." She snagged that photo, sighing as she regarded the shot of the men grilling. "The barbecue was the day after Thomas went to that party. I remember it now." She traced a shaking finger over my dad's face. "He was so tired, as they'd been up real late. He and your mother went to a work function."

I sat up straighter. That's what Annalise had mentioned. "The party," I hissed. "That's what I want to see. Do you think anyone took pictures of the party?"

"Not me. I wasn't there."

"But what if my dad had them? If someone had taken pictures from the work party..." I let my voice trail off, desperate hope coloring my tone.

She gestured to the pile. "Let's hunt."

I wanted to find those photos. I grabbed the next stack of pictures and methodically studied each one. There was no reason to believe there would be pictures of a party here in my grandparents' home, but my grandmother saved everything, so there was always a chance. If someone had taken pictures at the event, my dad might have held on to them ...

My heart stopped, then started again. I'd found it. A shot of my mother and father in front of a work banner at a company party for West Limos. Flipping to the back, I checked the date. Yep. The year it all went down. I gripped the edge of the photo as dark anger coiled through me. My mother took from me the person I loved most. My insides churned viciously as I studied the two of them. But it was only them posing for the camera, like some kind of company photographer had taken the picture.

I turned to the next one. A foursome. Sanders and Becky stood next to my parents. Sanders clutched his wife's shoulder tightly, and she smiled for the camera. My eyes roamed to my mother. I saw her looking to the right, just outside the frame.

Determined to follow her gaze somehow, I tore through the other pictures from the party. All in front of the banner, each one a little farther over, like the photographer was moving sideways. There were only a few more. As I lined them up, I could tell where my mother's eyes had drifted to just beyond the edge of the banner.

To a man playing a piano.

Luke Carlton.

Was Annalise right? Had my mother met her lover at my father's work party?

"I need to talk to Sanders again. See if he remembers anything from that night. Anything about Luke talking to my dad maybe. Anything that could make it clear what role Luke played."

But when I called Sanders a little later from the car, my dad's old friend didn't answer.

18

MICHAEL

I rapped on the window outside the detective's office. John Winston sat in his chair with his back to me, talking on the phone. He swiveled around, holding up a finger to ask me to wait.

As John wrapped up his call, I jammed my hands into my pockets, tension curling my muscles tight as the sounds of the police department filtered from behind me—the crackle of the radio, phone calls about cases, the shuffling of papers.

John nodded, then laughed, and at last he hung up the phone. Then he rose, opened the door, and let me in.

"How's everything?" John asked, clicking the door shut.

"It's fine." The two of us weren't known for small talk, so I took a seat in the wooden chair he offered to me.

"What have you got?" John asked. After Sanders didn't pick up, I had called John to tell him I had some details to share.

"Are you any closer to getting Luke? Closer to getting TJ?"

John sighed and scrubbed a hand across his jaw. "We're working on it every day. We're doing everything we can."

Frustration slid through my veins at how goddamn easily Luke Carlton had glided through life, avoiding arrest, covering his tracks, operating as a criminal so far undercover. "I don't know if it's a long shot, but I think"—I stopped, pausing before I said my mother's name because it tasted acrid—"Dora Prince met Luke at a work party," I said, then showed the detective the photos I'd found.

John nodded several times. "Yeah, I think you're right."

"You think I'm right?" I repeated, because I was hoping for something more.

"I've gotten similar information."

"So this isn't news to you?"

"I've been working leads on this case for a long time. This is one of them."

"Why didn't you tell me that's how they met?"

"Because it's not my job to tell you every detail. This is a police investigation. I'm grateful for all your help—don't get me wrong. But I have to be able to investigate, and sharing every detail with the family could slow me down on the way to answers." He took a beat and then leveled his gaze at me. "The answers we *both* want."

"Fine," I said, reminding myself that even though John was the gatekeeper, we had the same end goal. Ever since the police reopened the investigation this summer, thanks to a tip from Bianca Rosa, the hitman's long-ago girlfriend, I'd been laser focused on doing everything I could to help the case. So I tamped down my annoyance. "Let's put our heads together, then. I have some thoughts."

John nodded. "What's on your mind?"

I took my time before speaking, carefully weighing each word so that I could extract something from the detective. There was so much on my mind, so much I wanted to know—like why the Royal Sinners were so goddamn powerful, why they were stronger than the average street gang, and why they were smarter, nimbler, and had more firepower. But those were broader questions, and they wouldn't necessarily get me any closer to the answers I needed. Like the depth of the connection between my mother and the gang's leader. I needed specifics.

"The question we both want to know is *why*," I said. "We know my mother's lover is the head of the gang. We know the shooter was in the gang. We know the other accomplices are part of it too. What I'd like to know is *how* my mother got involved with the Sinners, and did it somehow start at my father's work? If she met Luke at a work party for my father's company, was Luke a regular there? He operates undercover, and that makes me question everything about where he's been and what he's done. Were the other guys in the gang involved in these work parties? Did they know my dad?" I held out my hands. "Maybe I'm reaching. But what if there's something more to it?"

John met my stare straight on. "That's what I want to know too. I want to know if your father's work is where they met, and if so, if that sheds new light on the accomplices. Luke played piano at a handful of these parties at your father's company. What does that tell us?" he asked rhetorically. "Not enough on its own, but now that we've learned that Luke is part of the Sinners, we have reason to believe he has knowledge about a number of gang-ordered hits over the years. That's why we want to know if your father's murder had a deeper connection to the gang. Was this just your mother's hit, or a part of something bigger with the Royal Sinners?"

19

BIANCA

A few weeks ago

I marched into the visiting room, the day after my son was arrested for selling stolen electronics.

Sat down across from Lee.

Stared hard at him. But I didn't have anger in my eyes. They were brimming with disappointment. And shame, too, over what he had done. It wasn't even the electronics. It was the stalking charge. The detective had told me about that. And dammit. That infuriated me, those damn messages that he sent to those women—the community center director and to Angie Carlton, the woman who raised that boy after his mother gave birth to him in prison —harassing them, scaring them. Messages to other mothers. Shame burrowed deep inside me, but so did determination. That had been my strong suit, my whole damn life —dogged determination. When I ran away, and when I came back, determined to raise this boy on my own, to teach him how to be a man, without any father figure to look up to. And to think, to goddamn think, he'd chosen those thugs to look up to. No way. No more. Not on my watch. This is not why I went to the police four months ago. Not for this.

"How the hell could you do that? I raised you better than this."

He nodded, gulping, saying nothing. His shoulders slumped, and I hoped to hell he was experiencing precisely how every last drop of remorse tasted. Bitter. Like something he never wanted to try again.

"Didn't I, Lee? Didn't I teach you better than this? Didn't I teach you so much better than this? I taught you not to be like your father. I taught you to make better choices."

In a small voice, a small, barely eighteen-year-old voice, he whispered, "You did, Mom."

I clenched my fists, fighting like hell not to let anger get the better of me. This was the moment when I would either keep him or lose him. Anger could not win. Love had to. Tough, fierce love. I reached for his hand and grabbed it. "You are *my* son. You are not your father's son. You are better than that, better than your blood. You know better, you were taught better. I expect you to start living better."

His shoulders shook. He nodded a few times, his lips quivering. In a wobbly voice, he asked, "What do I do now?"

The question came out so scared, so terrified. He was on the cusp. A boy who could travel one path and take on the true mantle of his birthright as the son of a murderer by following in his father's footsteps into a gang life, lured by the same damn men who were supposed to keep him out of that gang.

Or he could go the other way. Away from them. Away

from the criminals who broke their promise—surprise, surprise—and instead tried to corrupt him.

My son could choose redemption. Correction. Contrition.

Making up for the mistakes he'd made.

Tension radiated in me. But so did hope. I was flooded with it from head to toe.

I leaned back in the chair, crossed my arms, and did what I had tried to do for all these years. Teach him better. "Lee Rosa," I said, using the name I gave him at birth, the name he'd stopped using a few months ago in favor of his father's. "What do you think you should do?"

He drew a deep breath, dragged a hand over his head, and with the reluctant sigh, said, "Cooperate."

More hope. Because that was the first step. "Exactly. You should do the right thing. You should cooperate with the police. You need to tell them everything you know."

"Okay, Mom. I will." He squared his shoulders, swallowed, then raised his chin. "I'm not Lee Stefano. I'm Lee Rosa. I'm your son."

My heart squeezed, and I hoped to God he started acting like it.

20

JOHN

Michael asked more questions. "And I want to know if Luke knew about the murder. It seems likely now, don't you think?"

I spun around in my chair, pondering.

Yes, it would seem like Luke had to have known about the hit. It would seem, too, that Luke was deeply involved in the planning of it. He also had motive, and it would sure as hell seem as if Luke Carlton had gotten away with several other murders over the years, based on the information I'd obtained from my informants.

But evidence was evidence, and it needed to be hard.

We were closer to getting Luke, but there were things I simply couldn't share with Michael—details I couldn't speculate on with a witness or family member. Things like that the shooter's son, Lee, had started singing. We'd nabbed him a few weeks ago on grand theft of electronics, of all things. The kid was trying to follow in his dad's footsteps, living a life of crime. But a visit from his mother, who'd knocked some sense into him, had changed his tune.

Since then, he'd been cooperating.

He'd shared more about the two men who'd looked out for him after his daddy went to the big house—Kenny and TJ Nelson, his father's accomplices in the murder of Thomas Paige. Seems when Jerry went to prison eighteen years ago he'd asked his closest friends to keep an eye on his son, and to keep him out of a life of crime. For a while, they had, but Sinners are Sinners for a reason, and when the boy grew older they stopped honoring the promise to the incarcerated. Instead, they took Lee under their wing, started teaching the kid the ways of the street, first with fencing stolen goods.

That broken promise led Bianca to us, though she didn't know the names of the men.

But her son knew plenty.

Turned out, Lee knew some details about how the Royal Sinners operated, and he had some hunches about TJ's whereabouts these days. I was hoping to piece together enough information to find that slippery bastard and take him into custody too. I clenched my fists, thinking of TJ Nelson's rap sheet, and the long trail of evidence linking him to other crimes over the years. Some of my colleagues had gathered information about the gang as a whole, and the way the Royal Sinners had expanded in power, operating a lucrative drug ring throughout the city of Las Vegas and across the state.

TJ's involvement was clear, but connecting the Royal Sinners dots was proving more complicated than I'd expected. Did the hit have anything to do with the gang, or with things Thomas might have learned about the Sinners? Or was this simply what we'd thought all along, a crime designed so a woman could be with the man she loved?

Those questions kept me up at night, but I had witnesses to talk to and leads to chase down, which might bring me answers. As soon as I had the details, I'd get that fucker.

"Listen, I appreciate what you're doing," I said, taking my time with each word. I had to tread cautiously with Michael—men like him wanted to save the day. I couldn't tell him not to, but he did need to be smart. "You need to be careful, but I can't tell you not to look into things on your end using the resources I know you have. What I can tell you is I've heard that TJ had words with Thomas Paige a few weeks before he died. That conversation took place at your father's work." That was why it mattered to the investigation that Dora had likely met Luke at West Limos. I needed to tie Luke to TJ, and if I could just pull those threads a little tighter, I'd be able to tie it all together. "I'd like to know why, and what was said."

Michael nodded, an intense look in his eyes. "If you'd like to know, then I'd like to know too."

21

MICHAEL

On the way to the gym that evening, I tried to reach my father's friend once again. Becky answered, but when I asked for Sanders, she said, "He's busy for a few days, hon."

"Busy with what?" I asked, trying to sound casual rather than suspicious, even though I was starting to feel that way.

"He got called out of town. He has things he needs to get done before he finishes work," she said, as I turned on the blinker of my black BMW to exit the highway.

"Hmm. Okay. But I've got to see him soon, Becky. Can you have him call me as soon as he can?"

"Of course, love."

The line went dead.

As I hoisted a barbell a little later, I replayed the conversation with John, then the brief chat with Becky, trying to read between their words, to line them up like missing puzzle pieces alongside my conversation with Annalise earlier. And as I pushed up the heavy weight in my bench press, I zeroed in on some ideas, but they were fuzzy, hazy around the edges, and I didn't want to jump to conclusions. I lowered the bar, wondering if there was more to Becky's odd behavior, to Sanders's absence, and to the conversation TJ had with my father.

Now that—I'd sure as hell like to know more about that.

22

SANDERS

A few weeks ago

I folded. Again.

"You're killing me, mate. Absolutely killing me," I said, slumping dramatically on my friend's card table.

Donald scoffed. "If losing a dollar a hand is killing you, you ought to find a new hobby."

I raised my face. "Why do I come here and subject myself to this kind of torture?"

Becky rubbed my back. "It's called more than thirty years of friendship. Also, has anyone ever told you two that you're like an old married couple?" She pointed from Donald to me and back.

Donald and I both scoffed in unison.

"Becky, that's not true." I adopted a serious stare, looking at my friend. "Don, you forgot to take the trash out last night."

He straightened his spine. "San, for the thousandth time, pick up your socks."

Becky held out her hands wide. "Case closed." Then she leaned in and dropped a kiss on my cheek. "I need to take off. There's a water aerobics class calling my name. Next time, try to win, dear. Then we can make a bigger donation to the animal shelter."

"It's not like I'm trying to lose, but thanks for the tip," I said, then Donald dealt a new round. I wasn't a big gambler. We simply played for fun, and any winnings went to the shelter. Plain and simple.

Becky took off, and I watched her leave, feeling a tug on my heart. After all these years, I still felt that tug for her. That pull. I'd do anything for Becky, for our kids.

I turned around, playing another hand, when Donald boomed, "Look what the cat dragged in!"

When I looked up from the table, Michael Sloan was there.

A dart of tension shot down my spine.

I swallowed nervously.

Tried to remind myself I had nothing to be nervous about.

Not a thing.

Just act like normal.

Like everything is normal.

Because it is.

Michael joined us, as he had countless times in the past. A chip off the old block, he liked to chat with us, to catch up, to shoot the breeze about sports and music. Those were all normal topics, so I did my part to keep the conversation light, with predictions about the football season and discussions about some new bands coming to town. Michael won each round, like he always did, like his father before him.

Keep it normal, I reminded myself.

I cleared my throat, laughing at his winnings, keeping it

easy.

"Just like his dad. Thomas always beat us at poker," I said, and the thing is, saying that did feel normal.

Especially when Michael grinned, a hint of pride in his face. The kid—well, he was a man now, but he'd always be a kid to me—loved those comparisons, seemed to eat them up like candy.

"What can I say? I learned from the best," Michael said, then rubbed his fingers across his chest and blew on the nails.

Donald chuckled long and deep. "You did, kid. You definitely did."

When Donald's shift ended, the three of us headed to the Chinese buffet, grabbed some food, and debated which buffets in town were the best.

Yes, this was normal.

But I nearly choked when Donald shifted gears, pinning Michael with a serious stare. "Any news on the investigation?"

"None on my end. You heard anything?"

Donald scratched his head. "Nothing. I keep trying to invent a time travel machine so I can remember the conversations we had, in case there was a needle in the haystack. But about all I can recall is him mentioning once or twice at a poker game that there was some trouble brewing. Maybe it was around the time he was trying to get the promotion? That sounds about right."

"Was that all he said?" Michael looked ready to pounce.

Trouble.

That word nearly smothered me.

"Pretty much," Donald said, then looked to me. "Right, San? You'd know better than I would. Was there anything more?"

I shook my head, barely able to speak, as I pushed out a reply. "That's it. That was all."

23

MICHAEL

Present Day

But what sort of trouble?

As I lifted the barbell, I could recall my father mentioning something similar at one of our Chinese restaurant meals too. I just wished I knew what *sort* of trouble, and if that trouble was connected to Luke. I had nothing to go on now, since West Limos had come up clean in my research into the company. But the details nagged at me as I poked and prodded at my own memories of things my dad had said to me.

I wished I had Annalise's memory—precise and, not surprisingly, photographic. Mine was blurrier, and I often wondered if it was because of *how* I found out my dad was gone. The image splashed cruelly before my eyes, and I grimaced as I jammed the weights back in the holder. I sat up straight with my hands on my knees, trying to shake off the scene that sometimes replayed unexpectedly.

Taking measured breaths, I focused on the small details

around me now. The pounding music in my earbuds. The clang of barbells. The whir of bicycle machines.

They reset me to the present.

But the problem was the present was mired in so much uncertainty. I was on the outside, peeking in, trying to assemble the picture while only having access to the barest bits and pieces. I tried to fill in the blanks as I cycled through all the weights then headed to the rowing machine. Sixty sweaty minutes later, I called Mindy, my sounding board, as I drove home.

"Should we get Morris to look into the company my dad worked at too?" I asked, mentioning the private eye's name after I'd relayed my conversation with the detective.

"Hmm," Mindy said, seeming to mull over the idea. "I'm not so sure. Do you think that's relevant, or is that a rabbit hole? It's a bit of a different direction than having Morris tail Luke Carlton."

"I know," I said with a sigh. "That's the issue. Which path to send him down."

"Honestly, I think we need to keep him on Luke, since you know there's likely a connection with him to the murder after all, that he was more than just the clueless guy your mom was having an affair with. And I think you need to talk to the people your dad knew then. Donald, Sanders—those guys. I know you saw them a few weeks ago, but maybe now see if they know anything about the conversation with TJ."

"If I can even get Sanders to return a fucking call," I said with a huff, as I turned onto my street.

"Go see him, then."

But something about that suggestion seemed unwise. With Becky acting odd, I wasn't so sure how well her husband would take to a surprise visit. I shook my head, even though Mindy couldn't see me. "I've got to work

other angles. I'm going to see what I can dig up. I'll let you
know what I find."

I said goodbye, then pulled into the parking garage of
my building and headed up the elevator to my condo.
Once inside, I went straight for my computer, logging into
some of the databases that Ryan and I relied on for security
and background checks at work. I entered the name of the
limo company my father had worked for, but nothing new
surfaced. I'd been down this road before. When the investigation had been reopened, I'd looked into West Limos. I
wasn't suspicious, per se. Just being thorough. It was
owned by some guy named West Strauss. For years the
same guy had owned it from his home base in Dallas. Now
he was retired, living in Canada and kept busy fishing. But
he still owned a bunch of businesses around the country,
with managers at each to run the day-to-day operations.

I leaned back in my desk chair, sighing heavily. Maybe I
was reaching. Maybe the connection was simply that my
mother had happened to meet her lover when he'd been
playing the piano at a work party. She got to know him,
started selling drugs for his Royal Sinners to make some
cash on the side, then got greedy and wanted more dough
to cover her debts. She wanted to run away with her lover,
a new life for them both.

And killed her husband.

Yeah, that seemed as plausible as anything. The West
Limo connection was simply the way in which her world
collided with Luke Carlton's. Luke then became the
connection to the gang, the drugs, and the murder for hire.
Hell, maybe the conversation TJ had with my dad was
about my mother's affair, and had nothing to do with the
gang or the company.

I shut my laptop, padded to the kitchen, poured two
fingers of scotch, and let the liquor scorch a path down my

throat. I set the glass on the counter and headed for the shower.

Time to put aside the clues that remained cloudy. I had a trip to New York to get ready for, a woman to focus my energy on, and business to attend to.

As the water beat down on me, I bent my head under the spray, letting the heat soothe my sore muscles. I closed my eyes, and soon enough the questions stopped chasing each other. They circled the drain, and I visualized letting go of them. As the shower steamed up, my thoughts returned to that afternoon with Annalise.

For the first time all day, I let myself accept that I was going to have some kind of tryst with her. I was going to touch her in all the ways I craved. I could still smell her when I closed my eyes. She didn't smell like rain today. She'd smelled like longing. Like lust. Like the woman she'd become, not just the girl I fell in love with.

The woman was like a sexual jack-in-the-box. Wind her up and she exploded beautifully, like diamonds shattering into brilliant pieces. What would she sound like when I tasted her for the first time? How would she move beneath me when I finally had her?

I'd pictured her more times than I could count, but not in recent years. I'd denied myself that pleasure. Or really, that pain. I'd successfully shoved her out of my mind the day she unintentionally broke my heart in Marseilles. The shield had gone up, the walls had risen, and I'd resisted all thoughts of her.

Maybe I no longer had to resist.

Later, as I lay in bed, I told myself that this reunion was temporary. It was one snapshot, one moment, one chance. Then I'd move on.

I almost believed it.

24

LUKE

Twenty-One years ago

I stared at the letter from the symphony.

A thanks but no thanks from San Francisco.

I dropped it on top of the pile on the kitchen table in my mother's apartment.

I had a whole stack of them. I'd started compiling them after every inquiry. St. Paul. Dallas. Miami.

They sat on top of my rejection from Julliard from years ago.

From Carnegie Mellon too.

"Don't fret. You don't need to play in a symphony to be a success," my mom said from her spot across from me at the table.

"But it's what I've always wanted."

She took a bite of her apple, crunched it, then set it down. "No, you always wanted to play. Your dream was to play. You're doing that. You have the Nordstrom's gig. You have more Christmas parties than you can handle. You have a job teaching. Don't forget that," she said, giving me a smile. "That's what you wanted."

Maybe that was true once upon a time. When I was young. When I first discovered music. But that was before her car accident. Before the injury. Before all the endless medical bills. Before insurance refused to pay on a technicality.

I needed more work, better work, higher-paying work.

"It was, but we need more," I reminded her, my eyes straying to another stack. A stack of bills.

She simply smiled. "We'll find a way."

Such an idealist. She always had been. But idealism didn't keep the electricity on or satisfy landlords.

The only thing that did that was money.

Clenching my jaw, I looked away, thinking, contemplating, trying to figure out how the hell to deal with all those insurance claims.

Insurance. Damn insurance.

If I could find a way to stick it to the insurance company like they'd done to us, I would. I absolutely would.

* * *

A few months later, I landed a job playing the piano for a limo company's parties. The new client and I got along smashingly.

I had ideas for music, and the client had ideas for me. Over the next few years, those ideas stretched well beyond music. They reached to the streets, deep into the underbelly of the city.

It wasn't my first choice.

But at that point, my first choice was long gone.

This was my new choice.

And it turned out I was even better at this new gig than performing on the piano. The same skills I'd possessed that allowed me to read music, understand notes, and play symphonies could be applied to strategies, plans, and epic gains.

It wasn't Beethoven, it wasn't Bach. But this new world was my orchestra, and the men were my instrumentalists, playing the tunes to make beautiful music the color of green.

Soon enough, all the bills were paid, mother had her physical therapy, and I'd moved her into a new home in Las Vegas.

She was living her best life, and I was making it possible.

Insurance didn't win. I did, I had, and this new music sounded so good to my ears that I didn't ever want to stop playing it.

25

THOMAS

Eighteen years ago

Something didn't quite add up. I was no expert, but as I finished writing up my log of rides for the day, I grabbed last week's list to make sure I had the correct spelling of the client's name. But the man's name had been erased, as if the ride I had given him to the airport didn't exist.

I leaned back at the table in the break room and scratched my chin. Why would a ride suddenly go missing? I opened the binder and thumbed through the last few weeks. Here and there, a few others were missing too.

Flipping to the red tab, I checked out some of the other drivers' records. Sanders had been pulled in to handle a few airport rides. None of those were listed either. Maybe because Sanders was a mechanic?

I shook my head, as if I could make sense of the missing info. Perhaps I'd mention it to Paul, who ran the operations and oversaw all the drivers. Bringing attention to a discrepancy would surely put me in a good light, what with the potential for promotion on the horizon. Paul would have the final say in hiring me anyway, since the owner lived and worked in another state and was never on site.

I finished filling out the details, clocked out, then got into my car to head to my daughter's dance performance. Dora was meeting me there with the boys, except for Michael, who'd been studying at Becky's house with Annalise and was coming from there. As I arrived at the auditorium, I spotted Becky's car and saw my oldest son walking into the event center with his arm draped around his girlfriend. Michael leaned in and planted a kiss on her cheek. As they strolled inside, I pictured them like this a year or two from now, in college, going to a play or a concert, happy together.

But something was missing. Something was off. I rubbed the back of my neck, then an idea slammed into me. Something Michael would need. Something besides money. Not wanting to forget, I grabbed the notebook I kept beside me in the center console and wrote down my thoughts. Tomorrow, I'd make some calls, set things up for Michael. For now, I closed the notebook and headed inside to watch my daughter dance.

* * *

The next day when I filled out the log, more rides had pulled a disappearing act. As I packed up, I rapped on Paul's door, figuring now would be a good time to let him know. This would show initiative, that I cared, that I had the company's best interests at heart.

Paul furrowed his black eyebrows when I mentioned the missing rides. "That so?"

"Yes, sir."

Paul nodded and then smiled, a professional sort of grin. "That's good to know. Really appreciate you bringing this to our attention. We'll get it sorted out." Then Paul pointed a finger at me, like a gun. "That kind of attention to detail will get you far."

Excellent. That was everything I wanted. To go so much further.

26

MICHAEL

Three-fucking-thirty in the morning. Not when I wanted to be awake. Not when I wanted to be dealing with shit. But when the alarm sounded that there was trouble with one of our clients, I showed up.

I flew straight out of bed, into my clothes, and to the client's site. I was closer than Ryan, so I called my brother and said I'd handle the situation. White Box, a gentlemen's club, was just a few blocks off the Strip, making it just a few blocks from me. I pulled into the lot, parked my car, and ran a hand through my messy hair.

My armed guard was outside, lit up by the glow of the purple-and-white lights streaming from the art deco sign above the club, a sleek metal structure that oozed sexy class. The guard stood next to a plainclothes cop, along with Curtis, the VP and biz dev guy at White Box, who'd hired Sloan Protection Resources.

I said hello, then gestured to the premises. "So, what's the story?"

Curtis cleared his throat and went first. He was a beefy guy, exactly the type of man you'd physically want fronting a club, if you could choose a manager based on size. His face was like a block of wood, and so were his arms. His eyes were brown and warm, though, like a favorite uncle's. "We got word of some gang activity here on the premises," Curtis said, disgust in his tone as he recounted details of an attempted robbery and then the arrest of a young man with a *Protect Our Own* Royal Sinners tattoo. Apparently, the guy had tried to steal a watch worth five grand off another patron in the men's room. He'd brandished a knife, turning his crime into an armed robbery attempt. The cops came quickly, and the guy was in custody.

"Your patron, the guy with the watch—is he okay?" I asked.

"He's fine. Your man stopped things before it turned ugly," Curtis said, nodding to the armed guard I had supplied to the club.

I clapped my guy on the arm. "Good to hear."

I breathed easier knowing the incident was routine enough, and frankly the type of thing that happened now and again at these sorts of establishments. When you trafficked in sex and sin, you could sometimes attract the seedier element.

After another fifteen minutes, all was well enough, and Curtis strolled with me back to my car. "Thanks for coming by in the middle of the night to check it out. Charlie and I appreciate the service," Curtis said, referring to the owner of White Box. "He wanted me to extend his gratitude too."

"It's the least I can do. I'm sorry this happened, but I'm glad no one was hurt," I said.

"We're keeping a close eye out for this sort of stuff, and for gang trouble. It's been heating up lately all over town, so you can't be too safe."

"Couldn't agree more," I said, placing my hand on the

hood of my car, sensing an opportunity. I raised my chin. "Hey. Question for you."

"Shoot."

"Have you seen any other gang activity around here?" I asked. This gang was insidious and could sink its claws into businesses like a parasite on an unsuspecting host. I didn't want one of my clients to be that host. Selfishly, I couldn't help but wonder if the gang activity here could lead me to Luke or TJ. If the Royal Sinners were encroaching on this patch of land, circling it and threatening the innocent, maybe there was a chance to double down—help my clients, and find the men I was looking for.

Curtis shook his head. "Not too much. This is the first I'm aware of. Let's hope it's the last," he said, his voice determined.

"Let me know if you hear anything else."

Curtis nodded, his face solemn. "We've got high-end patrons here, and we don't want to mess around with that stuff, or the Royal Sinners. I'm with you on this."

"There's someone from the Sinners we've got our eyes on. Guy named TJ Nelson. He's wanted for some crimes over the years. Don't know a ton about him, but he has a gold earring. Scar on his right cheek. Tall, towering frame." I gave Curtis the scant details I was aware of. I didn't share Luke's name though. I didn't want to let on I was looking that high up within the gang. Besides, Luke wasn't likely to be seen in public as a gang member.

Curtis nodded. "I'll keep an eye out for him. Let you know if we spot him."

"Good," I said as I unlocked my car door.

"Get some sleep," Curtis said with a genial smile.

But sleep was nowhere to be found when I returned home, so I settled in to work, plowing through paperwork as dawn spread across the dark sky, casting pale pink morning light over Vegas from twenty stories high. I worked through contract approvals so I would be free to get on that plane and focus on the woman I wanted to be with. Sure, I had work to do in New York and meetings to attend that would keep me busy, but I didn't want to squander an ounce of my time with Annalise.

It was best to be ahead of the game, and I was.

That also meant I had enough time to see Donald before I jetted out of town.

* * *

My dad's oldest friend shook his head, thumbing through a deck of cards at his table at the Golden Nugget—empty for the moment, since it was early in the morning. "He never mentioned anything about someone named TJ coming by, not that I can recall," Donald said.

"Shit," I hissed. "I've got to figure this out. You sure? Not a word?"

Donald held up his hands. "We talked about lots of stuff, but I don't remember him mentioning it. 'Bout the only thing he said was that he was trying to get the new job and he thought he might have a lead on it when he found something that was missing at the company."

Something that was missing. If so, was that what TJ had come to talk to him about at work? I narrowed my eyes. "And he never said what that something was?"

Donald shook his head. "Sorry, kid. I barely remember what I had for breakfast most days. I hardly remember the specifics of a conversation that didn't stand out from two decades ago."

"Do you think Sanders knows? Since he worked there?"

Donald shrugged. "'S possible."

"Do you trust Sanders?" I asked pointedly, because the question had been gnawing at me.

"With my life." Donald tilted his head, studying me. "But why would you ask? Is there some reason you think you can't trust him?"

Yes. Because he's avoiding me. Because he's avoiding everyone. Because something is up. "No reason. Except I honestly don't know who to trust anymore."

Donald shot me a faint smile and nodded, then stepped around from behind the table and gripped my shoulder. "I hear ya, kid. All I can tell you is this—keep on digging, keep on asking. Your dad was like that too. He was focused and driven. You got that from him. Stay on it, and you'll find what you're looking for."

Focused and driven. My dad had used those words too to describe me—only my father had been talking about my quest to keep Annalise in my life. Those words were spelled out in the note I'd found in my dad's wallet, scattered across the driveway with credit cards and photos the night he'd died.

Annalise was once my dream, my one-time reality, and my endgame.

Then she was gone, reduced to a memory that haunted me. Now, she'd become real again, and it was time to meet her at the airport.

27

ANNALISE

"We will begin boarding Flight Twenty-Three to New York shortly."

I turned in the direction of the gate agent, checking my watch as I talked on the phone to my sister in Paris, nine hours ahead of me.

"How is Mom doing today? How was the doctor's appointment?" I paced the boarding area, scanning it for Michael, nerves skating across my skin. It was so weird to be traveling with him. This was what we had dreamed about when we were younger—this sort of freedom, including the freedom to change my flight. I'd been slated for a later one to New York, but had moved it up so we could fly together.

"Her day was all right, but not great, to be honest," Noelle said on the other end of the line. Our father had passed on a few years ago, and our mother lived alone in a small flat in Paris. That wouldn't be a problem ordinarily, except she'd had a bad fall a year ago, and her hip hadn't been the same since, so she relied on her two daughters. Noelle and I did our best to stay close, check in on her daily, and help with whatever she needed. These efforts were complicated by my frequent travel for work, but I picked up the slack when I was in town. "Her doctors are switching her to a new medication," Noelle added.

As my sister and I discussed side effects and dosages, I wandered through the noisy boarding area. Then the crowds cleared, and I spotted him.

My stone-cold heart thawed again. It shed its covering, and a grin tugged at my lips as Michael walked toward me, dressed in crisp black slacks and a light-green shirt, the top button undone. My eyes raked over him, snapshotting every detail, from his trim, tight waist, to his deliciously messy black hair, to the hint of stubble on his face. His ice-blue eyes lit up when our gazes met, and a slow, sexy smile spread across his handsome face.

As if a tropical sun caressed me, I warmed all over. Butterflies took flight inside my belly, surprising me. I'd expected lust, raging hormones, or the mad desire that Michael had unleashed in me the other night, but this was out of left field, this strange and new stomach flipping. It caught me off guard, especially when the butterflies soared to the stratosphere as he stopped less than a foot away from me, said nothing at all, and simply dropped a kiss on my cheek, which was the sexiest greeting he could have given me.

My focus on the call with Noelle was shot to hell. I was simply lost in this moment, as if all the travelers, all the noise, all the sounds of the world had blurred.

When Michael stepped away from me, I blinked and refocused, but I was still lightheaded, just from the sight of his face and the brush of his lips. "Take care of Mom. I'll be back soon to help out. Just a few days in New York for the shoot," I said to Noelle.

"Fly safely, *mon petit papillon*," my older sister said.

"Keep me posted on everything. Love you. Miss you. See you soon."

I ended the call, slipping the phone into my back pocket.

"Hi."

"Hi."

"Fancy meeting you here." My voice was laced with flirtation.

"What a surprise. I had no idea you were on this flight," he said, playing along, as if we'd just met.

"Perhaps we can sit together and catch up on the plane," I suggested, as if the two of us hadn't already made those plans.

"I like that idea." He leaned closer, his lips dangerously close as he said, "Maybe then I can whisper filthy things in your ear as we fly."

I wobbled, his words making me hot. My hand darted out, and I gripped his shirt, holding on. He looped an arm around my waist, steadying me.

"You'd like that, wouldn't you?" he murmured, as he roamed his eyes over me. I wore skinny jeans, heels, and a silky tank top that showed a peek of cleavage.

"Yes. So much. Would you?"

His eyes blazed darkly. "I would absolutely love getting you hot and bothered."

I brought my lips closer to his ear. "I'm going to let you in on a little secret. I'm already there."

A few minutes later, the gate agent's voice warbled across the tinny speakers, calling for first-class passengers. Michael swept his arm to the side, letting me lead the way.

As we stepped onto the plane, he asked, "How's your mom?"

The question surprised me, but I figured he must have heard the tail end of the conversation, picking up a few

French words that I'd taught him once upon a time. "She's okay. Well, she's not great. I was talking to my sister about her," I said and shared some more details as we settled into our seats.

Michael tipped his chin toward the bags that contained my camera gear, which I'd tucked under the seat in front of me. "What's the job in New York? More bikinis?"

"We have one more day for Veronica's at some very iconic New York locations. We've actually booked the New York Public Library and have some fantastic shots planned of the ladies lounging in their pj's on leather couches, reading old books. It's going to be very cool."

His eyes twinkled. "Can I have your job?"

"You want to lounge in your pj's and read in the library?" I asked, nudging him with my elbow.

"Yeah, that's it. Exactly."

"When Veronica's adds boxer briefs, perhaps I'll suggest you model them."

He leaned his head back and laughed, a deep, hearty sound that warmed my soul. I loved his laugh—he'd been so laid-back and carefree when I knew him before, quick with a joke or an easy comment. He was more serious now, so I craved these moments when he dropped his guard. When his chuckles slowed, he lowered his voice to a dirty whisper. "But you don't know if I wear boxer briefs."

I arched my eyebrow in a challenging stare. "No. But I fully intend to find out the answer to that, and to discover it . . ." I let my voice trail off, watching him linger on my every word with parted lips before I added, "Very soon."

He drew a sharp breath, and I zipped right back into the conversation. "Then after that, I have a boudoir session with a private client."

"Private client?"

"Just a woman who wanted to have some shots done as

a gift for her husband." The woman was the CEO of a sex-toy company, Joy Delivered, and she'd found me through a mutual contact—her brother worked and lived in Paris with his wife, and I had met them a few times at dinner with friends.

"Do a lot of women do that?"

"Enough to make it a good living for me," I said.

Michael shook his head in admiration. "Never knew boudoir shots were such a hit."

I nodded enthusiastically. "They've actually grown immensely popular in the last several years. More and more women do them. Some just do them for themselves."

He cocked his head, his eyes hooked on mine, then answered in a thoughtful voice, "That sounds very empowering."

"Yes! That's it exactly. Not everyone gets that, but you do," I said, grateful that he understood something few men truly got.

He tapped his temple. "I'm a feminist."

"It's hot," I said.

He smiled. "Ever shoot guys?"

"Shockingly, most men don't do boudoir sessions," I said in a deadpan voice. "But I have photographed a few couples."

"Really? That's pretty sexy. What about turning the tables though? Because I want a one-on-one with the photographer," he said, running his fingers across the ends of my hair, watching it fall from his hand onto my shoulder. "I want to be the one behind the camera, shooting photos of her looking gorgeous in anything and nothing." His blue eyes were fiery, intense. "Then I want to set down the camera and have her invite me to join her on the bed. And all the sensuality she poured into the pose, she gives to me."

I shuddered and swallowed. My throat was dry. My skin heated up. "I would do that," I whispered. "I would do that with you. I would give that to you."

The flight attendant began the announcements, and I closed my eyes and breathed deeply, trying to get some sort of hold on these raging hormones. But with him next to me, it was futile.

I resigned myself to being turned on the whole flight.

It was all his fault. That fucking hot, sexy man.

28

ANNALISE

Once we were airborne, Michael returned to the topic of my family. "How is your sister? Did she ever start the bakery like she wanted to?" he asked, and I loved that he remembered that little detail from our phone conversations years ago.

"Yes, she did. She runs it with her husband now, and she has three kids. So she's been busy." I pictured Noelle and Patrick up before dawn, peddling baguettes and croissants, and loving their little corner shop in Paris. I adored that bakery too.

"Does that mean you have to take care of your mom more?"

I shrugged. "Sometimes, but that's okay. My mom took care of me. It's only fair," I said, then softened my voice, placing my hand on his arm. "Is it weird to hear other people talk about their mothers?"

His eyes darkened briefly, then he shook his head. "No. It's the way it should be."

"Do you ever see her? I know you did at first, but then you didn't want to anymore." He'd told me that he'd visited her in prison a few times when he was in high school and college, but hadn't since.

His jaw was set hard, and he heaved a sigh. "Yeah, I used to, a long time ago, because I wanted to try—I don't know —maybe to understand what had happened, and why she'd done it. But soon enough it was clear there was no way to make sense of it. I couldn't be near her anymore. I don't think of her as my mother, and I haven't in years."

I ran my hand down his arm. "I understand why."

He turned his head and met my gaze. "Not everyone does," he said in a quiet voice.

"You mean other women?" I asked, and a brief burst of jealousy flared inside me at the prospect of him with other women, of him sharing such personal details with someone else that he'd once shared with me.

He ran a hand across his jaw, shaking his head. "Just people in general. My brother Ryan, and even Shan for a while. They wanted me to visit her, but I just couldn't."

"Do you think it's because you were closest to your father, or just because that's how you feel?" I asked as the plane began to level out, nearing its cruising altitude.

"Probably both."

"Do you think that will ever change? Your feelings for her?"

"I don't see how it could. Unless she was found to be not guilty, and that won't happen," he said with a scoff. "I believe there are other people who are also responsible, but she did this. So I don't see how I'd ever think of her as a mother again."

"Are you okay with that?" I asked quietly.

"Are *you* okay with that? With me feeling the way I do?"

I nodded resolutely and ran my fingers across the back of his neck. "Of course. It's your life. It's your choice." The tension seemed to lessen in his shoulders as I touched him, and I was struck with a memory as crisp as the images in front of me—a phone call years ago, a couple of months after I'd left Vegas and returned to France. It was one of the few times I'd heard him shed tears. His mother had just been found guilty of murder for hire, and had said her goodbyes to her family before she was taken away in the bus to prison. He was choked up, and it had shredded me to hear him recount the day. But my emotions were nothing compared to what he was feeling at age seventeen, his family pulverized by tragedy. The pain had started to fade from his voice over the next few calls and letters, and he'd told me, *Talking to you is one of the few things that makes me feel okay.*

Okay.

Such a small, flat word. But it was all he wanted, and it was enough. To feel okay. Somehow I'd given that to him. Perhaps I was doing the same now, helping him see that it was indeed okay to *not* want to be his mother's son.

"You sure?" he asked, and his voice was laced with nerves, like he desperately needed my reassurance.

I cupped his cheek and spoke confidently. "Yes. You're a man without a mother. And it's okay to be that way. It's like she died too, and your mourning for her just took a different shape."

His eyes locked onto mine, and he relaxed further. "Sometimes I wondered if I was too hard on her. Too angry. Too unforgiving. But then she admitted to Ryan that she did it. I don't need to forgive her."

"Some things are unforgivable. Obviously, this is one of those things," I said, letting my hand drift down from his face to rest on his leg. "Do you still miss your dad?"

"Sure. Of course. But you get used to it. It becomes part of your life, doesn't it? The missing," he said, as the flight attendants began to move about the cabin.

I nodded, and though he hadn't said my husband's name, I knew what he was getting at.

"Do you miss Julien?" he asked. Point-blank. Direct.

I swallowed, my heart rising up to my throat and sticking there. "Sometimes I do," I admitted quietly, looking down at the armrest, the in-flight magazine, the screen on the back of the seat in front of me. Then I gazed into Michael's eyes, clear and fixed on me. "But not right now. And not lately."

The crackle of the speaker interrupted our talk as the attendant announced that we were free to turn on computers and other approved devices. Neither he nor I made a move to do so.

Instead, we talked. We talked as we flew over Colorado, then Kansas, past Illinois and Ohio, through drinks and the afternoon lunch service, and through the movies that others watched. He told me about his family, catching me up on his brothers and sister. I remembered them all from when we were younger, and I savored every detail he shared. His sister's pregnancy was going well. Ryan was engaged to a beautiful philanthropist who made him happier than Michael had ever seen him. And his youngest brother, Colin, had started up a serious relationship with a social worker who had a teenage son. I loved hearing everything as I pictured the Paige-Princes—now the Sloans—in their new lives, healing from the damage that had ripped them apart years ago.

"What about you?" I asked, meeting his cool blue gaze. "They all sound so happy. So settled. Are you happy too?"

The corner of his lips curved up in the barest lopsided grin. "I'm happy now."

Now.

The word echoed. Reminding me that *now* was all

anyone ever had. This moment. To make the most of. No guilt—only pleasure, only passion, only the present.

I threaded my hand into the back of his hair, feeling those soft dark strands on my flesh, and he groaned. Low, barely audible. Just for me.

"Come closer and kiss me," I murmured, and he obliged, dipping his head and kissing me like we were the only two people on the plane—flying across the sky, leaving Vegas far behind, and heading to a new adventure.

29

MICHAEL

I had always been perfectly content to fly commercial. First class was great, but I'd never longed for a private jet. Not that I'd have minded one, but it was along the lines of a yacht or a mansion—nice to admire, but wholly unnecessary for my happiness.

That was no longer the case. A private jet was the *only* thing in the world I wanted right now. No, *want* was too small a word for it. I craved it like air. Because this kiss was different. It was as hot as all the others we'd shared, but it was something more too. It was crazed and beautiful. It was hungry and full of regret. For years gone by. For missed connections. For the past and for the present. It was as if everything that could have been between us was bottled up, stored, and aged to perfection, all in this one kiss. With her hand on the back of my head, she kissed me deeply, but tenderly too.

The wildness at the nightclub was gone. The frenzy of the dressing room had slunk away. Right now this was a kiss that made me a little drunk, like my body was buzzing with some kind of sweet opiate, and that opiate was her. I wanted to pull her on top of me, run my hands over her soft flesh, unzip her jeans, and then slide into her. Wanted to watch her fuck me here on the plane. To enjoy the view of her straddling me, riding me, slow and unhurried, lingering and lovely.

I loved and hated this moment.

This was just a fucking kiss.

But it was so much more.

I'd never kissed like this before. Fierce and greedy. Needy and dreamy.

I wanted to live in this kiss.

At some point, I broke the contact, because I had to. Because another second of her kisses would be too much. I brushed her hair away from her ear. "You keep doing that, and we're going to be putting on a show."

She grinned naughtily. "I think we already are," she said, glancing clandestinely over her shoulder.

"Tell me something," I whispered. "How do you say 'I want you so much'?"

"In French?"

I nodded.

"*Je te veux tellement.*"

I repeated it close to her ear, flicking the tip of my tongue over her earlobe as I said those words to her.

She shivered visibly. "*Mon dieu.* I love the way you say that."

I slid into another question. "How do you say 'Fuck me harder'?"

Shuddering, she whispered breathlessly, as if she were in the throes of passion, "*Baise-moi plus fort.*"

Lust slammed into me from all sides. I bent my head to her shoulder, dusting the barest kiss on her collarbone. "You'll be saying that later, won't you?"

She nodded, a small, sexy sigh escaping her lips. "I will."

Soon enough, the plane landed, and twenty minutes after that, we were in the town car I'd reserved. I raised the partition, and in seconds, her hands were on my pants, unzipping them.

Well, I wasn't going to say no to that.

30

MICHAEL

She was a sexy vixen. A fiery lover—a woman who liked to take and who evidently liked to give too, judging from how she rubbed her palm against the outline of my erection.

"Last night," she said, breathy and sexy, her lips near my neck, "I couldn't sleep. I was thinking of you. Of what you did to me in the dressing room."

"Yeah?"

She lifted her face to meet my eyes. She nodded, her lips now on my jaw as she slipped a soft hand under the waistband of my boxer briefs, then wrapped it around my hard cock.

I hitched in a breath, and time stood still as she grasped my hard length, skin against skin at last. It was relief and torture all at once. Her touch was electric. As the town car rolled along the concrete stretch of road away from the airport, she stroked my cock and whispered, her breath ghosting over my skin, "I couldn't stop thinking about you. All the things we didn't do."

I flexed my hips, thrusting up into her soft, nimble

hand. I didn't want her to ever stop. "Like what? What did you want most?"

She skimmed her hand lower, down to my balls, cupping them, playing with them. Oh hell, that was fantastic, especially as she dragged her nails across my skin.

"What do you think I wanted?" she countered.

I needed her to want me as desperately as I wanted her. It took every ounce of restraint not to answer her with *Suck me off.* Instead, I gritted my teeth and managed in a low rumble, "Tell me what you wanted. *Say it.*"

My chest rose and fell as she played with my dick then moved her hand up my shaft, rubbing a bead of liquid over the head. I groaned, closing my eyes as unholy pleasure swept through me.

With a tight grip, she twisted her hand, rubbing me up and down. I opened my eyes. Hers seemed to twinkle with lust and mischief. She had such a naughty side, and I wanted to explore that aspect of Annalise to the fullest. I had never known this part of her. All I knew when we were younger was that she liked everything I did to her, and that she came easily on my fingers, her moans and cries so sexy when her orgasm washed over her. I was learning that the woman with me now was dirtier, bolder, and so damn passionate.

She bent her head closer, pressing her forehead to mine, and whispered, "I want to taste you. Lick you. I want to feel your come in my throat. I want to swallow it all."

I thrust upward into her eager fist as her words scorched a path through my chest, spreading like fire throughout my body. She'd set me ablaze with the match of her lust.

"Did you get yourself off to that?" I asked. "Was that what did it for you—picturing your lips on my cock? Did you spread your legs wide for me and fuck yourself with your fingers?"

She panted as she pumped me faster. "Yes. I was naked on my bed, knees raised, legs spread, my hand between them, as I imagined taking you deep in my mouth."

My head fell back against the leather seat, hitting the headrest. That was the hottest image I'd ever pictured, and it was scored into my mind now. This naked beauty with her creamy skin, her sheets of red hair, her full breasts, and most of all, her abandon.

Her need.

"You tasted so good." She moaned on an upstroke, her lips parted and wet from licking them with the tip of her tongue. I wanted that red-hot mouth on me.

I commanded. "Show me how you did it."

In a flash, her red hair spilled across my thighs, and her head was between my legs. Her lips greeted my hard shaft with the warmest fucking hello I'd ever had.

"Annalise," I murmured, dragging a hand roughly through my hair, trying to absorb the enormity of this moment.

My girl.

My first love.

This wild woman.

I'd never had her mouth on me before. Now, as a man, I was finally able to experience the gloriousness of those lips, and in a whole new way. Because she'd never have blown me like this in high school.

This was an adult blow job.

Her warm, eager lips wrapped tightly around my cock. Then, in mere seconds, I was all the way in her mouth. She didn't bother with little kisses or lollipop licks of the head. She didn't brush her tongue along the underside of my shaft. No, she went full speed ahead like a hungry, starving creature. The head of my dick hit the back of her throat, and I cursed from the mind-blowing, blackout-inducing pleasure of her mouth.

My entire body vibrated with lust. My nerves were hot, my skin was sizzling, and my brain was lit up from this amazingly sensual woman. I roped my fingers through her hair, grasping her head tightly. Lifting an arm, she grabbed my other hand and guided it to the back of her head too.

That was hotter than hell. She wanted it hard and deep. She wanted me to hold her head, control her mouth, shove in far.

"What am I going to do with you?" I whispered, almost to myself, as I gave in to the way we both wanted it, my hands wrapping around her skull, her gorgeous dark-red hair spilling like silk through my fingers. She wanted me to keep her immobile as I fucked up into her mouth. She wanted me to be unforgiving in my desire.

The blow job was both too much, and never enough.

White-hot sparks sped through my bloodstream. Flexing my hips, I pumped into her as I held her in my grip in the back seat of a town car speeding into Manhattan. She hummed around my cock. The vibration—It made me dizzy. My skin burned. My organs heated. My brain was bathed in pleasure from the most fantastic trip of all—this kind of dirty intimacy with my Annalise. My eyes locked on her swollen lips, racing up and down on my shaft, then she was shifting on the leather seat, her hips rocking the slightest bit, like she needed to be fucked too.

I'd be taking care of her soon enough.

But first *this*. Her wicked, wonderful mouth. Her eager tongue. Her soft, talented hands that played with my balls as she sucked me without mercy and I fucked her mouth right back.

Unrelenting.

Until I started to lose control. My quads tightened, my spine ignited, and I was helpless to stop the rush. I thrust harder as my vision blurred. "*Coming,*" I grunted, barely even managing that one word of warning as my orgasm pulsed through me, fast and hot. I groaned her name, and came in her throat.

I shuddered and cursed.

As the aftershocks subsided, she released my dick from her mouth. She sat up, sighing happily as she ran a hand through her messy hair. She leaned back in the seat like she was spent.

I patted my thighs. "Get on me."

She climbed on me, straddling my thighs, her hands on my shoulders. "You know I've always wanted your tongue, Michael," she whispered against my lips.

"I know. You'll get it. You'll get it tonight. But for some reason, I like making you wait for it, getting you all worked up." I craved her taste fiercely, but I wanted to be able to spread her legs, to feel her bare skin pressed against my cheeks and give her room to wrap those sexy legs around my neck as I licked her sweet pussy.

As I worked open her zipper, I sighed in frustration. "These jeans are so damn tight." I could barely get them off. But I was up to the challenge, and I didn't really need them down far anyway. All I needed was just enough room to glide my fingers beneath the fabric of her light-blue panties.

Like that.

Oh, just like that. My fingers slid across her wetness, hot and slippery and fantastic.

"You're soaked."

"I know," she murmured as her fingers curled around my shoulders. "You turn me on. You drive me crazy."

I drew lingering, luxurious circles across her silky, hot

clit. She was near the edge already. A few strokes. A couple of circles. With some fast, fevered sweeps of my fingers, her hips were arching, swaying, rocking mindlessly against my hand until she cried out and came in less than sixty seconds.

Afterward, I kissed her face, her cheeks, her eyelids, the tip of her nose. Then her lips. That sweet, intoxicating mouth that had driven me wild. She opened her lips for me, her tongue seeking mine, and then we were kissing like we were drunk on each other, like we never wanted to stop.

But eventually we did, and I clasped my hand on her thigh. "Now listen. I have drinks with a client this evening. Then I'm taking you to dinner, and I would really appreciate it if you were wearing a skirt instead of jeans. Can you do that for me?"

She grinned coquettishly. "I can do better. I won't wear panties."

31

MICHAEL

Ten years ago

I shouldered my bag and scanned the arrivals and departures board, checking for my flight.

Delayed. For two hours.

I sighed and then shrugged. *What can you do?* I patted my carry-on. It was all I had brought on my short trip, and now I was returning to base. I had a paperback and music to listen to, so I'd find my gate, grab a seat, and pop in my earbuds as I turned the pages.

Heading for security, I reached into my pocket and took out my boarding pass and passport, and ten minutes later, I was on the other side at the small airport in Marseilles. As I strolled past a coffee shop, I focused on the tasks ahead for the week, and the work I had going on in my Army Intelligence division, doing my best to keep my mind off whether Annalise had responded to my letter yet. Maybe, just maybe, I'd find a reply from her on my return, and perhaps it would be the answer to my greatest wish—

her *yes*. It would be stained with tears of happiness, and it would smell like her.

The sensory memory ran through me of the girl I still loved, now a woman I desperately wanted to see again. I allowed myself that moment, then I blinked, refocused, and turned into the gift shop to grab a bottle of water. Soon enough, I'd have her answer. No need to linger on the unknown until it was certain.

After I paid for the drink and spun around to leave, I spotted the magazine racks. Most of the magazines were French and local, but there were also others, including *Vanity Fair*. From behind the column next to the racks, a woman stretched out her arm to grab an issue.

I only saw a sliver of her profile, the shape of her nose, but she was haltingly familiar.

My heart slammed against my ribs. It couldn't be. There was no way. And yet, *what if?* A fragile sort of hope raced in me as I took a tentative step toward her. I swallowed dryly, peering around the rack for a better look at the woman with the long red hair, flipping through a magazine.

And I knew.

The hair on my arms stood on end. Goosebumps scattered over my skin. She was my ghost, my memory, but she was all real now—creamy skin, green eyes, and red lips that I'd kissed more times than I could ever count.

Ma petite fraise.

My little strawberry. I'd called her that because of her hair, and because her lips tasted so sweet. I hadn't seen her in eight years, not since I put her on the flight back to Paris and said goodbye, my heart cratering as she flew across the ocean, far away from me.

I hadn't talked to her in five years, not since I was a sophomore in college.

But here she was, and if ever there was a sign, this was it. I'd never believed in them before, but I'd once believed in her. She was my religion. My first love.

My only love.

I took another step and then parted my lips and spoke —a dry crackling sound that became her name. "Annalise?"

She raised her chin, her eyes widening. Her expression changed from curiosity over who was asking her name to a wistful sort of wonder and surprise. She said my name like a question too, but it sounded more like amazement that we were both here. "Michael?"

I nodded. "Yeah." My chest warmed, like sunshine was spreading from the inside out. "In the flesh."

As if to test my statement, she dropped a quick kiss on each cheek, then wrapped her arms around me.

It was like falling back in time, landing softly on my favorite moment in the past. All those moments were with her. All my favorite times. She smelled like raindrops and passion, just like I'd remembered, and I inhaled her scent briefly before we separated.

I gestured to her, standing before me in the shop. "How are you?"

It was such an ordinary question, the kind you would ask an acquaintance, but after all these years, it was the only natural way to begin again. Even after I'd sent her a letter a week ago.

"My flight is late," she said, and I blinked at the sound of her voice. She no longer spoke with an accent. She sounded almost. . . American as she said more. "I was annoyed, but now I'm not. Her lips curved up in a wide, crazy smile.

Oh hell. I was grinning now too. Smiling like a fool. She still had that effect on me. My pulse thundered under my skin, hammered in my throat. She had to be saying yes. That must be her answer to my letter.

"Mine too. Late, that is. And I'm not at all annoyed now," I said, as hope rose inside me—the hope that we were flying in the same direction.

But when I asked, she said she was heading to Paris.

"Do you want to get a coffee?" she asked. "Or do you still detest coffee?"

"I would love to . . . get a tea," I said with a smile, and she laughed, and this was good. So good. Like old times. "You don't speak with an accent anymore?"

She shook her head. "Remember? I went to the American University in Paris," she said, and of course I remembered—we still wrote letters that first year of college. "It's helpful for international work to have perhaps a more neutral sound," she said, and I felt like there was more to it, but now wasn't the time to dive into the specifics of speech patterns and how they affected business.

We headed to an ordinary airport café, ordered black coffee for her and tea for me, and sat at a small iron table as travelers filtered past us, talking about their trips, their plans, what they needed before their planes took off. It was white noise, the elevator music to this surreal slice of time.

Sitting here with her.

I wanted to cup this moment in the palm of my hands, to carry it and treat it like a precious object, like it could become what I'd once longed for so terribly—a future with her.

I had so much I wanted to say. Things like *You're beautiful. I miss you. Why couldn't we find a way to stay together? Why did we have to drift apart? Did you get my letter, and will you please, please, please tell me it's the same for you?*

But when she lifted her hand to reach for her coffee, the breath escaped my chest in a cold rush.

The stone on her left hand was small, but shone brilliantly and horribly, slashing all my hopes.

My throat turned dry, and my chest pinched. I gestured toward the ring.

Annalise cast her eyes down at it, as if she just realized she was wearing it. She fiddled with it for a second then folded her hands in her lap. Out of sight. "I received your letter. I'm . . . engaged."

Two short sentences that punctured my lungs. It was something I should have prepared for. Something I always knew was a possibility. But my heart squeezed too tight, and I gasped for breath as nothing but hurt coursed through me. As quickly as it surged, though, I tried to shut it down. To remind myself that I'd been rolling the dice anyway when I sent the letter, and the dice had come up empty.

I inhaled deeply, let the air fill my lungs, then put on my best face. "Congratulations are in order, then. Who's the lucky guy?" I asked, taking the knife and digging it around in my chest a little more, carving out some of that beating organ.

"His name is Julien. We work together. He's . . . wonderful," she said, her voice faltering, as if she was embarrassed to admit that.

"I'm glad to hear it," I said, and I was, in a way, because she deserved someone wonderful. I'd just once believed that someone would be me. I'd believed it a week ago, a day ago, a few minutes ago.

I was a foolish romantic.

But really, what had I expected? That after not talking or writing for years, I would send a letter, and we'd magically run into each other then start back up again like some romantic movie?

Well, the thought had been front and center in my mind

for the last five minutes, sure. Because when you see the love of your life out of the blue in an airport, it feels like the stars are aligning.

Now, it felt like a cruel twist of fate.

I picked up my tea, took a drink, then set it down. We talked and caught up on each other's lives. We discussed our jobs and our families. She told me about Noelle, and I told her that Ryan and I were working for Army Intelligence, that Colin was finishing up college, acing every class, and that Shannon was slated to graduate soon too and was engaged to be married to her college sweetheart.

The ease with which we had always spoken about everything tugged at my heart, but it reminded me too of all that was lost.

Lost with her.

We wouldn't have this again. This was all there was, and I shouldn't feel so let down. I hadn't expected to see her. I didn't think I'd ever see her again in my whole life.

Tell that to my heart though. It was beating overtime for her, like it had been reawakened and was wishing desperately that this was a new beginning rather than another end.

Part of me wished I'd never sent that letter.

* * *

Dear Annalise,

I hope this letter finds its way to you safely, and that you are healthy and happy. It's been so long, too long, since I heard your voice or read your handwriting. I miss both with a deep ache inside me, one that never subsided. In spite of the time that has passed, I haven't stopped thinking of you, not once in all the years since we last spoke. I'm not exaggerating when I say a day hasn't gone by when I don't think of you with fondness, love, and desire, more than I even felt before, if that's possible. It seems utterly small to say I hope you are well, but I do wish that for you and your family.

I've finished college now (I graduated six months early and took off for the service) and am grateful for the scholarship from the Army that paid my way through school. Now it is my turn to give back, and I'm doing that, as it happens, in Europe. I'm working in Army Intelligence, and I have just been stationed in Germany. It's not France, of course, but it isn't an ocean away either. I am so much closer to you than I ever was before. Perhaps we can see each other again? Perhaps we can do more than see each other? Maybe even start over? I have always longed for you with everything in my heart. Je n'ai jamais cessé de t'aimer, ma petite fraise, my Annalise.

With all of my love,

Michael

32

ANNALISE

Ten years ago

I wasn't supposed to think he was handsome. I shouldn't be lingering on the memory of how he kissed, how I felt in his arms, or how damn good we had been together.

But as I sat across from Michael, my heart beat furiously, crashing against my skin, fighting valiantly to escape my plans, my future, my impending marriage. I laced my fingers together under the table, and I swore I was on the verge of crushing the bones in an effort to keep my hands in my lap, my butt in the seat, my lips to myself.

Some primal part of me was dying to lean across the table, hold his face in my hands, and kiss him like no time had passed.

Time, that cruel mistress. Time had played us for fools. I understood now why there was no forwarding address when the letter I'd sent him two years ago, after I graduated, was returned to me. He was already gone. Already serving his country.

It took everything I had to resist telling him I'd reached out a few years ago. Telling him about the letter I'd written him. The one that asked if he wanted to try again.

And when he sent me his, two damn years too late in some ways, I had to resist those words he'd written—*Je n'ai jamais cessé de t'aimer. I have never stopped loving you.*

Receiving that letter last week had been hard enough. Knowing how to respond was even tougher. Seeing him now was the most difficult part of all. Because as we talked, I slipped back into what we'd had in high school and that first year of college, and all that we'd been to each other.

All and everything.

I'd needed him for me to feel at home in America when I'd been alone, and he'd done more than that. He'd given me so much happiness. He'd needed me to survive the tragedy in his life, and I'd been there for him, even across the miles between us. I thought I would marry him. I thought I'd be with him forever. And I hated that it had been too hard to stay together when we were young and so dependent on our families.

Now we were older and could find a way, and that was what he'd been trying to say when he sent that letter.

Except . . . I toyed with the ring on my finger.

My heart climbed into my throat, lodging itself there. I wanted to cry, and I wanted *him*, and I wanted to not want him.

I was happy with Julien. I just wished seeing Michael wasn't so damn tempting.

And easy.

And good.

Soon enough, the clock ticked closer to boarding time. He walked me to my gate, and each step was a door closing, each second the final turn of the pages in a book. At my gate, we stopped, and unsaid words clung to the air like fog.

There was so much to say, and yet nothing that could be spoken. This was the last goodbye.

I swallowed my tears and choked back my emotions. "It was so good seeing you," I said, and wished my words didn't feel so inadequate.

He nodded. "And you."

I'll miss you. I'll think of you. I can't think of you. I can't miss you. You have to understand how hard this is.

He moved first, raising his arms, and I practically fell into his embrace then lingered for a few more seconds, breathing in his scent one last time before I pulled away.

The past was not my future. I couldn't look back.

No matter how much I wanted to in that moment.

33

MICHAEL

The jeans were gone. Mercifully.

In their place she wore a short green dress that hugged her fantastic body, showing off her breasts, her small waist, and those long, endless legs.

At the table in the far corner of a restaurant that Brent's brother had recommended, I couldn't take my eyes off the woman. Ask me a month ago if I'd be having sushi dinner in the Village, listening to Annalise tell stories about her sister, and I'd have said no way. She'd been just a mirage, a sepia-tinted photograph of days gone by. Now, she was eating a salmon roll, and I was having the best time. We weren't staying at the same hotel, so I'd picked her up at hers, the breath knocked clear out of my lungs when she'd answered the door.

In that dress.

And heels.

And, very likely, no panties.

But as much as I wanted her right then and there, I craved the anticipation too. I was a patient man, and I wanted to take her out to dinner. To savor every moment, from picking her up to walking to the restaurant to enjoying the meal. It was so simple, but this was what I'd dreamed of having with her. A freedom that wasn't possible when we were kids, and now it was all ours. No curfews, no rules, no regulations. A real date with this woman, and as the evening unfurled, a new sensation spread through me, a freedom from all my cares I hadn't felt in years. An case.

"One time when I was helping out at Noelle's bakery, an American woman came to the counter, and she tried so hard to speak in French," Annalise said with a smile, continuing her tales of working with her sister from time to time.

"I bet you hate when they do that."

She clasped her hand to her chest. "Me? No. Why would you say that?"

"Doesn't it make the French people crazy when we try to speak French?"

"No," she said, shaking her head. Then a guilty little grin appeared on her face. "Only if it's very bad French."

I laughed as I picked up a yellowtail slice and swirled it in soy sauce. "Was her French very bad? Tell the truth."

She held up her thumb and index finger. "Only a little. It wasn't good, but she tried, so she got credit for that. She said she wanted *un yaourt abricot*, but she pronounced *yaourt* like *tarte*."

"In her defense, 'yogurt' is one of the hardest French words to say."

She gave me a curious look. "You know *yaourt* is 'yogurt'?"

"You taught me some French words," I said, then popped the sushi in my mouth.

"Did I teach you *yaourt*?"

I nodded as I finished chewing. "Isn't 'yogurt' an important word to know?"

She set down her chopsticks, crossed her arms, and fixed me with a stare. "I taught you words like 'kiss' and 'come' and 'fuck.' I did not teach you 'yogurt.'"

"Must have picked it up on my own, then, when I was in France. I spent a few weekends there."

Something dark passed through her eyes. "I remember," she said, sadness coloring her tone. She reached for my hand. "I remember seeing you at the airport."

I straightened. "You do?"

"Of course. How could I ever forget?"

I shrugged, wincing. The memory still hurt. I hadn't forgotten a single detail.

"I remember everything about it," she said softly but confidently. Her bright green eyes held me captive, never looking away. "I remember the way your hair was shorter, how you looked at me in the gift shop, and the hurt in your eyes when you saw my ring. You have to know I never wanted to hurt you."

"I know," I choked out, and the memory of that day slid in front of me, in all its hope and heartbreak.

"I hated feeling like I broke your heart, but I had no idea you were going to send me that letter," she said, and her voice sounded like she was shattering now too.

"Of course you didn't know."

"I opened it with nervous fingers. Part of me hoped it would say all that it *did* say, but I was so conflicted for wanting that. I loved my husband, Michael. I want you to know that." She inhaled deeply, as if she needed the air to fuel her. "But I thought about you every day in college. I missed you every day. Getting over you was nearly impossible." She took a beat, like she was preparing to say something hard. "I wrote you a letter when I graduated."

I flinched, completely unprepared for her to say that. "You did?"

Sadness flickered across her lovely eyes. "I did."

"What did it say?" I asked, desperation in my tone.

"That I'd finished. That I was free. That I wanted to see you again."

Like a blow to the gut, I could barely breathe for several seconds, as the realization sank in, hard and cruel. I'd missed her letter. We were star-crossed lovers. "Fate had a field day with us, it seems," I said, humorless. "I never received it."

"I know," she said, resigned. "No forwarding address. You were already in the Army, I presumed."

"I was," I said, and the corollary to that was I wouldn't have been able to see her anyway. The United States, rightfully so, owned me then.

"And that's when I *had* to move on, Michael," she continued. "That's when it was time to march fully forward. And then two years later—two years too late—you blasted back into my life with that letter that was a thing of beauty, and I was unprepared for how much your words would stir up my feelings again."

She ran her fingers across my palm. Her touch was comforting and maddening. Because it felt right, and like the only touch I'd ever want. "I just want you to know it wasn't easy to get over you the first time, and it was gut-wrenching to let you walk away in Marseilles."

"Why are you telling me this now, Annalise?" I asked, clasping her hand tighter, needing her answer.

"Because I told you that you're the first man I've been with since my husband died, but you're also the only man I've even thought about. I let go of you years ago because I had to, and then when I was finally able to think about this again," she said, gesturing from me to her, "you were the only one who I could even imagine sharing this with."

The only one.

A rush of heat flooded me at those three words. I wanted to be the only one for her, even if I was only able to have her for a short moment in time. I would take what I could get, and I would savor it. She was here right now, with me and no one else.

"You have no idea how glad I am that I'm the one you thought of, Annalise," I whispered.

A smile tugged at her lips.

Then, I went for it. Just let it all out. A hope, a wish, a what-if question. "Do you ever wonder what would have happened that day if you weren't engaged? If you'd never have met him?"

"No. I don't think about it. I don't have to wonder," she said, her tone steady and certain as she looked straight at me, the rest of the restaurant fading into a blur. "Because I know what would have happened."

My hands shook and my heart stuttered as I rasped out, "What would have happened?"

She leaned in closer, placing a hand on my cheek. "I'd have stolen you. Taken you away from the Army. Brought you home with me to Paris. Kept you all for myself all these years and made up for lost time," she said, and my heart beat furiously, slamming against my chest, loving her words.

"Stop saying those things," I whispered, shaking my head.

"What things?"

"Things that make this harder for me."

"Why is it hard for you?"

I drew a breath. "Because you say things like that and it

makes me want to steal you away. Maybe this is my only chance."

"What if it is?"

That was the question, wasn't it? What if this night, this trip, these hours were all we had? I didn't know if I could risk putting any more of my heart on the line for her. One thing was certain—my original notion that one touch and she'd be out of my system was well and truly gone. "Then we make the most of it."

She nodded. "We are making the most of it. Right now."

Before I tumbled into the land of no return with her, before I gave her every part of my heart and soul, I cleared my throat. "Are you ever going to finish the story about the yogurt?"

She laughed, her head leaning back, her long elegant neck exposed. "She couldn't pronounce *yaourt,* so it came out like *tarte,* and we gave her an apricot tarte. She seemed quite happy about that." She picked up her chopsticks and grabbed a piece of sushi.

I laughed softly. "A tarte sounds better than yogurt."

"My sister's bakery makes the best apricot tartes. Come to Paris sometime and find out."

I arched an eyebrow. "Come to Paris for a tarte?"

She jutted up a shoulder. "Or more."

"Like what? What else should I have with the tarte?"

She set down her chopsticks, the sushi untouched, then tilted her head and murmured, "*Me.* You should have me."

My blood heated, and my head swam with dirty thoughts. This meal seemed wholly unnecessary. I had no more interest in fish and rice. I could subsist on her, on this talking, these confessions, and these touches that promised what was to come.

I was ready to call for the check, but the waitress was

nowhere to be seen. I glanced around, then tossed my napkin on the table, stood up, and reached for her hand.

She rose, not even asking a single question. I led her past a table, around the corner, and down the hallway. I knocked on the door of one of the restrooms. No one answered, so I turned the knob, pulled her inside, and locked the door.

"*Michael,*" she said, all sexy and low.

"Yes?"

"What are you going to do?"

I lifted her up and set her on the sink cabinet. "Have my dessert now. I want you so much. I've wanted you for so damn long, and now you're here with me, and everything that comes out of your mouth makes me crave you even more." My voice was rough and hungry as I ran my fingertip across her bottom lip.

Her breath rushed over me. "It does?"

"So much. So unbelievably much." I dragged my finger down her neck. In its wake, goosebumps rose on her skin as I traveled along her throat, down her chest, between her breasts. I reached her waist and squeezed her hip. Touching her was such a privilege, such a complete and utter gift. "Lift your dress. Let me see you."

Trembling, she reached for the hem and lifted it, and all the air rushed from my lungs as I stared, just fucking stared like a starving man at her beautiful, wet pink pussy.

"So fucking pretty." I ran a finger through that slippery wetness. "I've wanted to taste you forever. I've wanted to have your sweetness on my mouth. Will you give it to me?"

"Please take it," she said on a pant, arching her back, raising her hips.

I kneeled, pressed my hands on her thighs, and took my first taste. I groaned the second I touched her. She was heaven on my tongue.

She gasped and clutched my head, her fingers threading through my hair. I was intoxicated—utterly buzzed on her. My mind turned hazy with pleasure and possibility, with the sheer magnitude of this sensual dream becoming my visceral reality at last. She was better than all my fantasies. She was real and wet and hot, and she wanted me as much as I wanted her.

My bones hummed, and my mind ignited as I flicked my tongue against the soft rise of her clit. She moaned, a long, delicious sound that seemed to vibrate through her whole body. I kissed her pussy deeply and then drew her swollen clit into my mouth, sucking it between my lips. She bucked against me, seeking more, and I gave it to her.

I gave her everything, and I was sure I'd never want this with anyone but her.

Ever.

34

ANNALISE

His lips. His tongue. His hands gripping my thighs, holding me tight.

At once it was all too much and not enough. I felt like I was ready to fly to the moon, to launch into orbit, and I still wanted to ride higher, go farther. Everything was silvery as my body dissolved into his touch. He caressed me with his masterful tongue then sucked hard on my clit. In some kind of delicious harmony, I moved with him, rocking into him, hips shifting, keeping a sensual pace with him as he ate me out on the edge of the sink in the restroom.

The lights were low, a soft blue glimmer against the black tiles on the wall, and somehow the glow fit. This was a decadently lit space for a deliciously dirty deed—sex in a restaurant bathroom. I didn't care where we were. I hadn't thought I would survive a minute longer without some kind of contact, and bless this man, he *knew*. He knew precisely how to meet my needs and exactly how to lick, kiss, suck, and drive me wild. I felt untamed with him, on the edge of control, ready to let it all go. My hands curled tighter around his head, my fingers laced through his hair. I looked down, and the sight of his face between my legs, devouring me, made me wetter, hotter.

I moaned his name, loved the way it felt on my tongue, the shape it took on my lips. Loved how he licked faster and hungrier each time I said it. We were like a feedback loop. His name fell from my mouth, and he consumed me. Like he was drinking me up. Like I was the only one he'd ever wanted.

I felt that way right now. Nothing could compare.

Pleasure climbed up my legs like vines, spreading across my whole body, filling me with a desire so deep and so far, I felt like it would never end. This feeling—this mad, crazy bliss—was everything. Gripping his head, I moved with him, moaning and sighing with every stroke of his tongue, every kiss of his lips, and soon I melted into him, boneless and mindless with pleasure. I was losing touch with the world around me as my pulse beat rapidly across every inch of my skin, as heat flared in my chest, and my face flushed as I chased my climax. There it was, rising up, swelling, and my nerves blazed. My hold on reality shattered as I thrust into his face, coming and coming and coming.

I squeezed my eyes and sealed my lips, trying desperately to quiet the little noises that escaped. And I shook. My body just fucking shook from the orgasm that thundered through me, blowing my mind, blasting my once-cold world into nothing but scorching heat and lust.

All I wanted was more of him. All of him. I wanted to feel everything with him. Everything I'd denied myself, and everything good in the world.

As my release ebbed, Michael rose, cupped my cheeks, and whispered, "You taste divine. *Ma petite fraise.*"

"Take me back to your room," I whispered, revealing the depth of my desire for him. "Spend the night making love to me. I need you so much."

35

MICHAEL

The door fell closed with a loud creak. In seconds, my hands were on her face, her breasts, her waist. Everywhere.

I pressed her to the wall of the foyer, trapping her with my body, touching her all over, as if I could memorize the feel of her curves.

As I lifted her arms over her head, pinning her wrists, I couldn't help but wonder if this was an all too vivid dream. Everything with her felt so insanely good it bordered on unreal.

How many times had I fantasized about this? How many nights had I taken her to bed in my mind? She was a jewel, brilliant and beautiful, her eyes sparkling. Her body was lush and warm, and her hungry lips hunted for my mouth. Her breath, her pants, her noises played in my ears like a sultry song.

My lips were fused to hers; her body was sealed tight to mine.

I kissed her like the world was ending, but it was only the beginning of something entirely new between us. I couldn't get close enough to her, and I could barely accept that she—my what-if girl, though she was all woman—was moaning softly in my mouth, pressing her breasts to my chest.

With my hand caging hers above her head, I pushed against her, craving this frenzied foreplay of clothed bodies, of clawing at each other to get close. I wanted her with a desire that couldn't be measured. It felt like the kind of want that could scale mountains, invade countries, and send men and women to the moon. I broke the kiss, breathless, and held her face in my hand, getting lost in her emerald eyes.

"I've dreamed about this for so long. I can't believe it's real," I said, fighting so hard to hold in all the other feelings. If she knew how much and how deeply the need to be with her had defined me, had driven me to learn new ways of living, I might scare her away.

My muscles tensed from the restraint inside me as I reined in all the words I wanted to say. It was too soon, too much to share.

"But I'm real, Michael," she said, breaking free of my grip to place her hands on my face. "Feel me. Touch me. I'm here."

I closed my eyes, and my skin turned electric from the tender possession in her touch. No one had ever made me feel this way. All the other women were right. They had been completely right in their assessment when they'd said to me, *You're in love with someone else.*

I was.

Irrevocably.

This was my fate in life, to fall in love with the same woman over and over.

A rush of air escaped my lungs with the sharp, clear realization. I was in love with Annalise once more. I'd been madly in love with her before, and now it was happening all over again as I fell for the woman she had become—for her fragile but strong heart, her open mind, her willingness to try, her compassion, and her understanding of me.

I was dying to tell her, to imprint on her flesh, *I'm in love with you.*

Instead, when I opened my eyes, I chose my words carefully. "All I want is to touch you. To feel how real you are." I tugged off her dress, drinking in the sight of her in a black bra and nothing else.

A groan rumbled up my chest, then I dropped my face to her collarbone and slid my hand between her legs, the temperature in me soaring as I touched her silky heat. Lightly I stroked, teasing her, drawing out gasps and moans, sexy little sighs and sweet, heady murmurs. I pushed the cup of her bra down over one breast, freeing a nipple and sucking it deep, then nipping her.

With each bite across her flesh, I imagined tattooing her with words. The words I wouldn't give voice to, I left as marks. A kiss on her throat. A long suck on the swell of her breast. A pinch of my teeth on her neck. Each one said, *I'm so in love with you.*

"Michael?"

My name was a question. I looked up, dazed from touching her. She spread her hands across my chest, her fingers toying with the buttons on my shirt. "I don't want to use a condom. I want to feel you completely. I'm on the pill, and I'm safe," she said, meeting my eyes. Hers shone with desire.

My mind and body latched onto the image of sliding into her, no barriers.

I swallowed thickly, nodding. "I'm safe. I haven't been with anyone in a year."

Her eyes went wide. "You haven't?"

"That surprises you?"

As she worked open the buttons on my shirt, she said, "You're so handsome, I can't imagine you would be alone."

"I'm not a player, Annalise," I said roughly, as her long fingers undressed me.

"No, you're not a player. You've never been one. You always had your eyes on the woman you were with, and only her." She said it generally, as if the statement applied to my approach to relationships, and it did. If she only knew how precisely that fit her.

"Look at you," she murmured as she opened my shirt. Dipping her face to my chest, she planted kisses on my pecs, biting a nipple. I hissed in a breath. "You are so strong," she said, dragging her fingernails across my muscles as she pushed off my shirt.

"You're going to ruin me with all your compliments."

"Your body," she continued, as her eyes roamed over my chest and arms. "I love it. I love looking at you. I love touching you."

And I loved being touched by her. More than anything in the world. Especially when her hands went *there*, to my belt, unbuckling it then unzipping my jeans. I helped push them down then off my feet, along with my shoes.

I glanced at her, then back at myself. "Feels like we've been here before. I'm kind of thinking we want to get to the next level of naked."

She laughed. "You mean the completely naked level?"

"Yes, that one," I said, and led her to the bed. I sat on the edge of the mattress and looped my hands behind her back, unhooking her bra, letting it fall to the floor. My hands shot out and cupped her breasts, pinching the nipples as she arched into me. I raised my face and stared up at her, still in awe that she wasn't a mirage.

"You're here," I said in disbelief.

"I'm here," she echoed.

Naked before me, totally revealed, and the most beautiful thing I'd ever seen. I wanted to kiss every inch of her body, to catalog each feature, from the tiny little appendix scar on her belly, to the small spray of freckles on her chest, to the strength in her legs.

"I . . . This isn't fair. Please take your clothes off."

I stood and shoved down my boxers. Her eyes blazed darkly as she stared at my cock, licking her lips. *Fuck.* I wanted to live in this moment, to return to it again and again—her unabashed lust. Her deep desire. Her stare made me hotter, made me burn. I reached down and stroked my cock, letting her watch and loving her reaction.

"Are you thinking of me?" she asked naughtily. "When you do that?"

"Now. And always."

She trembled and then joined in, wrapping her hand over mine, stroking along with me. "I think of you so much. I'm so worked up being near you. So wound up. You drive me crazy with want."

I gripped her shoulders, guided her to the bed, and regarded her naked frame as she lay back on the sheets, resting on her elbows. "So beautiful. All I want is to make you feel good."

"You already do," she said, then raised her knees and let them fall open.

I was helpless to resist. I bent down and buried my face between her thighs once more, kissing and licking her sweetness, rubbing my stubble all over her slick, wet heat. She moaned and rocked her hips into me, faster, harder, then just wilder. Her hips shot up as I thrust my fingers inside her and sucked her sweet clit between my lips until she came, flooding my tongue, her pleasure all over my face.

Seconds later I crawled up her, wedged myself between

her legs, and dragged the head of my cock through her heat.

She gasped, her head falling back against the pillow, her lips parted.

"So greedy," I said as I toyed with her. This was what I'd craved for so long. The chance to be with her. The thrill of fucking the woman I'd never stopped loving.

"Please don't tease me. I need you. I need you now," she said, so desperate, so sexy, so beautiful.

"*Je te veux tellement,*" I said, repeating the phrase she'd shared on the plane.

She trembled, whispering desperately, "Say it again."

"*Je te veux tellement,*" I said roughly.

"You're even sexier when you speak my language."

"I'm only speaking the truth. I want you so much. So fucking much."

"Have me. Take me."

I pushed inside her in one hot, tight thrust.

Then the earth stopped spinning. The stars melted away from the sky. Gravity had no hold on me, because I was falling, falling, falling into her.

After all these years. After all this time. It was exquisite and so unbelievably good. She gasped, her breath spilling out as she made the first move, her hips rising up, her legs wrapping around me.

"Closer. Come closer," she whispered, and I lowered myself, our chests nearly touching as I braced on my elbows, flexing forward in slow, steady thrusts, taking my time, savoring the feel of her sweet, bare pussy.

Our heated bodies moved together. I was lit up everywhere, my entire being electrified as I pushed in and out, then deeper, hitting her right where she went wild, her back bowing off the bed, her mouth falling open with a beautiful groan that became my name.

"Say it," I growled. "Say it now."

"*Baise-moi plus fort.*"

God, it was music from her. It was heady and thrilling to hear her say those words.

"I knew you'd sound crazy for me when you said it like this," I groaned, then buried my face in her neck, kissing, biting, marking.

"I am. I'm crazy for you," she said, and then it was her turn to nip. She went for my collarbone, and I nearly exploded. I loved her roughness, and she knew it because seconds later her hands were on my shoulders, then she dragged her nails down my back, digging into my flesh.

"Let me feel you all over me," I said as I fucked her faster, harder.

She ran her nails down to my ass, curling her hands around me. I pushed deeper, the start of my orgasm barreling through my body. She arched up, grabbing my head, crushing my mouth in a crazed, fierce kiss, full of teeth and tongue and madness. Then she let go, my name tumbling from her lips in a raptured cry as she shattered beneath me, arms and legs grabbing, twisting, tugging me even closer, like she'd never get enough.

Her need for me set me off, igniting a mind-blowing orgasm that blurred my vision and torched my veins as I followed her there, into perfect fucking bliss.

Like heaven on earth.

I collapsed on her, a sweaty, tangled mess of limbs and lips and desire, sated at last.

She ran her hands through my hair and sighed softly against me. It was unequivocally the best night of my life, but I also winced inside with the awareness of how much harder it would be to say goodbye now that I'd experienced all of her.

Until she said the next words.

36

ANNALISE

Wow.

Just wow.

That was out of this world.

I lay on the bed in a sea of rumpled sheets, Michael's strong arms wrapped around my sweat-slicked body, my heart beating like a hummingbird, and I blinked open my eyes.

All my senses were heightened, and I felt new, like I was experiencing being alive again after a deep, dreamless sleep.

Breathe in, breathe out.

Each inhalation sent air rushing through my blood, waking me up, nudging me, reminding me that this was life, this was sex, and this was good.

It had been so much more than good.

I'd seen stars, tasted heaven, breathed rarefied air. My skin tingled all over, and my blood pulsed hot and fast from my climax. I'd never come like that before. I felt it humming in my bones. Skimming across my skin.

And hammering in my heart, insisting on being heard. I

wanted more of him. So much that the thought of not having him again already hurt—like a phantom pain, a promise of how it would feel if I let him go. The prospect of flying home in a few days and leaving this bliss behind made my chest ache, like it had been carved out once more.

I was tired of hollowness. Tired of hurting. I wanted more of the good. I turned in his arms, facing him. "Michael . . ." My voice sounded hoarse to my own ears— all that moaning his name had taken a toll. "I'm going to need so much more of that from you."

My gaze locked on his, watching the slow spread of his smile, the way it stretched across his whole face, how his blue eyes seemed to flicker with happiness.

He kissed my cheek, whispering soft and sexy, "With me, you can have everything."

The sentiment made me shudder, and yet I wasn't talking about more sex, per se. Or even more sex in the next few days. I pressed a hand to his naked chest, needing to make sure he understood *exactly*. "What I mean is . . ." I stopped to let a breath fill my lungs, fueling my admission. "I want to see you again. I don't want this—whatever it is— to end when we leave New York."

His features froze. His lips were parted, his jaw was set, and his eyes were vulnerable. He didn't move, as if he was slowly absorbing my request. Soon enough, though, he found words. His question came out as a scratch, his voice gravelly. "You do?"

I nodded vigorously. "I do. Maybe that is crazy. Do you think it's crazy?"

He shook his head. "*No!*" flew off his tongue.

The speed of his response emboldened me. That, combined with the endorphins still rushing through my system, drove me on. "I just . . ." I began, running my fingers through the fine hairs on his chest. "I just would be so sad to leave New York and not see you again. And I don't have a plan, or an agenda, or anything beyond the here and now. All I know is I want to see more of you. Which probably sounds . . ." My voice trailed away, lost in the noises of late-night New York floating through the window.

"Sounds what?" he asked, prompting me.

"You probably think it sounds too hard, since I'm in Paris and you're in Las Vegas, and that's how it was before," I said, worried that we were facing the same obstacles, those very ones that had splintered us years before.

That sexy smile returned, tugging at his lips as he shook his head. "No. It's not crazy at all. We're not the same as we were before. The distance—it's not as daunting. We have the means to deal with it."

I nodded. "Yes, we do. And all I know is that I don't want this to end."

He pulled me closer, held me tighter. "That's enough for me to fly across an ocean for you."

He dusted my lips with his—a soft, sweet kiss that was both gentle and thrilling at once. On his lips, I swore I could taste his happiness, and I kissed him again, taking some of it for myself.

We chatted in bed, talking about friends and family, work and music, photographs and security. I wanted to savor these moments with Michael. This time with him was the sweetest thing I'd experienced in a long time, and I wanted to revel in it.

Soon enough, our lips found each other again, and we kissed, slow and lazy, the kind of kiss that made me wetter and him harder, that led to fingers slipped between legs and dirty words when he said, "Get on your hands and knees. I want to take you that way."

I didn't need to be asked twice. I wanted to be fucked

that way by him, with my palms flat against the navy-blue comforter, my knees sinking down, and my ass in the air. Michael ran a hand down my back, inch by torturously slow inch, each touch making me wriggle and writhe.

"Mmm," he murmured, his big palm tracing my flesh, pushing my spine low, forcing me to raise my ass higher. "Look at you. Look at my Annalise. So fucking wet. So fucking hot. So needy for me."

Like a sparkler igniting, those dirty words set off a fresh wave of desire within me. Heat pooled between my legs as I lowered myself to my elbows, my breath coming fast. "I do need you. I need you in me, Michael."

He dragged his fingers through my sex, and I moaned, closing my eyes, giving in to the fevered rush in my body, surrendering to my desire to be fucked.

Sheets rustled behind me as he moved, straightened up on his knees, and positioned himself. When he rubbed the head of his cock against me, a wild cry ripped from my throat. "Fuck me. Hard. Take me. I'm yours."

And he took, fucking me as I'd never experienced before—rough and beautifully cruel, fingers digging into my flesh, hands gripping my breasts and pinching my nipples, teeth nipping my back and shoulders. Deeply buried inside me, he fucked me savagely. I moved with him, moaned with him, slammed my pelvis back on his cock, letting him know that the more he filled me, the hungrier I was. Sliding a hand up my backbone, he grabbed my hair, wrapping it around his fist. I gasped, and the noise turned into a long, animalistic cry as he yanked.

"Rougher. Harder," I bit out.

I wanted to be bruised, to feel used, to be fucked so hard I felt him for days. Michael Sloan was more than willing to give me all of himself, to plunder my body with his cock, to take me mercilessly until my hands grappled at the sheets, clutching and twisting as pleasure spiked then slammed into me.

A shattering.

No warning.

Just a rapturous crash as my climax rattled my body, jarring my bones. It shocked me, the power of this kind of orgasm. With a final thrust, growling my name in my ear, he came. I'd never felt anyone go so deep inside me. Never felt so in tune with my body.

But it was more than that. I'd never felt this kind of physical connection. Raw and hungry.

And boundless too.

That may have been what surprised me the most—the endlessness of this pleasure. I supposed that was how any sort of new passion felt. But there, in the dark of the night, in the middle of a city of millions, tucked away in a hotel room, I believed in its promise.

I believed in fate too.

In second chances.

As he spooned me, brushing soft kisses against the back of my neck, right there, right then seemed precisely why I'd landed a job in Vegas, and why I'd said yes to the New York gig. As if the cruel mistress of circumstances who had toyed with us and yanked us apart when we were younger was working in our favor now.

Bringing us back together in a whole new way.

After that rough, punishing sex that bruised my hips and made me sore everywhere, I was sure I'd fall asleep sated. I did. For a bit.

But sometime in the middle of the night, I woke. Not with a start, but with a slow, unhurried shift of my hips. His erection grazed my backside, and I wiggled my rear against him.

Without speaking, Michael slid his hand along the back of my thigh and shifted my knee to make room.

"Yes. Please. You've made me insatiable."

"Good, I like you that way. Hungry for me," he said against my neck as he eased inside me. He made it a lazy and luxurious coming together, as the warm pleasure in me hummed, tension coiling, and I climbed to the edge once again. I cried out his name, and then out of nowhere, a sob escaped my lips, mingling with my noises, obscuring the sound.

A tear slid down my cheek.

I wiped it away quickly. Judging from the way he grunted and shoved deep in me, he didn't notice. I was overcome as a storm of emotions swelled, gripping my chest, squeezing my heart like an invisible hand.

My heart was fracturing at the same time as it was stitched back together. Sex with Michael was both wondrous and bittersweet.

And I understood precisely why I felt so fucking good, and so fucking confused at the same time.

"It's so good with you, Annalise," he said a minute later.

"I know. It is. It's so good."

It was unlike anything I'd ever felt. It was better. It was the best.

That was the problem.

37

ANNALISE

The beautiful blonde, who wore an emerald-green satin push-up bra and matching lace panties, stretched on her belly on the white duvet—heels in the air, lips red and pouty.

Casey Sullivan had one of the best smiles I had ever photographed. The woman also knew how to give "come fuck me" eyes to the camera. She was thinking of her husband, Nate, so she said it was easy to gaze at the lens that way—like she loved him and wanted him at the same damn time. We were finishing up the last series of shots at the boudoir studio space.

Afterward, I showed her some of the pictures on the back of the camera.

Casey shrugged into a robe and peered at the images, and she squealed in delight as we flipped through the frames. "These are amazing," she said, then ran her hand over the outline of her belly. "You can't tell I had a baby six months ago."

I shook my head. "You look radiant and beautiful. The camera loves you because you're so happy and in love."

Casey met my eyes. "You can see all that from how I look at the camera?"

"Of course. It's in your eyes. Everything is."

Casey narrowed hers and studied me. "Hmm. What's in yours, then?" she asked playfully.

A red flush crept across my cheeks.

Sex, hot sex, and more sex. Dinners, days, sleepless nights. Idle chats, deep conversations, sweet nothings, and so much coming together. The last two days and nights in Manhattan had passed in a blissful blur. I'd canceled my hotel room and stayed with Michael. Yesterday, I'd finished my shoot for Veronica's while Michael had worked with clients, and last night we'd gone to dinner and a club. And there had been hours when we hadn't left the room at all. New York with Michael was a great escape from the past and the present.

The only trouble was it almost seemed too good to be true. Too deep, too quick, too intense. I couldn't believe we were here after all this time, and I couldn't help the part of myself that was scared, after all I'd been through, all *we'd* been through, to feel so much so fast.

"You're happy too." The declaration came from Casey, and my heart skittered.

"Of course I'm happy," I said in my best cheery tone, keeping things businesslike. "I love what I do."

"But I can see a sadness in your eyes too. Is something holding you back from truly being happy?" Casey pressed.

I swallowed and fiddled with my camera. The woman was too observant—that was supposed to be my job. I didn't answer.

"If something holds you back from your happiness, you should try to move through it," Casey said softly.

I looked up, my client's gentle words threading into me. "Spoken from experience?"

"Sort of. I had to get over my fear that my husband and I would risk our friendship if we became more."

"And you didn't, clearly."

"We didn't, but we had to face it and take a leap of faith. I think whatever is making you sad, you should face it," she said wisely.

On the cab ride back to the hotel, I lingered on her advice. Rubbing my thumb against the outline of the lens in my camera bag, I realized Casey was right. I had to face this thing, this nagging voice, this knot in my stomach that stood in the way.

My fear of what closeness might lead to. How hard that made it to live in the moment.

That night I dressed in jeans, heels, and a soft black sweater, and perched on the edge of the bed before we headed out for dinner. I waited for Michael to emerge from the shower, and when he did, my heart thundered. His hair was damp and a white towel hung on his hips, revealing his flat, toned stomach and the trail of hair that led to my favorite place. God, I wanted him so badly, in ways that went beyond the physical.

"I'm scared," I blurted out, ripping off the Band-Aid.

He sat next to me on the bed, gazing at me intently. "About what?"

This was the hard part. The deep, dark truth. "Because it's so good with you."

His lips twitched and he looked down, then back up at me, schooling his expression. "The sex, you mean?"

I nodded. "That. Yes. It's amazing. It's better than anything I've ever had." His grin lit up the room, as I continued, "But that's only the start. It's not just the sex, Michael. It's how we are. You and me. Our connection. And I want to embrace every second, but sometimes . . ."

"You worry," he whispered, finishing the thought.

"I do. Sometimes it's hard to jump in because I think of all the things that could happen . . ." I slowed my words to run my fingers along the back of his neck and into the soft strands of his damp hair.

"I'm right there with you. We just have to let ourselves feel, and take it one day at a time. That's what I've learned, Annalise," he said, leaning his head back against my hand and closing his eyes, almost as if he was demonstrating how to feel again.

How had he gotten to be so wise? Where was the carefree, easy guy I fell for decades ago? But of course, I knew the answer. He'd had to let go of who he was. He'd had to walk through all his own grief too.

As my fingers toyed with his hair, I asked, "You learned that because of your father?"

"Yes. Once I stopped missing him so much and being so angry about everything that happened, I chose to live in the moment and try to appreciate every day. I learned to just have a good time hanging out with family. Enjoy work. A good hard run. That's the only way through everything. Keep on living—keep on feeling."

"I want to feel. With you," I told him honestly. I'd survived the grief, and now it was time to live.

Go all in.

So when I went to dinner with him that night, I chose to relish every ounce of the happiness, to lose myself in the joy of being with this man I cared for so deeply. When we returned to his room for our last night together, I knew there was one more thing to do. One more way to give my whole heart to moving on and having faith.

"Take my picture," I said. His brows raised in question as I handed him my camera. "I'm turning the tables, like you said. I'm always the one behind the camera. I want to be the subject, and I want you to photograph me, getting naked for you. That's what I want to feel tonight—what it's like to give myself to you."

His eyes blazed darkly, shining with desire and something else—something I'd wanted desperately when we were younger. Something that scared the hell out of me now. But maybe if I was on the other side of the camera, I could handle everything I saw in him, and let him see the parts of me no one else was privy to.

38

MICHAEL

I wasn't a photographer, but I didn't need to be to know she was a breathtaking subject. Gorgeous, real, and heart-breaking. Written in her eyes was a mix of emotions—trepidation, courage, excitement, determination . . . I tried to capture them all as she tugged her black sweater over her head, then unbuttoned her jeans.

She didn't pose or mug for the camera. She simply *did*, and I simply shot.

She reached for the zipper of her jeans and worked it open.

"Mmm. It's getting harder to concentrate," I murmured as I snapped a shot of her undressing.

She laughed, and I caught that on film too. "*Harder*. Haha," she said with a flirty smile. That was captured for posterity also—her playful side shining through. I caught every moment of her getting ready for me.

Her eyes met the lens, as if she were able to peer into it to see me. Even though I was the one with the camera, somehow I felt studied at the same damn time. She was so *knowing*, observant down to her marrow, even when she was the one being photographed. Those green irises held me captive as she gazed at me, taking her time undressing, pushing the denim of her jeans down one hip, then the other, giving me a strip show.

She wiggled her eyebrows. Licked her lips.

My chest rumbled as my dick hardened. "That's what I was talking about earlier. You enjoying yourself."

"I am."

"I want you to enjoy yourself with me."

"I do." She let her jeans fall to the floor. She stood in her black bra and panties, and I snapped an image of that too, as my skin grew hotter and desire flashed inside me.

"You like it when I take your picture?"

She nodded.

"Then lie back on the bed. Hair on the pillow. That's one of my favorite looks of yours. All those crazy red strands spilling across the white pillowcase."

"Tell me why you like that," she said, scooting back on the bed, assuming the pose.

"Because you're vulnerable and raw. Because you look real and sexy, and you look like you want me."

She swallowed, and I snapped quickly, cataloging her reactions. "I do want you."

"Let yourself want me," I said quietly, capturing more as she reached back to unhook her bra, her breasts spilling free.

"Fuck," I muttered, my erection straining against my jeans. "I'm so fucking turned on. Can't concentrate on the picture."

"Don't concentrate. Just shoot," she said, as she tucked her thumbs into her underwear, and I continued snapping shots, my length thickening as a heavy need thrummed in me. The need to have her. To take her.

She pushed down her panties, revealing the soft auburn

landing strip. My mouth watered. I wanted to rub my face against it, to feel her slickness on my jaw. To taste her heat on my tongue. I groaned but somehow managed to click again and again, as she skimmed off her panties and lay naked on the hotel bed.

"Open your legs," I instructed.

She raised her knees and let them fall open.

Gripping the camera harder, I swallowed thickly. "Don't let anyone else ever take your picture like this," I said, as possessiveness rushed through me. I hated the thought of anyone ever seeing these photos, let alone seeing her naked. Thank God the pictures were on *her* camera, which meant they'd be safe where they belonged.

"Never," she said in a heated whisper. "No one ever has," she added. "This is only for you."

I inhaled sharply, her meaning registering. She was giving me something her husband had never had. Something that was a first.

I couldn't take it anymore.

In a flash, I set the camera on the bureau and unbuttoned my shirt.

With her index finger, she beckoned me. I recorded that image in my mind—her calling me to her side. Me heeding her wish. I'd play those few seconds over and over again. "Come to me," she said. "Join me. Fuck me like you wanted to when you were taking the pictures."

I shoved off my jeans. "On your stomach, then," I said, and didn't take my eyes off her as she flipped to her belly. With her cheek pressed against the pillow, she watched me. Watched me as I stripped off my boxers and as I reached to stroke my cock, hissing in a breath because it felt so fucking good to touch myself as she stared, her eyes flaming with lust. But something else too. Longing, desire, and also a new kind of freedom. Like she was finally letting herself feel everything.

She lifted her rear, inviting me home.

"*You*," I gritted out as I climbed on the bed and brought my dick to her ass, rubbing it against the soft flesh of her rear. She moaned, rising up into me as my hard length slid between her cheeks, like a filthy tease of what I wanted to do to her someday. She pushed back, and I filed that reaction away in the dirty vault to bring out again when we were both ready. For now, I moved lower, gliding the head of my dick against her heat. She was slick and wet and so damn ready for me.

"I want you so much. I love wanting you. It feels so good," she said, her eyes looking back at me, and I fell even harder for her as she let herself open up to me and to pleasure and to this chance to feel again, to live again, and hell, I hoped maybe, just maybe, to love again. I covered her with my body, and she let out the sexiest purr, then the most intoxicating moan as I pushed the head of my dick into her slippery sweet entrance. I sank inside in one slow, deep, decadent thrust.

"Did you like it when I took your picture?" I asked once I was fully seated in her.

"God, yes," she panted.

I pushed deeper. "Why? Why did you like it so much?"

She moaned. "Because I love being naked with you. I love being with you. You make me feel so good."

"Just let me make you feel this way. *Let me.*"

"I will. I am. Oh God, please."

As I fucked her like that, slow and unhurried, she moved with me, shifting her hips, aligning her body, sliding against me. I cupped her tits, squeezing, then pinched her nipples.

She gasped as I tugged at them, and that drove me.

Burying myself as deep as I could go, I gripped her hair in my hand.

"Yes," she said, urging me on, and I knew she meant both the fucking and the tugging. I wrapped those gorgeous red strands around my fist.

Yanking her hair, I pulled her head back, raising it off the pillow.

I gave it to her the way she wanted. Driving in deep. Gripping her hard. Fucking her relentlessly.

With each thrust, she cried out in pleasure. With each pinch, she groaned my name. With every nip of my teeth, she became wetter.

And I was consumed. Utterly consumed.

Sex with her was a revelation. It was as if I'd discovered life on another planet, to know that it was possible to have this kind of sex. Savage yet tender. Cruel but gentle. To know she wanted it the same way. Her sounds told me she wanted to feel it everywhere. In her body. On her skin. In her heart. Oh God, I hoped she wanted me in her heart. So deep that I could never be removed. Like I was the end of the line for her. Just like she was for me. *Always.*

Love me, I wanted to say. *Just fucking love me.*

But I couldn't say that. Not now. Not yet. Instead, with her hair tight in my hand, and her throat exposed, I gripped her shoulder, digging my thumb into her collarbone.

"Just like that, just like that," she cried out, this time in French, in that heated way she spoke when she was close to the edge. Her pussy clenched around my shaft, so tight, so fucking perfect.

"And this?" I asked, biting down on her shoulder. *Love me.*

"Oh God."

I thrust harder. Brought my lips to the shell of her ear

and spoke harshly. "Do you want me to leave marks? Ones that say you're mine? I want to fuck you till you're mine."

"Yes. Yes. Yes," she urged, and I let myself believe she was answering my greatest wish. *I'm yours.*

I pressed my lips hard to her neck, my teeth biting down, digging in as she went crazy beneath me, rocking and thrusting and losing all control as she cried out and came undone in a fevered frenzy.

My body tightened, and my vision blurred. The rarest pleasure, the kind that came from total carnal bliss, surged in my bones, igniting me until I came long and deep inside the woman I loved.

I just fucking loved her.

And it was so goddamn hard not to tell her, in her language or mine. I tried to swallow the words, to choke them down, but the moment got the better of me. "*Je suis fou amoureux de toi. Tellement fou que je pense à toi, tout le temps, et je ne peux pas m'en empêcher,*" I whispered, barely scratching the surface of how I felt.

She tensed all over. Then she scooted out from under me, her hands on my chest, her eyes meeting mine. "You speak French. You speak perfect French."

Fuck.

I hadn't meant to say it in French. To tell her I'm mad about her. Crazy for her. That I can't stop this feeling. And I hadn't meant to let on that I'd understood everything I'd heard her say in her native tongue.

39

MICHAEL

Sixteen years ago

As I rounded the corner of the long hallway in the languages building, I opened the note yet again. The one I'd found scattered in my driveway, wreckage from my father's wallet. Like a treasure hunter, I had salvaged it, clutched it in my hand, gripped it tight that night, like a precious thing. And it was. I'd held onto it ever since. I probably always would.

I folded the note and tucked it back into my wallet when I reached room 403.

Freshman year French.

I wrapped my hand around the knob and opened the door, then my eyes roamed across the sea of desks. Nerves whipped through me. I wasn't a natural at languages. I was good at business, at strategy. Those were my skills. But I'd taken a night class during my senior year of high school, and I was committed to seeing this through. This note was part of the plan—the plan I'd discussed and hatched with my dad. The plan to apply to school in France, to be with Annalise, to make a life with her.

Reminder: Tell Michael he's signed up for French classes in the evening. A gift to him. He needs to learn the language for when he goes to school there. He needs to learn French for Annalise. So he can find his way back to her.

I hadn't been able to get into college in France the first time around, and she'd had no luck in the United States.

But I could keep trying. Because . . . there was always someday.

It was my father's wish for me, and I would fulfill it.

I stepped into the classroom, daunted but ready, and started working my ass off to learn another language.

Six years later, at age twenty-four, I was fluent. During those six years, Annalise and I had lost touch, but by the time I was done with school, on my own, serving my country, I was ready to find my way back to her.

So I tracked her down and sent her the letter. *Je n'ai jamais cessé de t'aimer.*

40

MICHAEL

She sat up in bed, staring at me like I'd skydived in from another planet and landed kaput on her bed.

"Michael?" She raised an eyebrow.

I rubbed my hand over my jaw. "Yeah?"

"Did you just have a conversation with me in French?"

My shoulders tightened, and I silently cursed myself. There was no denying it. I'd done nothing wrong, but I couldn't pretend I hadn't said those things. "Not a whole conversation. Just a few words," I said, desperately trying to sidestep.

"How did you know what to say?"

My heart slammed against my chest. I didn't want to tell her. Not yet. I didn't want to expose myself like this. I didn't want to reveal the full extent of what I'd done for her. That my desire to find her again, to be with her again, had driven me to learn a whole new language. "It was just a few words. That's all," I said, then glanced at the clock on the nightstand. "You have an early flight. Let's get some sleep."

"Okay," she said in a strained voice.

I turned out the light. "Come here. Come closer," I murmured, and wrapped my arms around her.

"I'm already close."

She snuggled into me, giving in on this count.

"Michael," she said, her tone pleading as she pressed her warm body to mine, skin to skin.

I kissed her hair. "Not now."

"I want to know."

"Just let me hold you."

She sighed, relenting. "Thank you."

"For?"

"For taking my picture."

I smiled into her neck and kissed her there, inhaling her scent. "I want you to be happy. Tell me you won't regret this. Or me."

She shook her head. "I don't regret you. I could never regret you. But I want to know—"

I whispered into her hair. "Shh…"

I just couldn't go there tonight. I would break.

41

ANNALISE

His breathing evened out, and soon he was asleep. I stared at the bright green letters on the hotel clock. After midnight. I had a five a.m. wake-up call, and the world's earliest flight to Paris.

Back home.

My chest ached. I missed him already.

I hadn't realized when I sought him out how much I needed *this*. Contact. Emotion. Passion. I'd been so shut down, but one flip of the switch from him, and the electricity was powered on, bright and shining, lighting up a whole city.

Perhaps that was why I'd searched for him when I went to Vegas. Because now I was free to roam, to return to wondering *what-if*. To my first love.

Such a big love.

Maybe I'd always been destined to find my way to him again. I'd told myself he was safe, but I wasn't looking for safety, as I'd quickly learned in a few short days with him. I was on the hunt for connection, for that thread between two people. I may not have realized it that afternoon at the

Bellagio, but I knew it now, and I had discovered the mother lode with him.

But tonight I had something new to noodle on. A twist. A surprise.

Something I hadn't expected.

His sudden fluency.

It perplexed me that he'd spoken to me in French, then tried to deny it. There was nothing wrong with him knowing my language, but I was so damn curious for details. How he'd learned it. Why he'd hidden it.

And if he'd done so for the same reasons I'd made similar choices. I'd chosen to refine my English at university, but not simply for the sake of fluency. I'd done it so that I could sound as American as I could, so I'd have the chance to come back here someday, to have an easier time of finding work, to converse fully and easily with Americans.

To fit seamlessly into his world.

A lump formed in my throat, tightening as I thought of the past, of how much we'd wanted to stay together, but of how damn hard it was. And how time and distance had pulled us apart.

Still, I desperately wanted to know more.

But the clock told me it was too late to press.

* * *

The next morning, I showered, stuffed my toiletries into my suitcase, and checked that my car service was on the way. But I couldn't seem to let go of what I'd learned about Michael last night.

Perhaps it was the former journalist in me, the part of me that chased answers, that hunted for truths.

I checked my watch. Ten more minutes. I couldn't wait.

I blurted out, "Why did you hide from me that you know French? It's driving me crazy. I want to know."

"I don't really know it well."

But he looked away from me as he grabbed the handle of my suitcase, rolled my bag to the door, and reached for the door handle, his cool blue eyes glancing anywhere but my face.

That was my answer, but I wanted the confirmation. I followed him, shouldering my purse, then stopped him from opening the door. I placed my hand on his arm, then ran my fingers up to his hair. I turned him to face me. Pressed my forehead to his. And spoke to him in French, rapid-fire. "You're amazing, and I adore you. I want to see you over and over. I want you to do everything to me and with me. You make me feel happy again, and when you come to Paris, I will show you everything, and you can have me in alleys and staircases, and we can fuck in museums and in restaurant bathrooms, and then you can make love to me in bed. You can talk dirty to me and tell me how much you want me, and I will tell you the same, because I do. So much I ache for you now."

He trembled and bit his lip like he was holding in all the things he wanted to say.

Determination spurred me on. "And you make me feel again. I feel things for you I haven't felt in years. Or for anyone. Do you know how terrifying that is for me?" I said, laying my heart bare. I was heading to the airport in ten minutes, jetting away from him once again. What did I have to lose? I'd already lost him once, so rolling the dice on this truth from my heart was a chance I had to take.

His eyes squeezed shut, his expression pained. Then he opened them and met my gaze.

"Yes," he admitted. "I know. And I want all of that too."

I inhaled deeply and cupped his cheeks. "Why didn't you just tell me?"

I was dying to know the answer.

42

MICHAEL

Because it revealed everything, that was why. Because it showed all my cards. It told her the full extent of my feelings, then and now.

Slumping against the door, I dragged a hand through my hair.

And then stopped.

Stopped keeping it all inside.

Stopped biting my tongue.

"Why didn't I tell you I learned French for you?" I tossed out the question like an attorney on cross-examination. "Why didn't I admit I spent six years studying your language because I was in love with you?"

I'd wanted to hide it, to keep it from her. I hadn't been sure I was ready to share everything when we were just finding our way again. But those words, those things she said . . . I couldn't help but reciprocate.

She pressed her hand to her chest. "You learned French for me?"

"You make it sound foolish."

She shook her head. "No. I'm just processing. It's big. That's a big thing. How did you do it?"

"I started freshman year of college. It was my father's idea. He even wrote me a note about it," I said softly, so my voice wouldn't break. "He knew me better than anyone. He knew you were all I wanted. He wanted me to be with you. And I still have the note," I said, reaching into my back pocket, opening my wallet, and taking out the worn, threadbare sheet of lined paper with his last words.

Annalise covered her mouth. Her bright eyes glistened with tears. "Your father wanted you to learn the language for me?"

I nodded and swallowed thickly. "He was practical, and he was romantic. He knew I wanted to be with you. He wanted me to be fully prepared, including the ability to speak the language and get a job. So I could live and work and be in France with you." I rubbed my hand across the back of my neck. "I took classes in college. I used to think I was doing it for him. And maybe, in some ways, that was how it started. A way to feel connected to the man who was gone. But I didn't let myself believe that for too long."

"It wasn't for him?" she asked softly.

I shook my head. "No. His note might have been the reason I started, but you were the reason I never stopped. I wanted to be with you."

"I wanted it just as much. You have to know that," she said, her bright green eyes wide open and honest, not shying away. "Michael," she said, soft and tender. "That's why I learned to speak without an accent."

"It is?"

She nodded. "I went to the American University in Paris to be surrounded by English speakers. I needed to refine my language skills so I could speak like a native for business. So I'd fit into your world, if I could find my way back to you."

My heart hammered in my chest from her admission, from the things we'd both done.

But once again, what we'd done hadn't been enough to bring us back together then.

"You do fit in." I glanced at my watch, trying to avoid this deeper dive. "Your car will be here in five minutes."

"I know, but this conversation is important."

It is, but I didn't know how long I would last. There was so much more to it, so much more it revealed on my end.

I grabbed her suitcase, opened the door again, and headed with her to the elevator banks. I pushed the button and then met her curious gaze. This was so damn hard. Putting myself out there. I waited for her to go next.

"I knew you had started taking classes, but I had no idea you'd become fluent. After we lost touch, why did you continue learning it?" she asked as we stepped inside the elevator.

That was the question. And the answer would reveal everything.

I drew a deep breath, weighing.

Ah hell. What did I stand to lose now? She was getting on a plane, leaving again. She might as well know. The elevator doors slid closed, and I fixed her with a serious stare. "Because I never got over you. I never stopped loving you. Even when we fell apart, I wanted to find my way back to you."

There it was.

My heart. Served up. Given to her once again.

Her lips parted. She stepped closer. "I wanted that too," she said, placing a hand on my chest as the car chugged downward. "Don't you know that?"

But that was the thing. I didn't know. "No. How would I have known? We didn't talk anymore."

"I thought about you all the time. I saved up every cent I earned from my job at a café. I was setting it all aside to see you again."

"You did?" I asked, surprised. She was shocking me too with her admissions, with the realization that we'd both been trying from afar for a someday.

She nodded. "Yes. The year we tried to stay together and then through the rest of university. I wanted the same thing, Michael. I wanted to find a way back to you. That's why I had sent you the letter you never received."

The car cranked its way to the lobby, closer to goodbye. With each floor we passed, my emotions tightened, rising to the surface.

Perhaps it was her letter. Maybe it was knowing the wish to be together again had never been one-sided. I'd kept such a tight lid on my emotions since Marseilles, squeezing them in, stuffing them into an airtight box, denying I felt anything for her still. I was tired of it. I was in love with her. I wanted her to know the full scope of my love, how far and deep it went. How it consumed me. Drove me. Carried me through the days and nights. The last time I saw her, I lost her. I might not have had a chance with her then, but I had a chance with her now. I wanted her to know.

The doors opened, and I walked through the lobby and out to the crowded avenue, already thick with morning traffic and the din of horns and screech of tires. I peered down the street. Her car wasn't here yet. I turned to her. My God, she was beautiful, and she was here, and I wanted her to know who she was to me.

Everything.

"Annalise, I learned French so I could be with you. I

wanted to be able to be with you wherever you were. It was all for you."

She nodded, listening. Waiting for me to say more.

I gripped her shoulder. "I know how to say *I love you* and *I want you* and *You're the only woman I've ever loved*. I know how to say a million other things like"—I switched to French—"you came back into my life now, and it's the same you, the same girl I fell in love with eighteen years ago, and it's the same me. It's the same us. But it's better because we've both lived. We're strong, but more fragile. We're tough, but still vulnerable. And I want to love you. Because . . ." I said, placing a hand on her cheek, her red hair blowing in the breeze.

Her tongue darted out, and she licked her lips, anticipation evident in the set of her jaw, the look in her eyes.

I swallowed, saying the last of my piece. "Because I've been in love with you forever. I've been in love with you for eighteen years."

She pressed her teeth into her bottom lip, her shoulders rising and falling.

"And it's driving me insane," I said. "I hold the words inside. But every time I'm with you, I want to shout the truth of how I feel for you. That I love you, I'm in love with you, and I've never ever stopped."

My admission echoed down the avenue, ringing across the entire city.

Trying desperately to read her reaction, to find out if this was a one-way path again, I searched her face. In her worried eyes, I saw fear and uncertainty. I wanted to kick myself. Perhaps I should have waited. Held back until we were on solid ground, until we were far enough along that I was sure she loved me too.

"I," she whispered, and her voice sounded feathery, like it came from another part of her. "I . . ."

Her car pulled up. The driver cut the engine.

"You need to go," I said, tipping my chin toward the black vehicle.

She wrapped a hand around my bicep. It felt too good. I couldn't be tricked by the feel of her. "You have to know how I feel for you now. I feel so much for you. Tell me you know. You *have* to know."

My head understood that of course she couldn't mirror my exact words. Of course she hadn't been in love with me while she was with Julien. But my heart wanted all of her, the whole time. Even though I knew that was hardly fair.

"Look, I didn't say this for you to reciprocate. I said it to be honest. Because it was eating me up. And I want you to know—I love you, and that's just a fact of my existence." I waved at the car and shot her a rueful look. "And you need to go. That's a fact of yours."

She placed her fingers on my cheeks, held my face in her hands, and kissed me. "I will miss you so much."

That was all for now, and it had to be enough.

Seconds later, I lifted her suitcase into the trunk and walked in the other direction, not looking back.

43

SANDERS

Four months ago

When I heard the siren, I cursed and banged a fist against the steering wheel. With a frustrated sigh, I flicked on my blinker and pulled to the shoulder of the highway.

A yawn erupted from my mouth. I was so tired from the drive. So damn exhausted from so many hours spent trying to finish up these last few runs to make the money I needed. Fucking college loans. Goddamn bills. Too many doctor appointments for my back. They all added up to the need for more greenbacks, so I'd taken on more runs like this one. I'd barely slept on this quick trip to California, and I'd just wanted to get home to Vegas sooner after visiting my sister in the Golden State. As I cut the engine, I peered in my rearview mirror to see the man open the door of his state trooper sedan and walk toward me.

The last person I wanted to see was an officer of the law.

The absolute last person.

I should have relied on the tried-and-true tricks for a long drive.

Gum. Coffee. Loud music.

Maybe even tried one of those damn apps my sons were always telling me to use to avoid the speed traps. But smartphones were a pain, and I'd always followed the speed limit.

Until now.

Because I'd wanted to get home to sleep in my own bed next to my wife. So I'd gunned the engine.

I lowered the window, trying to put on my best *just an average fella* smile. A working joe, just like the trooper. Because I was.

Boots crunched over the gravel on the side of the road.

"Afternoon," the officer said, his voice cool, his eyes obscured behind aviator shades. "License and registration, please."

"Sorry about that, sir. I was going a little too fast," I said, opting for patent honesty, hoping it might do the trick.

"Yeah, I'd say," the officer remarked, humorless. The young man studied me from behind his sunglasses, then whipped them off. I felt naked and exposed, and I blinked several times, unsure of why I was under such scrutiny. The trooper scrubbed a hand over his chin as I reached for my wallet in the center console. It slipped from my fingers, and I gripped it more steadily, shaking my head. Damn, I needed to get some sleep.

I fished in my wallet, then handed the cop my ID.

The cop raised his chin. His mouth curved up, and his eyes narrowed as he glanced from the ID to me, then back again.

"Funny thing, Mr. Doyle," the cop began in a drawl. He clucked his tongue and tapped his finger on the ID. "Your eyes don't look so bloodshot in this photo."

I sat bolt upright. "Come again?"

The cop cocked his head. "You been drinking? Smoking maybe? You look like you might have been enjoying some substances."

My jaw tightened, and I shook my head, fear prickling along my skin. "No, sir." I'd never done that, never would. But when the cop's eyes roamed the car, spotting my bag in the back seat, the man arched an eyebrow. "What have you got in there?"

"Just my stuff."

"What were you up to? Where have you been?"

"Visiting my sister. In California."

"In California?" His eyebrows rose, like it was so ridiculous an Irishman might have a sister in the States.

"We moved here with our parents when we were teenagers," I said. "Never lost the accent."

"Fascinating," he said, his tone telling me it wasn't fascinating at all, and he was clearly doubting me.

He tipped his forehead to the back seat. "Mind if I have a look?"

"What are you looking for, may I ask?" My voice was etched with worry, nerves skating over my skin.

"Whatever you're on," the cop said smugly.

I held up my hands, heart thumping wildly. "I'm not on anything. I swear."

Doubtful eyes stared back at me. "You were swerving in and out of the lanes like you're drunk or high. Your eyes are bloodshot."

"I'm just tired. Been driving a lot. Trying to get home and sleep in my own bed."

"If you're just tired, you won't mind if I have a look around."

My stomach plummeted. "Go ahead," I said, trying to sound like I wasn't terrified.

Five minutes later, the cop gave me a sharp, knowing stare. "You want to start talking about what you're transporting across state lines?"

For more than eighteen years, I had been making these runs. I'd been flawless. I hadn't asked questions. I hadn't wanted to know. I'd simply taken the packages and brought them to the addresses I'd been given.

I'd never been pulled over, never been questioned. And now, four months from retirement, I was nabbed.

That was just my luck.

For the first time, I felt the cold grip of fear that the authorities would find out everything I'd done.

44

MICHAEL

The grocery store. The piano shop. His house.

That was what the private detective had said Luke Carlton's daily life consisted of.

Since Annalise had returned to Paris and I was back in Vegas, I narrowed my focus on the investigation and conducted some recon of my own.

I pulled into the parking lot at Luke's regular grocery store on his usual evening to shop. Maybe it was an act of desperation. But hell, this guy was slippery. And I didn't care for slippery. I wanted the man to be caught. Put behind bars. Locked the fuck up.

Maybe I could find a clue. The detail that would tip the scales on the side of justice. I sat in my car and waited, like I was the private eye.

And hell, if this job didn't suck.

But Luke was like clockwork, and at six p.m., he walked through the front doors of the store. I got out of my car and kept a decent pace behind him, clenching my fists.

How could that man—that Royal Sinner—have such an ordinary, average life?

Luke pushed a cart through the aisles, buying bananas, a whole chicken, some cereal, toilet paper, potato chips, orange juice, and a can of white beans.

Each aisle Luke wandered down, I was tempted to confront the fucker. To grab him by the collar of his short-sleeve button-down shirt, slam him against the canned peas, and ask him what the fuck he had done eighteen years ago. How he'd gotten away with it. How he was still getting away with everything.

But somewhere between the bathroom supplies and the salty snacks, I slowed my pursuit and tamped down the treacherous ball of anger inside me. Talking to Luke, confronting Luke, spitting on the man's face—none of that would help solve the crime. Those would only serve to mess with the investigation. To tip him off.

I turned around, marched to my car, and yanked open the door. Once inside, I dropped my head to the steering wheel and cursed up a blue streak.

When I looked up, Luke was depositing grocery bags in the trunk of his car a few rows over. Shrugging, I decided to follow him when he left. Keeping a reasonable distance, I drove behind him for a few miles on a long stretch of road, stopping at traffic lights, never going above the speed limit. Luke turned into a strip mall, and I followed too, watching as the man parked and headed into a piano shop.

The bastard probably needed more sheet music.

I loathed him for that too.

For his boring fucking life.

* * *

Work consumed me. The next few days roared by in a sea of trouble, triage, and shitstorms. I'd been called to one of the financial firms that employed us for private security to deal with some threats against the building. Then Ryan and I tackled an issue with one of our banks involving an attempted robbery of an armed vehicle. Bad mojo was going around daily, and I was tense, poised for the next shoe to drop. It was like one of those weeks where bad things happen in threes.

The next one would come any second . . .

And it happened on a Thursday night.

We were working late at the office when the call came. I answered the office line on speaker. "Michael Sloan here."

"Hey, Mr. Sloan. We had more gang trouble at White Box." It was our on-the-ground guy at the club.

I groaned as Ryan looked up from some contracts.

"What happened?"

"Actually, it all worked out," the man said, and I breathed more easily as my guy recounted what went down. "Some dude from the Royal Sinners tried to solicit one of the dancers."

"But that happens all the time at a club," I pointed out as Ryan nodded silently, following along.

"True. But he wasn't just trying to get her to go home with him. He wanted her to be part of a prostitution ring."

"Jesus," I said, seething.

"But don't worry. We handled it. Threw the guy out."

"Good," Ryan chimed in.

"Thanks for the heads-up. Glad it was all taken care of," I said, and when I hung up, I met Ryan's eyes.

We were thinking the same thing.

"We should go there and touch base. Check in," Ryan said.

I nodded. White Box was far too important a client.

Fifteen minutes later, we walked through the main doors and quickly found Curtis and Charlie at the sleek silver bar. Women in next to nothing danced onstage, and scantily clad waitresses delivered highballs and scotches, as low techno music thumped through the club. Patrons lounged on red velvet couches, mostly businessmen, judging by the sheer number of suits and ties. In the far corner, a group of men puffed on expensive cigars in the smoking lounge.

"Everything work out okay?" Ryan asked after saying hello to Curtis and clapping Charlie on the back.

"All good now," Charlie said, then huffed in frustration. "I can't stand those street thugs trying to recruit the women here. That's not the business we're in." He counted off on his fingers. "They are dancers, plain and simple. And my dancers are salaried. They have health insurance. I even have a retirement plan for them. That isn't how I run this place. They aren't ladies of the night."

"Sorry that happened," I said.

Charlie waved me off. "No apologies needed. It comes with the territory. But I will be breathing easier at night when the authorities finally break up the gangs. What do you think we can do as private business owners to combat the problem?"

I eyed Ryan, and a look passed between us. These guys were speaking our language. We loved having a client who cared so much, who wanted the same things we did.

We spent the next thirty minutes strategizing, brainstorming, and discussing best practices for private citizens and companies to handle the problem.

When we were through, Curtis glanced at his boss, and Charlie nodded, giving him permission to say what was on his mind.

"This is why we want to do more work with you," Curtis said. "We want you to handle security for our clubs in Phoenix, Dallas, and Miami."

More business sounded good, so I took Ryan out for a

celebratory round of poker and beer afterward. That was a welcome end to a shitty work week.

With so much trouble still on the streets, we decided it made sense for us to start carrying again. We both had concealed weapons permits and knew how to be safe. With crime on the uptick, it was a necessary precaution.

I said goodbye to my brother. As Ryan headed home to his bride-to-be, a pang of sadness hit me. I was happy for Ryan, and I also couldn't help but want that for myself.

With one woman in particular.

As I arrived home, my phone buzzed. It was Friday morning in France, and there was a note from Annalise lighting up my screen.

45

ANNALISE

I ran my finger over the computer screen, tracing the contour of my own body. I'd turned the image of myself on a hotel bed into an arty black-and-white photograph. In it, I looked at the photographer out of the corner of one eye, one knee raised, hair spilling down my back.

From my desk by the floor-to-ceiling window in my apartment, I adjusted the contrast a bit more, then I leaned back in my chair, crossed my arms, and studied the screen.

Trying to understand more fully what I was seeing.

What I was feeling.

Here in this photo, I felt . . . like myself again. For the first time. So odd that a nude photo, a shot of me turned on beyond all reason, would make me feel that way.

Like I knew who I was once more.

Like I knew myself again.

But it did, only it wasn't entirely because of me.

I moved closer, the world narrowing to this image and me.

Another look. Another angle.

And then, in a burst of understanding I *knew*.

I felt like myself again because of Michael.

Because he was the one who'd seen this photo. And more so, because he was the one who'd seen me.

And that meant everything.

Because he was the one I wanted to share myself with.

And my God, I hadn't felt that in ages.

But I did. I felt it with him, that desire to share.

Myself.

My past, my present, and perhaps my future with him.

I pushed away from my chair and roamed around my flat, a flare of energy igniting me. It was as if I was understanding the world again.

And I needed to move.

To go beyond this small space, these walls.

To drink in the city around me.

An idea seized me, and in minutes my purse was slung on my shoulder, flats were on my feet, and the metro was rattling its way to one of my favorite spots in the city. One of the passages of Paris.

I got off the train, lifting my face to the sky, then looking around.

Everywhere. Just looking.

Taking in Paris anew.

All the places I loved.

In the passage I headed to a map shop, stopping outside the window to stare at the vast collection of maps of the world. I'd always loved history and geography. That was one of the reasons I'd become a photojournalist. To see the big world beyond this city. I ran my finger over a map in the window, tracing a line over Italy, to Turkey, over to Singapore . . . all the places I'd been.

I looked at my watch. I was due at my mother's in two hours to help her with dinner and to fix her broken sink. That gave me time to walk past some of my old haunts.

My city.

My home.

I strolled past a café I loved, stopping for an espresso, savoring every sip, as I watched my countrymen and women stroll by, laughing, arguing, loving. I paid the check, then tapped my regular table for good luck. I wandered across my favorite bridge on the Seine, marveling at the gray ribbon of water that snaked through Paris, then along the antique shops and art dealers near the Musée d'Orsay, one of my most beloved spots in the city, and past the sidewalk dealers by the river, peddling postcards.

Everything I adored.

Everything I'd barely noticed lately.

But I was seeing it all again.

Almost for the first time.

And as I took in the familiar and the new, I was struck with another flash of clarity.

I wanted to share this city with Michael.

It was good to feel again. Good to want again. Good to live and share and maybe even love again.

When I arrived at my mother's later that afternoon, I knocked then let myself in. She was reading a book on her couch and when she saw me she set down the book and greeted me with a hug and a warm hello. "How was your day, *mon petit papillon?*"

"It was completely necessary," I answered, and my mother raised an eyebrow at my response.

"I took myself on a tour of Paris," I explained.

"Ah, did you see the Arc de Triomphe?" she teased.

I laughed, then gathered carrots and potatoes from her fridge, chopping them as I talked. "I saw the places I used to love. Places I wasn't sure I could love again."

She lifted an eyebrow. "Just places?"

"They're more than places," I said, because they were.

"I had a feeling you were going to say something like that."

"Places I want to share. Places I want to go. The ones I saw today and others." I set down the knife and clasped her hands, my heart expanding in my chest, cracking open. Everything I hadn't fully accepted in New York, I was accepting here. And it felt incredible to understand my heart, why it was thundering in my chest. And to tell *someone*. In a way, it was fitting to tell my mother first. She'd been wanting my happiness for my whole life. "I want to feel again, *Maman. Everything.*"

Her smile brimmed with love. "You will. Perhaps you already are."

We talked more as I finished dinner, then fixed the sink, chatting about the news of the day. Later, I fell asleep on the couch. When I woke up the next morning, I stretched, brushed my teeth, and said goodbye.

Outside, as the sun rose in the Paris sky, I snapped a photo of a coffee éclair in a bakery window. Then I sent a message with it to Michael.

Annalise: Are coffee éclairs on your hell-no list too? Wait. Don't tell me. I want to discover all the things about you I don't know. I want to share this city with you. I want to learn what you love. Will you let me?

46

MICHAEL

As we finished a quick early walk-through of Ryan and Sophie's ceremony, slated for next month at Mandalay Bay's outdoor terrace, my cell phone buzzed, and my new Pavlovian response kicked in, a dart of lust flaring in me.

My phone had been glued to my side since I'd left New York, but even more so after Annalise's note the other night. *That note.* It was a window opening and sunshine pouring in, and of course I'd said yes. In the last couple of days, there'd been a shift in our communication back-and-forth. She sent me sweet little messages throughout the day, and often included photos too, pictures of her life in Paris. And she captioned them all.

In French.

I answered them. In French.

That wasn't all though. She also gave really good naked Skype strip shows. The best, actually. Last night, for instance, she'd shown me precisely how a cheektini looked on her succulent ass. She'd modeled no less than a dozen, sliding them on, gliding them off.

I missed seeing her, holding her, but I was okay with

how things were. Because at least we had something. I
didn't try to define it, or pressure her for more. Just
voicing my own feelings on the street before she left had
been enough for now. I was no longer carrying that hard
knot of tension inside me, that secret knowledge that I was
a man wildly in love with a woman. My feelings were out
in the open, and somehow that made things better, especially when she sent her note. *I want to discover all the things
about you I don't know.*

But as I pulled my phone from my pocket, it was my
private investigator's name that flashed across the screen.
It had been a quiet several days on that front since I'd
returned from New York, but Morris had messaged me the
other day to say that he had some leads and hoped to get
some solid intel soon.

Soon couldn't come fast enough, especially after my
pointless pursuit of Luke several nights ago.

"Michael," the man said in a gruff, gravelly tone befit-
ting a PI. "I got something for you."

I straightened and glanced over at Ryan and Sophie,
who were wrapped up in each other, laughing, whispering.
They probably wouldn't care that I was busy on the phone.
I walked away from them and down the aisle that would be
covered in peach tulip petals for the wedding.

"Tell me what you've got."

"Meet me in person in thirty minutes. There's a diner
off the highway. It's busy enough, but far enough away
too."

Morris gave me the address, and I repeated it. When I
hung up, I headed over to the happy couple and dropped a
hand on Sophie's shoulder. "Hey, I need to take off, but I'm
all set on what I need to do for the ceremony."

"What's going on? Client stuff on a Saturday?" Ryan
asked, his brow knitting.

I cut off his concern. "Nothing work-related. Just something I need to do."

I didn't want to say anything in front of Sophie. Not that I was worried it would get back to John, but the fewer people who knew about my own investigation, the better chance I had of gaining information. I'd learned that over the years in this business.

"Fine, fine. Just take off," Sophie said with a pout, shooing me away. "We were going to invite you to get a bite to eat, but now we won't."

I smiled and pressed my palms together as if in prayer. "Rain check?"

She waved a hand as if wiping away my transgression. "You are forgiven. Oh, wait. Are you going to bring Annalise to the wedding?"

That hadn't even occurred to me. "I don't know. I hadn't thought about it."

"Think about it. It would be so nice."

It would but instead of lingering on that idea, I shifted my attention to Ryan. "I don't believe I've even said much about Annalise, and now you're telling Sophie to invite her to the wedding?"

Ryan shrugged. "You don't have to say much. Your constant texting, emailing, and Skyping says it for you. Oh, and the fact that you were madly in love with her in high school."

I shook my head. "I seriously need to go."

"Bring her," Sophie called out as I turned on my heel.

"It's more than a month away," I shouted back.

"Invite her now. Gives her time to plan!"

I laughed once more, not giving anything away. But as I headed to the parking garage, I found myself considering it further. If we were really doing this long-distance thing, and it seemed we were, why not bring her to my brother's wedding? We'd already been tossing out options for my first trip to see her in a week or so. Maybe we could plan the next one too.

For now, though, I shifted gears, calling Mindy and picking her up along the way.

"My fingers are crossed for big news," I said as I held open the car door for my friend.

She wrapped her index and middle fingers together. "Me too."

At the diner, Morris was working his way through a mug of coffee when I slid across from him, shaking his hand in greeting. Mindy said hello too, and sat next to me. Fifties music played on the sound system, and waitresses took orders decked out in pink diner uniforms.

"This place has great fries. You should get some," Morris said, sliding a well-worn menu to the two of us before scrubbing a hand across his jaw.

"Far be it from me to refuse great fries. Want to split a plate, Mindy?"

The blonde nodded. "That I do."

After we ordered, I raised my chin. "So, what have we got?"

Morris took a deep breath, dipped a hand into his messenger bag, and pulled out a manila folder. It was so old-school, and I kind of loved the Philip Marlowe vibe. The guy just needed a fedora to finish the look.

Taking his time, he flipped open the folder and stabbed his finger against a photograph. It was upside-down, but I could tell what it was. I glanced at Mindy then at Morris, then leaned closer to study the picture, my muscles coiled, tension threaded tightly inside me. "The piano shop? The place where he buys sheet music?" I asked in a hushed tone.

Morris nodded.

"Okay. What of it?" Mindy asked.

Morris raised both eyebrows. "I've been casing it. And our target. All day long. All night long. Stuff cops don't have the manpower or resources to do."

"And?"

"There's a lot more that goes on in the back of the store than sheet music."

I swallowed. "Like what?" I asked, so fucking eager for information.

"It's where the Royal Sinners fence all their stolen goods. It's their goddamn fucking headquarters. Everything runs through there. Electronics, phones, watches, all sorts of stolen shit. As well as guns. They've got themselves a huge illegal gun sales operation they're running from this joint." He lowered his voice even more, licked his lips, then made his pronouncement. "Bust out the big guns—you've got your man."

Time froze . . . then sped up. My fingertips tingled, and the possibility of justice tore through me. A smile spread across my face, morphing into a thrilled grin. I looked at Mindy, and she beamed too. We raised our hands, smacked palms, and treated Morris to a cheeseburger and the best fries in Vegas as he shared the rest of the details.

Later, Mindy and I went to meet John at a Starbucks.

"This is good stuff," the detective said, his eyes glinting with excitement.

"Is it enough?"

"I can't make any promises, but if I can't at least get him in custody with this, someone should take away my badge."

Mindy laughed, and John turned his attention to her, as if he was seeing her for the first time. Maybe even checking her out.

47

THOMAS

Eighteen years ago

Any day now, I would learn if I'd landed the promotion. The increase in salary made me even hungrier for the job, and I was sure I'd nailed the interview with my boss. Paul had seemed impressed and had asked me a ton of questions about how I'd uncovered the discrepancy, and what they could do to prevent those sort of accounting errors in the future.

"We should have an answer in a few days," Paul said at the end of the interview, then extended a hand and flashed a toothy grin before walking me to the door.

The next day, I entered my last ride of the day in the logbook in the break room. After a hearty swig of my coffee, I set the mug down, closed the binder, and stood up to leave, when I was joined by a young guy. I didn't know the fellow's name, but I'd seen him around, operating as sort of a jack-of-all-trades. He had a short Mohawk and a gold earring in his right ear, and he helped out Paul from time to time.

"Hey," I said, with a nod of my chin.

"Hey," the guy replied. He wore a black T-shirt, and had arms like iron and height like a basketball player. "Got a minute?"

I stopped in my tracks. "Sure. What do you need?"

The guy scratched his chin and then waved broadly to the break room. "Listen. I get that sometimes things might seem odd around here." He tilted his head to one side. "Was this written down?" Then the other side. "Was this *not* written down? It can be confusing remembering if every-thing was there, if it wasn't there."

I frowned. "You work closely with Paul?"

The guy nodded, then flashed a smile. "That I do, and listen," he said, clamping his hand on my arm, "let me give you some advice. Things here are more complicated than they seem. I had to learn that the hard way, but I learned it. You're just better off if you don't let all those details worry you."

"I'm not worried," I said, straightening and shrugging the guy off my arm.

The man clapped me on the back. "Good. Because there is nothing to worry about whatsoever."

I raised a brow at his last comment. The man was clearly delivering a message. One I wasn't sure how to take. "Okay, then. So we're good."

"We are good. Just remember," the man said, tapping my broad chest, "you have any questions, you ask me. I'm here to help." He lowered his voice. "The key to lasting a long time here, to getting the good gigs, is to know what's important and what's not important. I want to help you get there. Let me help you."

I wasn't sure I bought his routine, but best not to let on.

I nodded and said, "Sure," even though I was pretty damn certain I wouldn't be turning to this guy for help. "What did you say your name was?"

"TJ." He repeated it. "TJ."

I rubbed my hand across the back of my neck and thanked him, then headed off to meet Sanders and Donald for our Saturday afternoon poker game at Sanders's house. Once I arrived, I settled in at the table, grabbed a beer, and caught up with my buddies as Donald dealt, focusing on the cards, tuning out a lot of our work talk, as he often did.

"How was the interview? Think you'll get it?" Sanders asked.

I shrugged hopefully. "Hope so. I think he was impressed with some of the things I brought up for improvement, as well as how I can apply what I've been learning in night school." Sanders sat up straighter and raised an eyebrow as I elaborated. "There were some extra trips and missing trips in the logbook. Seemed like a problem area to me. But then after the interview some guy made a big deal about how there was nothing to worry about. Whatever that means," I said, still doubtful about the whole incident.

"Was he talking about the missing trips?" Sanders asked as he perused his cards.

"He didn't really say, but it sure seemed that way."

"Huh." Sanders scrubbed a hand across his jaw.

Conversation halted as Annalise popped into the kitchen. "Oh, hello!" She gave a quick wave to each of her host family's guests—to Donald and to me. "I'm going to get a snack," she said, and reached for an apple in the fruit bowl on the counter.

"Hey, Annalise," I said, tipping an imaginary hat. She was leaving in a month or so, heading back to Paris, and Michael and I were concocting a way for them to stay together. "Good to see you. Michael said you have plans with him later today, right?"

She nodded. "Yes. We're going to the movies."

"Want a ride over when we're done here?"

"I would love that. Thank you."

As she left, Sanders shook his head and smirked.

"What are you laughing at?"

"Those two. So young and in love."

"It's nice to see," I said, then winked. "Does it remind you of Dora and me?"

Donald snorted. "Ha. Not exactly."

It was no secret among my friends that my marriage had run into some trouble. Dora had been distant, distracted lately. Not to mention harping on me about money all the time. I wouldn't have minded more, but it's not like I was pissing it away. We played cards for pennies, and I worked my ass off to save everything I made.

"I know, right?" I said, shaking my head, half amused, half irritated. "She's been all over me about money. But we're getting by, and I feel good about this promotion. Besides, I told her if she wants money, she should just smother me and collect the life insurance."

Sanders cracked up, and Donald raised his beer. "Let's hope she doesn't take you up on it," he joked.

I laughed. "Yeah, she thought it was funny too. Besides, everything is fine. I've got plans in place for all the kids, and college, and life. It's all good. She doesn't need to worry. I'll get the promotion, I'll show them what I can bring to the table, and it will all work out fine."

48

SANDERS

Eighteen years ago

I took a long gulp of my beer to cover up the nerves flaring inside me.

The rides. Those damn missing rides.

I knew about the rides. I knew why they didn't exist in the books. But unlike my buddy, I didn't fucking ask questions at work. The company had been good to me, plain and simple. No reason to sniff around and ask about things. The less you asked, the better off you were. Head down, nose to the grindstone, mind your own business.

That's what I did. Did the jobs, took the cash, paid the bills.

And saved some extra for the future. Hell, that's all I wanted to do. Provide a comfortable future for my Becky.

So I took on the extra work to make it happen.

It was starting to make retirement possible someday. Someday down the road, but I could feel that day coming.

And hell, did I ever want to tell my friend how to get in on the action.

Call him over, lower my voice, and say, *You didn't hear this from me, but . . .*

Because the company offered ample opportunity for making money. I wished I could tell Thomas how to do it. Share the secrets.

But the man was too good. He wasn't one for breaking the rules, let alone bending the rules.

Ever.

As Becky wandered past the kitchen on her way to the garden in the backyard, I caught a glimpse of my wife.

Her smile, the hope in her eyes.

A man had to do what a man had to do. Every man had to take care of his family in his own way.

I met Thomas's eyes and nodded. "Yup. It will all be fine."

49

THOMAS

Eighteen years ago

"How was your day, Mr. Paige?" Annalise asked, as she slid into the front seat next to me an hour later.

"Not too bad. Yours?" I turned on the engine. She was such a sweet girl, and I was so damn happy that Michael had found her.

"It was good. I'm *good to go* for the history test," she said with a wide smile, using one of the Americanized phrases she'd learned during her stay. "And did you have a good morning at work? You work hard for a Saturday."

I tapped the dash as I pulled out of the driveway and rolled down the street. "Doing my best. And yes, work was good."

"But there is something you worry about?" she asked, tilting her head. "I was not eavesdropping, but I heard some of your conversation as I walked into the kitchen. I hope you don't mind me asking."

I smiled and shook my head. "Nope. Don't mind at all. I

admire your curiosity. You'd make a good journalist someday."

She smiled widely. "Thank you. That's what I hope to do. With my photos."

"You'll do great. And to answer your question," I said as I flipped on the blinker and turned right, "there's just something odd I noticed at work, so I mentioned it."

I shared a few details with her, since she was such a good listener.

"Maybe there is a reason for it all? There has to be. Things don't just disappear," she said. "You are probably onto something. Some connection."

I nodded. "That's what I think too."

I slowed at a red light near the strip mall. I glanced over and my eyes narrowed briefly, catching the silhouette of a man walking into the nearby piano store. Holy crap. The guy looked like TJ. Big and broad and toweringly tall. Annalise's eyes followed mine.

"Do you know him?"

"I think so," I said, peering out the window.

The man turned around before heading inside. No doubt. The arms, the height. That was TJ.

And I never would have expected to see him here.

"Funny. Some guy who works with me just went into the piano shop. He gave me a hard time earlier today. I'd never have pegged him as a musician."

She flashed a smile. "People surprise you. They do things we don't expect."

50

DORA

Eighteen years ago

As my husband stripped off his button-down shirt, I fiddled with a necklace on my bureau, averting my eyes. I could hardly look at him anymore. I didn't want him. I'd had no interest in him since I'd fallen in love with another man.

I hadn't planned to. But Luke had given me so much. He'd given me hope. He'd helped me find a way to make more money, to earn well beyond my meager seamstress wages and Thomas's paychecks. The cash I'd amassed from my side business had helped me make ends meet and then some. Luke understood that. He wanted the same things. He was driven, and since he knew I'd needed more, he'd helped me find a way to get it. Something Thomas wouldn't do. Ever since that night I'd met Luke at the work party—not Narcotics Anonymous, like I'd told my sweet Ryan—he'd understood my deepest needs. To provide for my children. To give them the opportunities I'd never had.

So what if I had to bend some rules to make it happen? Break some laws, even?

Luke was wonderful and sweet and paid attention to all my needs. I longed to be with him. Ached to have a life with him. I was sure he was my future, especially now. I ran a hand over my stomach, still flat, but not for long.

Could I go through with it? I'd lined up all the players. Luke had helped me find the right men, connecting me with a broker who was flawless at arranging hits.

I knew TJ, had sold to him and his cousin. I knew Stefano well too, since he was my supplier.

My stomach churned at the thought, but I pushed those feelings aside, denying them. I was tired, so damn tired of scraping by. Besides, I wanted to raise my family with Luke. Was that so wrong? How could it be, now that God had put this baby in my belly?

Still, my chest heaved as I placed the simple necklace Luke had given me in the bottom drawer of my jewelry chest. I'd wear it when we ran off, when we escaped at last. A symbol of my freedom from this hard life.

"Everything okay?" Thomas asked, that all too familiar concern in his voice. He tried to look out for me, even now. He had no idea, no idea about a damn thing, and I wished he'd stop being nice to me.

I pressed my lips together and nodded. "Just fine."

I ran a hand over my stomach, a fresh wave of nausea kicking in. I gritted my teeth, not wanting to let on. I'd had morning sickness that lasted all day long with my other pregnancies. No surprise I'd have it again with this one. I hadn't slept with my husband in months, so I'd never had any doubt about who this baby's daddy was.

This baby was my reason.

I'd gotten in too deep with the drugs and the gang and the selling. But now, I had a way out. If I could pull this off

—and Luke had assured me that Jerry Stefano was the best hitman in the business—then we had a chance.

And we had a plan.

A perfect plan. A perfect crime. That would lead to a perfect life.

Everything would fall into place.

Luke had promised he'd leave town with me. We'd escape with the life insurance money and go to Arizona, Florida, Texas . . . anywhere. Start a new life with the man I adored. Be with him, my new baby, and all my kids. All five of my children under one roof with the man I loved madly. And with his mother. He'd take care of all of us, and I'd take care of my babies.

That was my dream. My big, wonderful, perfect dream.

I could taste it. I could sense it.

It wouldn't be easy, but it was my only choice. It would be worth it, the end result, the freedom.

Thomas came up behind me and placed a hand on my back. "Come to bed. You're so tired these days. Get some rest."

He kissed my hair, and I shuddered.

Once more, I wondered if I could go through with this.

51

ANNALISE

"The piano store?"

To say I was surprised was an understatement. More like shocked, but also excited. The latter because Thomas had driven past the piano store once while giving me a ride, and made a passing comment about a guy from work that we saw there being an unlikely musician. But I'd never have thought it was the epicenter of the local gang that had ripped Michael's family to pieces.

I gripped the edge of the iron latticework table in my fifth-floor flat and stared at him with wide eyes through the computer screen. "I drove past there. With your father. We drove past it one day."

He sat up tall. "You did? Why?" he asked from the other side of the world. He was in his condo, the steel counters of his kitchen framing the video screen.

"You and I went to the movies one Saturday afternoon, but before that your father had come over to play poker with Sanders and Donald. He drove me to your house. Do you remember?"

It was all so clear in my mind. It wasn't as if I had been

lingering on that particular memory, but now that Michael mentioned the piano shop, that day splashed to the surface of my thoughts with a particular clarity.

"That's where the Royal Sinners run the operation from," he said in a breathless whisper.

"A piano store. That's so clandestine," I said.

He nodded. "My private detective found out last night. Apparently, they run everything through there. Do you remember anything else from when you drove past it? Did my dad say anything unusual?"

I shook my head. "No. Not at all. He simply noticed someone from work going inside the store. He didn't give a name, but I remember the man was big and broad and incredibly tall."

Michael's eyes narrowed, and he hissed the name. "TJ. Must have been TJ."

I clasped my hand over my mouth, shock coursing through me. I collected myself, then said, "That was TJ? Your father was surprised that he was at the piano store. That was really all he said about the place. But before then, we were chatting about his work."

Michael gestured for me to tell him more. "About the promotion he was hoping for? He always told me he was hoping to impress the guy who ran the company. But nothing came of it. Obviously."

I cycled back to that day, the pieces coming back to me. "I overheard him and the others at the house that day talking about 'extra work trips.' I believe he said someone at work told him to stop asking so many questions. Oh, and when we drove past the store, he said the guy heading into the shop had been giving him a hard time at work, but that was all."

Michael's eyes went wide. "That's got to be the missing link. That must be how it's all connected. If TJ worked there too, the Royal Sinners must have been operating somehow at the limo company." He scrubbed a hand over his jaw. "We looked into his employer when the case reopened, and the cops did too, but nothing came up as a cause for concern. Even the guy who ran the place—he was squeaky clean, and now he's long gone. Retired in Canada. Not a single blip or issue, but hell," he said, stopping to blow out a long stream of air. "That's how they operate. Under the radar."

"Yes. If they run it out of a piano store and have been avoiding capture for years, they're smart. But you've figured it out," I said with a smile, because I was so damn proud of him. His work had gotten the investigation that much closer.

Michael paced in front of the screen. "Everything from the Sinners must have been flowing through my dad's company, I bet. Maybe the owner didn't even know, and it was all right under his nose. And that's how my mother met Luke in the first place. At a work party. I found pictures. So Luke must've been running everything—all these illegal operations—through the back of the piano shop, but it was actually being funneled through West Limos. The drugs and the guns. And my mother was a part of it, since she was involved in selling drugs. That must be why the investigation was reopened. My mother was behind it all, but there were other people who had a hand in offing my dad. Christ," he said, dragging a hand through his hair.

I nodded sadly. "He said something about finding some discrepancies at work. Rides or items that were missing. Maybe they were missing because the Sinners were transporting guns or drugs through the company. And your dad found out about it."

He snapped his fingers and pointed at me, his eyes

lighting up with that *aha* moment. "You know you're beautiful and brilliant?"

"So are you."

"I need to tell John."

I waved him off. "Go, go. This is important. I'll see you soon," I said, and I was ready. Ready to have him come see me here in Paris, to have him in my home, to share some of my life here with him. I wanted to show him the local bakery, wander through the alleys, through the shops, take him to my favorite places in Paris. To make new memories with Michael.

"Nothing could stop me from seeing you."

52

LUKE

Play me some Beethoven.

That's what my mother had always said to me when she needed an escape from her troubles.

Beethoven had been that for her.

And for years I'd given her that escape through the choices I'd made.

As I flipped on the blinker to turn into the cemetery, the rising crescendo of "Ode to Joy" filled my car, reverberating off the windows, reaching the far corners of my vehicle. I was bathed in music. It encased me.

It drowned out my thoughts.

Thoughts of my own orchestra, and how it had been falling apart.

Thoughts of the men under my control who'd become increasingly uncontrollable.

Thoughts of my sweet wife, Angie. Innocent Angie, who knew nothing of my life, just as my mother had known nothing before. As it should be when it came to the women you love.

And briefly, thoughts of Dora.

Every now and then, I thought of her.

Rarely though.

The life we'd planned, the life I'd wanted with her—to run away, raise our kid, bring my mother along—had fallen to pieces.

But Carltons were strong.

Carltons rose up.

So that's what I'd done.

I'd taken my son out of town, protected him, looked out for him, and taken my mother too, until she breathed her last breath several years ago.

Now, I parked the car as the final notes rang loud and true in my head.

Turning off the music, I got out of my car, a simple hatchback that fit the façade I'd carefully crafted of mild-mannered piano teacher. I shut the door, and headed to my mother's grave.

Trudging across the grass, I could still hear the music. I could always hear music.

When I reached the headstone, I kneeled, set down the tulips, and pressed my fingers to my lips, then to the cold stone.

I sighed, then told her I was worried. "Too many questions, Mother. They are asking too many questions. But I've made it this far. Twenty years in this life. Twenty years taking care of my family this way. I'll make it twenty more." I scrubbed a hand across my chin, reflecting on how I'd pulled it off. And the answer was remarkably simple —routine.

A front.

An act.

"But was it an act?" I asked her. I shook my head adamantly. Deep in my heart, I knew none of my life was an act. I *was* a family man. I loved my children. I adored my wife. And I cherished the memories of my mother.

That was how I'd pulled it off. By being true to who I was—a man who loved his family.

And a man had to do what a man had to do.

I rose, said goodbye, and continued on my day.

53

JOHN

Missing rides.

That was an interesting development.

One that I tucked away, knowing I'd look into it soon.

Very soon.

But right now?

I had what I needed when my partner dropped a new stack of photos on my desk early the next morning.

The final nail in the coffin, so to speak.

"This is it, isn't it?" I asked, that sense of calm starting to set in, the sense that things were going in the right direction.

He parked himself in the chair across from me. "This is it," he echoed.

We flipped through the pictures in silence at first, the images doing all the talking, and they were worth so many thousands of words.

At last. At long last.

Shots of Luke in the parking lot of a gas station off the highway thirty minutes from town. Checking out a shipment of stolen guns.

I raised my face, released a satisfying breath, and met Manny's gaze. "Guess he goes to a few more places than the grocery store and the piano shop."

"Just a few," Manny said.

After my best friend had been paralyzed by a drive-by gang shooting when I was fourteen, I had vowed to always do my part to keep this town safe. Sure, Luke Carlton had done so much more than sell guns. But all I needed was probable cause to bring the man in. Thanks to Michael's tip, coupled with months of investigation, and now these photos, we had the necessary evidence.

I could smell justice in the air.

* * *

No one was home. We knocked on the door of Luke Carlton's house at a quarter past ten in the morning. But the sound of my fist rapping on the wood echoed without an answer.

I turned around, scanning for Luke's car on the street. I hadn't seen it when I'd pulled up, but even so, I looked once more. He was slippery. He'd skirted the law for a long damn time.

But I didn't have him yet.

And I needed him.

I leaned to the right, trying to catch a glimpse through the window into the home. It looked just the same as it had when I was here over the summer. I'd interviewed Luke when the case was reopened. The man claimed to know nothing. He played up the whole fear factor, sticking to his story of being terrified the Royal Sinners would come after him.

So ironic.

My jaw clenched as I remembered his routine, the way he'd tried to distance himself from his army on the street.

In truth, they were in his back pocket, and the man probably figured he was still getting away with it. That his long, time-honored practice of hiding behind his fake life and pushing others to take the blame would keep working. Hell, even the handful of gang arrests made recently were for other crimes—none were related to the murder.

And so Luke kept going about his business.

If he stuck to his schedule, and he sure seemed like the type, that meant I might need to track him down at the piano shop this evening. But as we returned to the car, then headed out of the neighborhood, Manny and I debated whether arresting the man at that place was the smartest approach.

"That would be like walking into . . . well, into target practice," I said.

The shop was the center of their gun trade, and if I wanted to keep this arrest as quiet as I possibly could until I had TJ too, I needed a different way in.

I zeroed in on a brand-new approach.

* * *

When evening rolled around, Manny headed inside the grocery store, strolled around the aisles, and reported back via text.

A small sense of satisfaction took root inside me.

Yes.

Criminals had patterns.

Life-long criminals tended to stick to them.

And Luke Carlton was indeed a man of routine. That routine was his camouflage. It had shielded him for years. His clockwork schedule had made him appear one way to the world, and that masquerade made it possible for him to live a life of crime undetected.

With my senses on high alert, homed in on every detail, I got into position. I waited by the automatic doors of the supermarket—ready.

Truly, I'd been ready for this for a long time.

Tension coiled in me, but a kind of excitement too. This was why I did what I did. The chance to clean up the streets. Put the bad guys behind bars.

The air was charged with electricity, with possibility.

The doors slid open, and my partner crossed from the tiled floor of the grocery store onto the sidewalk.

Briefly, a small knot of guilt wormed its way through me as I thought of Marcus, the courageous boy who'd helped us start down this path. Marcus and the rest of his family would be safer, though, I reminded myself. The sooner I could dismantle the Royal Sinners, the better off everybody in this town would be.

Sixty seconds later, Luke Carlton neared the exit of the grocery store. It was a little after six on a weekday evening. He carried two bags of groceries. He wore jeans and a short-sleeved shirt. His gray hair was freshly combed, as if he'd taken a shower before he ran his errands.

Luke didn't notice the two men in slacks and button-downs loitering outside the local market. He kept walking, his keys in one hand, whistling under his breath. Sounded like Beethoven, something he'd probably taught to a young student recently.

I burned with frustration over the freedom this man had enjoyed for so many years. But it was also Luke's Achilles' heel. He thought he could keep it up indefinitely, living like an average, ordinary guy.

I stepped away from the brick wall I'd been leaning

against and stepped in the path of the head of a dangerous street gang.

"Pardon me," he said, shifting to the right to avoid me. Funny how Luke didn't even look up. If he had, he might have recognized the detective he'd lied to a few months ago.

Fucking mild-mannered piano teacher, my ass. But the guy had pulled it off, living a double life for years. That was about to be blown wide open.

"Good to see you again, Luke Carlton. You're under arrest," I said.

The second the words left my mouth, Luke dropped his grocery bags and bolted. It was an instant reaction—he took off along the sidewalk of the cavernous store, running like hell.

I went after him, sidestepping the groceries that had spilled from the bags. Luke had more speed than I would ever have expected. He ran past a line of shopping carts, grabbing the handle of one and yanking it out onto the sidewalk.

I dodged the cart, and my partner was right behind me as Luke rounded the corner, heading for the back lot. Luke seemed hell-bent on escape, and I completely understood his drive. The man had lived a scot-free life for two decades. That could drive a man to run like hell.

Even though the bastard was fast, he wasn't fast enough. No fucking way was I letting Luke Carlton get away from me in the back-parking lot of a grocery store.

With my heart pumping, my feet pounding, and my breath coming in fast, powerful spurts, I neared him. Ten feet, five feet away now. I closed the distance across the asphalt, stretched out my arm, grabbed the back of his shirt, and tackled him.

Luke twisted in my arms. "Let me go. You've got the wrong man."

He was like an eel, flinging and swishing and desperately coiling his body. But I wasn't letting go. I yanked Luke up as Manny reached us, pinned both wrists, pushed him against a dumpster, and slapped on the handcuffs.

I breathed out hard. "As I was saying. Luke Carlton, you're under arrest for illegal gun trafficking." Then I rattled off a litany of violations that this man had committed over the years, from selling guns without background checks, to peddling weapons to convicted felons, to giving firearms to fugitives.

And I read him his Miranda rights.

Then at last, we took him in.

54

LUKE

The questions from the detectives were relentless.

Irritating, frankly too.

I let Beethoven's Fifth Symphony play in my head as they peppered me with inquiry after inquiry.

"Did you meet Dora Prince at Narcotics Anonymous?"

I crossed my arms in the interrogation room, and nodded a yes. They didn't need the truth. That I'd met her at work. Met her at the West Limos party. Met her, romanced her, fell in love with her.

All that was true. I'd planned to marry Dora Prince.

To take my mother and Dora and her children and our child and go so far away. Maybe Texas. More likely Florida. To live in the sun, to listen to music, to play Bach and Mozart and "Chopsticks" too. To teach our children how to play.

But life doesn't work out the way we plan, does it?

Rarely.

The detective went again. "Why did you say you were terrified of Jerry Stefano?"

Oh, I don't know, why would anyone say that? Because

there's no one better to pin all the blame on than the man already behind bars?

Turn him into the boogeyman and protect yourself.

I didn't answer.

Another question came my way. "Why did you leave Vegas after your son was born?"

Silence. I remained cloaked in it. I knew my Miranda rights. In my head I answered, *Because I wanted out.*

"Why did you come back?"

Silently once more, *Because money runs out.* Money doesn't grow on trees.

"Were you involved in the planning of the murder of Thomas Paige?"

I stared at the detective.

Seriously? Did he think I'd answer *that*?

But I answered the way I'd always answered. With a lie. "No."

By now, it felt true. It exuded truth. I'd said it so many times it felt like a part of my very heart. As far as I was concerned, it was the whole truth.

55

LEE

I counted off another day.

Another day closer to freedom.

A freedom I craved desperately.

What a stupid shit I'd been.

Thinking this made me a man.

Taking a piss in public.

Wearing a onesie.

And waiting.

All the never-ending waiting.

The only thing that made it bearable was books. The ones my mom brought. Stories passed the time. Stories took me away from this concrete hell.

And so did my remorse.

"You'll be out soon," my mom said when she came to see me that morning.

"I can't wait," I said, and I meant it, but not simply because I hated it here. I meant it because I wanted something else more.

A second chance.

A chance to show her I wasn't living as Jerry Stefano's

son. That I wasn't following in a criminal's footsteps. That I could turn away from that life that had once lured me, from the ways of the street that Kenny and TJ had taught me.

I wasn't my father's son.

I was hers.

And I wanted to show her that I could make changes.

She'd lined up plans for me to take a community college class when I got out. I never liked school, but I'd have to man up and do it.

I laughed to myself. School had to be better than being behind bars.

We talked some more, and when the visit was up, she asked if I'd seen the detective lately. "No, but when I do, I'll cooperate."

"I love you, Lee."

"I love you, Mom."

A little while later, the detective came in, and I took my mom's words to heart once more. No longer did I protect my own in the Royal Sinners. I protected my mom.

And I would do that by sharing what I knew.

"Any chance you want to tell me where TJ Nelson likes to hang out?"

I named a few spots, including one that made the detective's eyebrows dance.

"That so?"

"Yup." It was the truth, and his eyes seemed to spark.

When he rose to leave, I cleared my throat. "Detective."

"Yes?"

"You can call me Lee Rosa."

He cracked a sliver of a smile. "Good to know, Lee."

56

MICHAEL

Michael

I answered John's call immediately.

"I need your help, Michael," he said, wasting no time.

"Lay it on me," I said from my desk.

"I think I know where to nab TJ. But bringing him in will require some stealth. The man's already wanted, so I need the element of surprise, but I know how to pull it off."

I was all too happy to help.

* * *

"You want us to set a trap?" Curtis asked.

"Yeah. I would really like that," John said, his tone somehow casual but also intensely serious.

My eyes swept from John to the two men I was making this request to. Leaning against the back of a royal-blue lounge chair, Curtis scratched his square jaw with his thumb, glancing at Charlie before answering. "So we've got to bring those scumbags back into our business?" he asked, arching an eyebrow skeptically as he waved a hand around the club, quiet now during the day. Jazz music hummed from the same speakers that played dance music after midnight.

John nodded. His arms were crossed. "I know it's not what you want, but if we bring him in—and I've got the warrant for his arrest—we can dismantle the gang. He's the last linchpin left, now that we've got their head guy. One of my witnesses has named the places he's been seen."

Curtis shook his head. "This isn't one of them."

"No. But by using the guy who started trouble here a few weeks ago with the knife in the bathroom, we think we can lure him. That guy is willing to cooperate to get out of his own trouble by inviting TJ here. Making it look like just a regular night out. Once he's here, you make the call, and we'll bring him in."

Charlie blew out a long stream of air. "I don't like bringing them in here. We've been trying to keep guys like that out. I don't want any guns in my club."

"I hear you loud and clear," John said. "But we're close, so close to blasting them apart. We'll have plainclothes cops here. They will be the only ones with weapons, besides my men and myself. We'll do thorough checks at the door to make sure. And Michael's team will ramp up security. We will keep your business safe."

Charlie hummed and raised his chin at John. "I heard you speak at the benefit a few months ago."

My ears pricked. I hadn't attended that event, but both Ryan and Colin had. It was a fundraiser for the local community center where Colin volunteered. His girlfriend, Elle, ran it. Colin's company was one of the main donors, and so was White Box. These guys were committed to cleaning up the city, and I hoped they'd take this chance, even if it put them at risk.

"You had a friend who was injured when you were younger," Charlie said, meeting John's eyes.

The detective nodded.

"I know what that's like," he said through tight lips. "I lost one of my brothers when I was younger. To street crime too. That loss changed me. Led me to make some choices I wasn't so proud of. Now I'm trying to live a better life, in his name. He would have wanted us to do this."

Curtis nodded and patted Charlie's shoulder. "He would have. He really would have."

Charlie turned back to them. "We will help you."

* * *

The waiting was miserable. Minutes ticked by as if they were hours. The days were elongated, and I walked through town as if in a surreal dream. I was glued to my phone, just in case there was news. In case Morris or Mindy or John or Ryan or Annalise or my White Box guys called.

Waiting sucked. Waiting was torture. But I understood this was the safest way to bring in TJ. The fucking mastermind of multiple hits had gotten away with so much, but with Luke now behind bars and facing a possible trial, and TJ's cousin Kenny arrested, and many of their guys on the streets locked up too, the power structure of the Royal Sinners was cratering. They were caving in on themselves. TJ was the last man standing, and once he was down, I could breathe again.

I was slated to fly to Paris in a few days, and I had half a mind to cancel the trip. But I didn't want or need to do that. I wasn't the guy who'd be making the arrest. I was simply the man waiting for justice for my family. Justice would happen, one way or another, I was sure. We had waited long enough.

I went to the gym late one night, hoping a workout would burn off some of the tension. At the end of my weights session, my phone rang.

57

JOHN

I was playing pinball with my future brother-in-law when the call came—Sophie liked that Ryan and I were hanging out, trying to get to know each other better, since we'd be family and all. I'd just sent a silver ball screaming up the board and into the waiting maw of Jabba the Hutt at my favorite game in the arcade hall not far from White Box. The phone trilled.

Immediately, I let go of the buttons, saw my colleague's name flashing across the screen, and answered the call from my guy on site at the club. "He's here."

I wanted to punch the sky. "I'm on my way. Don't let him out of your sight."

Soon, I walked through the door of the club, the neon lights bright and beckoning. Once inside, I nodded to Curtis, who watched over the joint like a sentry. Curtis tipped his forehead to the cigar lounge.

I conveyed a silent thanks with my eyes, found my colleagues, and made my way to the lounge, two men behind me. I peered in through the glass window into the small room. A cloud of smoke engulfed three guys, and one of them laughed.

The man was bigger, brawnier, and tougher than the others, and even though I had never laid eyes on him before, I recognized TJ Nelson in seconds. The gold earring. The arms the size of barrels. The missing tooth now capped with a gleaming white one. And the tattoo on his right bicep.

Protect our own.

The last puzzle piece. The last man standing. Inhaling deeply, I reached for the door handle, turned it, and entered the dark, smoky room. There was no way out. Three pairs of eyes met me, and TJ's were the hardest— dark brown, cold, and full of hate.

He didn't say a word, just raised his chin, waiting for me to go first.

"TJ Nelson?"

"Maybe. Depends who you are," the man said, his voice deep and menacing.

"I'm the man you've been avoiding for eighteen years. But your lucky streak ends tonight," I said, moving quickly, brandishing my badge.

TJ's hands darted behind his jacket, like he was hunting for a weapon, but I was faster, drawing my gun from my holster and aiming it. Since the other men had helped to lure him in and were actually working for us on this, I was sure TJ didn't stand a chance—even when the broker wielded a long, gleaming knife.

Still.

I didn't waver, keeping my focus on him, careful but ready.

His eyes turned to slits, and he raised the weapon. For a second, my blood went cold. The club had a metal detector for guns, but somehow TJ had managed to slip this knife through. This was precisely why I had needed to trap the guy, capture him in a corner, someplace my suspect would let down his guard.

"You don't know who you're messing with," TJ hissed as he lifted the weapon higher.

"But I do. I absolutely do," I said coolly, keeping the gun trained on the man I wanted behind bars.

TJ tried to stand up from the leather couch, but in a flash, my partners moved in, quickly overpowering him, each man pinning an arm. One grabbed the knife, and the other cuffed him.

Then, as I tucked my gun away, I said the words I'd wanted to announce for so long. "I have a warrant for your arrest for the murder of Thomas Paige. You have the right to remain silent. Anything you say can and will be used against you in a court of law. You have the right to an attorney. If you cannot afford an attorney, one will be appointed for you."

TJ's eyes widened. The expression on his face was cold white fear.

Good.

As it should be.

As it absolutely should be.

58

MICHAEL

Many glasses of champagne were raised. In the kitchen of my grandparents' house, the very home that the Sloan siblings had bought for them a few years ago as our way of saying thanks, I lifted a glass. Cleared my throat. Said words I'd longed to say out loud.

"To justice. At long last," I said.

"Hear! Hear!" It was a chorus sounded by everyone.

My grandmother nodded as a tear slipped from her eye. We clinked glasses, Brent, Ryan, Sophie, Elle, my grandparents, even Mindy was with us. I tapped my glass to the lowball glass of Diet Coke Colin held, and to the water glass in my pregnant sister's hand. I suspected John would be in attendance at the next event, but for now he was still busy working, and I was glad of that. I hoped that Marcus would come back soon to join us. Maybe for Christmas.

"At last," Victoria echoed, and we all drank.

There was something incredibly odd about celebrating an arrest. And yet, it wasn't the least bit bizarre.

Since my world had been wrenched upside down and shattered eighteen years ago, I'd grown accustomed to these unexpected moments. In a family that had seen their father killed by their mother, that same mother in prison, and a half-brother born behind bars, life remained unexpected.

Celebrations could take on the strangest forms, moving well beyond the usual festive occasions of birthdays, anniversaries, and weddings.

I knocked back a hearty gulp of champagne and wrapped an arm around my grandmother. She looked up at me and flashed a smile brimming with relief.

That was what this feeling was.

The long, overdue exhalation.

It was blissful relief, hard-earned justice, and delicious victory. Nothing would ever change the course our lives had taken that fateful night, but at last, there was the promise of peace once again.

Shannon beamed, and Brent rubbed his hand on her belly. Sophie began slicing the cherry pie she'd made for the occasion, as Ryan once again thanked her for the key part she'd played in helping decode the names of the accomplices. Colin wrapped his arms around Elle and kissed her cheek, then whispered something in her ear. She shot him the sweetest smile, and for a moment, I found myself wondering if Colin would be down on one knee soon too, popping the question to the woman he loved.

Love.

There was so much of it here in this house. We had a surplus when it came to love. My brothers and sister. Their husbands, girlfriends, and fiancées. My grandparents. Even the dog had joined in, rubbing his side against my grandmother's leg.

After I'd taken a bite of pie, my phone buzzed. Grabbing it from my back pocket, I felt my heart warm as I found a new photo from my woman.

A shot of her legs. It looked like she was sitting at a sidewalk café, and I could picture her perfectly—watching the world go by, observing it all, drinking it in, and thinking of me.

Annalise: Waiting for you. Not much longer.

I'd be seeing her in mere days. The past was behind me. The present was free of its weight. The future was in my grasp, on the other side of an ocean, waiting for me. I could have it, taste it, touch it, love it.

Love her, if she'd let me. I hoped, and I hoped, and I hoped that she was ready.

She was the love of my life, and I'd been given a second chance with her.

And if this whole situation's long time coming had taught me anything, it was that I needed to seize it.

59

ANNALISE

Over the last few days, Michael and I had wandered across Paris, seeing museums, stopping at bakeries, popping into shops, strolling along the Seine, and flipping through vintage postcards at the street-side dealers.

Today, we made our way to the Marché aux Puces at Porte de Vanves, a massive weekend flea market spread across many blocks.

I took his hand, threading my fingers through his. He glanced down at our joined hands and dropped a kiss on my cheek. I shuddered at the sparks that raced through me, just from a little kiss. He was so affectionate. Holding my hand. Wrapping an arm around me. Planting kisses on my face. Anywhere and everywhere. I loved walking through Paris with him touching me so possessively, as if he was telling all the world that I belonged to him.

"My father and mother used to bring me here when I was younger. To this flea market," I reminisced as we weaved through the crowds of shoppers along this stretch of vendors. "They loved to bargain shop. My father would come here to buy tools and skeleton keys and dusty old books. Funny thing is, he never actually used them. We had to donate them all when he passed away."

"Why did he want them?"

"Honestly, I think he loved to haggle."

Michael nodded. "Now that makes sense. I'm quite good at haggling. You should see me in action. It's amazing that Ryan thinks he's the negotiator of our firm, but really it's me. I make sure we get the best deals."

I squeezed his fingers. "Will you haggle for me, then?"

He arched an eyebrow, and we stopped, other bargain hunters bumping and nudging us as they pushed past.

He lowered his mouth to my ear. "Does that turn you on?"

I shivered in response. "I'm pretty much always turned on when I'm with you."

"Let's go," he said, his voice gritty, dirty.

Suddenly, the flea market had become foreplay, and Michael proved how much when he snagged a blue-and-white ceramic teapot that had caught my eye for twenty euros, down from its original fifty.

As we strolled away, he whispered to me, "Did it work?"

"Hot and bothered."

"Let's see how much."

I tipped my head to a café across the street, the words *Bouledogue* painted across the front in red letters, alongside an illustration of a canine of the same breed. Once inside, we took the staircase to the basement where restaurant bathrooms were usually located. Michael rapped on the door. Empty.

He tugged me inside, locked the door, and hung the canvas bag with the teapot from a hook.

He thumbed the hem of my skirt. "I love that you wear skirts with me now."

"I've learned my lesson."

Wrapping an arm around me, he tilted up my chin so I looked at him. His eyes searched mine, full of so much passion that I heated up all over, my skin tingling. He pushed a strand of hair away from my face and kissed a path along my jawline. My legs turned to jelly. My knees went weak, and heat pooled between my legs. One kiss, one touch, and I was ready.

He ran a hand along the inside of my thigh, and I quivered, melting into him. He gripped my waist and backed me up so I was pressed against the door. Cupping my jaw in his hand, he gazed into my eyes. My mouth fell open, and the entirety of the universe narrowed to his beautiful face, to the way he stared at me, drawing out the anticipation. To his words as he said, "Now let me fuck you, my love."

My eyes floated closed. His need for me was so intense it nearly overwhelmed me. But I knew precisely how he felt—the same need drove me. Made me want to smash into him, grind my body against his, bring him close and then closer still. My hands worked open his jeans, unzipping them, freeing his cock. The aching desire to be filled by him spread to every bone, every nerve, every cell. I ran my hand along his hard length, thrilling at the feel—the skin so damn soft, while he was so incredibly hard.

Then his hands grabbed my ass, and I let go of him. In seconds he'd lifted me, wrapped my legs around his waist, and tugged my panties to the side.

"Michael, do I have to be quiet?"

He shook his head as he rubbed his cock against my wetness, sending an electrical charge through me. "I don't care who knows that you're in heaven when I fuck you." He eased inside me, and that current surged, igniting me, crackling through my being. My head fell back, and I moaned. Loudly.

Heaven.

That was precisely what this was. Sex with Michael was a faraway land of ecstasy, of endless fiery pleasure. "It's so good, there's no way I can be quiet," I murmured.

"Then moan. Cry. Scream. It doesn't matter to me. Fucking you is something only I get to do, and I don't care who knows how completely consumed you are."

"I am. I am consumed."

His fingers dug into my ass as he thrust. Deeper. Harder. Farther.

He pumped, swiveling his hips, pushing, his cock moving in sharp jabs that sent ripples of desire everywhere. Each one was more powerful than the last. He dipped his face to my neck, whispering my name as he fucked me. Whispering kisses across my skin that made me shiver. That made me burn. "You knew it would be like this with us, right?"

I nodded on a breathless pant as he stroked inside me. "Yes, I knew."

His breath came fast, ragged against my skin. "I can't hold back from wanting you like this. From fucking you everywhere. From making you come."

His hips moved in relentless thrusts, and my back slammed against the wood. My body sought more of him, chasing the release. "Michael," I groaned. "I need to come so badly."

"Come on me, my love," he said, and I knew from his pace, from the low timbre of his voice, that his climax was imminent too. I knew also from this deep, exquisite ache in my body, and most of all from the mad fury in my heart, that he was fucking me into falling all the way. That his words and his deeds and his care and his love made it impossible not to fall for him again.

With his dirty voice in my ear, I broke. My orgasm crashed over me, swept through me, stole my senses.

I cried out.

He grunted, with a deep, powerful thrust. His climax followed mine, our bodies shuddering, our hearts beating fast. A minute later he lowered me, holding my waist, letting me find my land legs again.

When I did, I cupped his cheeks and looked deeply in his eyes. "I'm falling."

He sighed happily, as if I'd taken the weight of the world off his shoulders. His eyes shimmered with something that looked like joy. "Then I'll catch you."

I pressed my face to his jawline, rubbing my cheek against his stubble, terrified and elated at the same damn time.

Terrified that now that I loved again, I could lose again, and that my heart couldn't be put back together a second time.

60

MICHAEL

We crossed the Seine on the walk to my hotel, stopping to gaze at the slate-gray river and the city unfolding on each side. Fog drifted over the water, curling like smoke as night fell on Paris. Streetlamps cast their halo glow on the sidewalks.

My trip only lasted four days, and was fast coming to an end. Too fast. I was quickly learning there would never be enough time with Annalise. I'd booked a hotel room for this first visit, not wanting to presume I'd stay at her place, and we'd spent our nights at the hotel together and our days traveling across the city, our own little vacation.

It was a dream come true.

Especially when Annalise tilted her face to look at me, a sweet smile on her red lips. "How are we going to do this, Michael?"

I brushed a thumb across her cheek. Not touching her was impossible. "Like we've been doing," I said, since I wasn't going to let time zones be an issue.

"Does the distance scare you?"

I shook my head. "Nothing scares me now that you're back in my life."

"I don't want us to fall apart. I don't want us to lose touch," she said, gripping my shirt. "I want a chance with you. A real chance."

"We'll make this work. You'll come see me, I'll come see you, and we'll meet in the middle."

She grinned, her bright smile lighting up her emerald eyes. "We will meet in the middle."

*　*　*

A glass display case stacked with chocolate tartes, raspberry cakes, and flaky croissants beckoned to me. Across from the hotel, the Roussillon bakery had long lines, but boasted the arrondissement's speediest bakers, or so Annalise had told me. "The line moves quickly."

"Good. Because I'm hungry. You keep me working hard all night long," I said with a wink.

She nudged me. "And you love my workouts."

"I do. And right now, I'd love breakfast," I said, my mouth watering as I surveyed the shelves of baked goods, from baguettes and rolls to éclairs and strawberry pastries.

When we reached the cashier, Annalise ordered a baguette and a coffee éclair. The woman stuffed a loaf into a white paper bag, then wrapped an éclair in paper and twisted the ends.

"*Pour vous?*" she asked me.

"I would like an apricot tarte and a yogurt," I said in my best French. I was rewarded with a grin and the treat.

Outside, we parked ourselves at a small wooden table.

"Now the test. You hate coffee, but do you like coffee éclairs?"

"Let's find out."

As a cool breeze blew by and a hint of gray swelled the sky, she slid the éclair to me. I bit into it, savoring the sweetness. I hummed around the flaky pastry, and wiggled my eyebrows.

"So that's a yes?"

I nodded. "Big yes. You keeping a list of my favorite things?"

"Perhaps I am," she said, and my heart thumped harder, simply because she'd truly wanted to know. She'd followed through. She was curious about my everyday wants and wishes.

We traded bites of the tarte, shared the yogurt, and pulled off chunks of bread as Parisians strolled by on a Sunday morning. Soon the sky darkened, and raindrops splashed across the cobbled sidewalk.

We tossed the remnants of our late breakfast into a trash can, and I offered her a hand. "You know what's good to do in the rain?"

"I do," she said, cupping my cheeks and kissing me as the world around us turned gray and wet and cool.

I moved my lips to her ear. "You smell like falling rain."

"Do you like it?"

"I love it," I said, lacing my fingers through her hair and inhaling her, so glad I didn't have to rely on a letter to get my fix.

She pulled back to look at me as if she was searching my face, studying my eyes, uncovering new truths about me, and maybe herself too. "I think this is more than falling."

My heart beat faster, soaring to the sky, and I could hardly believe that life could be so good, so sweet. It was even better when we returned to the room and spent the next few hours in bed, taking our time, discovering even more, falling even deeper.

61

ANNALISE

A small fire blazed in the fireplace, warming the centuries-old building that housed the tiny restaurant not far from the Eiffel Tower. Framed artwork of eggs, asparagus, and tomatoes lined one white wall. Another wall was red brick. White cloths draped the tables.

It was Michael's last night here, and already I missed him. The empty ache had started before he even left. I wanted him here. Wanted him to stay. I'd loved every moment with him.

Right now, I simply loved watching him talk to Patrick, Noelle's husband. With the dinner plates cleared away and the dessert served, they were discussing French politics and world affairs. It was so sexy to hear him so deep in conversation, a glass of red wine in his hand, his blue button-down shirt revealing a small patch of skin at his throat that I wanted to kiss.

My lips longed to press against his chest. My fingers itched to undress him. My heart ached to have him close.

Especially since he fit in so well with my family.

I understood even better why he'd learned French—to

be able to talk like this, to be a part of my life. It was such a heady thing, such a romantic endeavor. I'd marveled at what he'd done, and now I witnessed it. This meal with my sister, my mother, and Patrick was one of the first times I'd heard him speak my language for this long.

He'd talked to my mother too during the meal, and she'd plied him with questions about Las Vegas. Was the Strip larger than life? *Yes.* Were the hotels as big as they seemed? *Absolutely.* Was the city full of sin? He'd answered yes to that one too, a sad smile on his face.

I was amazed how much he loved his home, in spite of all the pain he'd gone through there. But that was behind him now that the last man had been taken in. We hadn't spent much time diving into the details of the final arrests. Michael seemed to want to move on, and I couldn't fault him for not wanting to dwell on it. Perhaps that was part of why he appeared so carefree again, so much like the man I'd known when I was younger, yet so much like a new man too. Strong, protective, and yet vulnerable. I'd never known someone to put his heart on the line the way Michael had for me.

"He's a good man."

I turned to meet my mother's light-green eyes. Her voice was soft, a whisper just for me.

I nodded. "He is."

My mother's hand, wrinkled from years, pressed to my forearm. "I'm glad you're letting yourself be happy."

"Me too."

Her knowing eyes stared back at me. "Have you told him how you feel?"

"Sure. He knows how I feel," I said.

My mother squeezed my arm. "No. Have you told him you're in love with him too?"

I froze with the glass of wine on the way to my lips. I

was just starting to admit it to myself, but hearing it out loud? Knowing that someone so close to me could see it, had noticed the connection between us? It was becoming real.

"You should tell him," my mother urged.

I parted my lips, but words didn't come. I wasn't sure what to say, or if I could give voice to all these questions stirring inside me. Was I ready to take that final leap?

"Tell him soon," my mother whispered, then she pressed a kiss to my cheek before continuing. "And I know it's not a one-way street. I see the way you look at him. I see how you lean close to him. How your world seems to be his world."

A lump rose in my throat. My eyes welled with tears, but none fell.

After the check came and Michael insisted on paying, my mother announced loudly that Patrick and Noelle would walk her home.

Noelle nodded vigorously. "Yes. We'll help her up the steps."

"Go," my mother said, shooing us along. "Your flat is around the corner."

We said our goodbyes, and Michael and I turned the other direction. "Do you want to come to my place?" I asked.

"If you're sure."

I stopped on the street, reached for his hand, then looked him in the eyes. "I want you to see where I live. You're not just some man I'm slinking away to a hotel room to be with. You've had dinner with my family. I want you in my home. You're part of my heart. Part of my life."

He pressed his forehead to mine. His breath ghosted across my skin. His arms looped around me. With him, I felt so much potential, so much possibility, so much future.

I took him to my home.

62

MICHAEL

Annalise unlocked the green door. It creaked open, and pride shimmered in her eyes. Her irises danced as she held out her arm and led me through the narrow foyer into the small kitchen.

"My home," she said, beaming.

I cataloged the room. Red espresso cups. Sky-blue dishes in the dish rack, and a clean sink.

We wandered into a tiny living room, and before I could look around, she gestured to French doors that opened into a small den.

"This is my office," she said proudly, and showed me some of the framed photos on the wall, shots she'd taken over the years. There were a few images from the Middle East that had won her awards, but mostly the photos were of simpler things.

A lemon-yellow dresser.

A crowded street-side café.

A leaf blowing across the sidewalk. Even a few of her black-and-white boudoir shots.

"You really are talented," I said.

Then I spun around and took in her living room for the first time.

My gaze immediately zoomed in on a framed photo on her built-in bookcase of her husband, holding a handful of maps under his arm.

One photo. That was all. But it was enough to remind me of Marseilles.

Her hand ran up my arm. It was warm and comforting, but right now I didn't want it.

My reaction was emotional, not rational. It was passionate, not thoughtful. I could have devised a million logical explanations to settle my brain and cool my nerves. But I was shaken.

And she noticed. "Does it bother you?" she asked, indicating the picture.

I told the bitter truth. "Yes." It wasn't my proudest moment. "And I feel like a complete ass for saying that and feeling that."

"You're not," she said, shaking her head.

"I just wish . . ." I didn't finish the thought. But filling in the missing words was easy—*I just wish you didn't have a photo of your first husband.*

"Michael," she said, her voice soft. "I have photos of you too. I had an entire photo album of our year together in Las Vegas. I took it to university. I even looked at it the other day before you came here, along with the photos I took of you at Caesars. One of those photos is on my desktop right now until I decide how I want to frame it or crop it."

I dragged a hand through my hair, and for the first time wondered if Julien had felt this way too. If he'd been crazed enough to want to have this woman all to himself, to erase her history and mark her only with him. I would have wholly understood. Because this intense need to be her *only*, as selfish and single-minded as it was, gnawed at me.

And I didn't want to say anything more. I didn't want to say the wrong thing. My jaw ticked, and I held all these dark wishes inside me.

But Annalise missed nothing. "Michael, I have a past. It's real, and it's a part of me. Just like ours is. You and I found our way back to each other, and there's nowhere else I'd rather be. Just because I cared about him doesn't mean I can't feel everything for you."

Ah hell. I was a complete jerk for feeling this way. I was envious of a dead man. I was eaten up by the fact that she'd had a husband. Who. Had. Died.

I was alive.

What the fuck was wrong with me?

"I'm sorry," I muttered, though I knew that wasn't enough. Perhaps I was too stubborn. Too narrow. I knew it was irrational, but this woman—she was it for me. She was *all* for me. And that feeling inside me, of never wanting to be without her, made me rash.

"Do you still love him?" My throat was raw as I gave voice to my darkest fear.

"Michael," she said, imploring. "Stop. Just stop. He is gone, and I'm not in love with a ghost. I'm here. And I'm falling in love with you now."

I swallowed, collecting myself. I drew a deep breath, trying to let it out while taking in what she'd just said. That's what I should be focusing on. But my chest churned with black and white and gray emotions, and I didn't know how to wrestle them to the ground and have them make sense.

We left soon afterward, heading back to the hotel.

Annalise could sense my mood, sense that I needed to get away from memories of the past, back to neutral ground and where we were now. It was my last night in Paris, and I wanted to reconnect with her.

At the hotel, I made love to her, letting the sex blot out the blackness in my heart, the ugly jealousy in my soul. But something continued to nag at me.

I didn't want to be her second best, and yet I felt like the runner-up. The whole truth of what bothered me boiled down to this—she could have chosen me in Marseilles, and she didn't.

And so when she asked me once more what was wrong, the dam broke.

In bed, I turned to her, and said it. Cruel, terrible words. "You could have picked me."

She blinked. "Excuse me?"

"Ten years ago. You weren't married yet. You could have called off the engagement and run away with me," I said, and once I saw the expression on her face, I knew I'd said the wrong thing.

She recoiled. "Is that who you want me to be?"

Did I? It was a valid question. "A woman who loved me? Yes." But that was an emotional answer. Only an emotional one.

She sighed. "Michael, I hadn't seen or even spoken to you in years. Imagine that. Picture that. Picture our life together like that. If I'd left him for you. I'd made a commitment, and we were at different places in our lives then. I missed you. I loved you. But our time wasn't then. And if we're fixed on the past, we won't live now."

I clenched my teeth, as she leveled her assessment straight at my heart.

And it was all too true.

I should have said I was sorry.

But what hurt the most wasn't that she was likely right.

It was that I wished I could go home and ask my father's advice. Wished things could have been different starting eighteen years ago.

63

ANNALISE

As I raced down to the Métro a few days later, on the way to a photoshoot at a client's Montmartre flat, I was annoyed. I was still so damn annoyed, as my train rattled into the station and I stepped through the doors. I was frustrated as I gripped the pole and the subway rumbled away. I didn't want to have to constantly justify my past to Michael. He'd have to accept it at some point if we were truly going to be together and pull off this transcontinental relationship. Wasn't it hard enough to manage a long-distance love without this added layer of . . . bullshit?

I huffed and stared off, searching the faces of the other people in the car, wondering if everyone on this train was as goddamn frustrated as I was.

Michael had tried to be cool after we'd left my apartment. But I wasn't a fool. I'd read his emotions and sensed his distance back at the hotel. He'd pulled away from me that last night, and everything since then had been bittersweet.

I wanted the sweet, hold the bitter, please.

And I didn't want to make apologies for having loved before. For having made a choice. To be honorable. To be a woman of my word.

I reached my destination, climbing the many stairs out of the station, and walked along the curving, hilly streets to find my client's home. All the while, I tried to force Michael out of my brain. There was no room for annoyance now.

I raised the iron knocker at the door and was greeted by a stunning fortysomething woman with black hair.

"Come in, come in," the woman said in a smoky, sexy voice, excitement in her tone. "I've been counting down the hours until the shoot."

As I captured images of the boudoir session, the woman told me that she'd been divorced and was remarrying. The photos were a gift for her soon-to-be husband. In the images, she appeared both sultry and joyful. This woman had moved on.

Why couldn't Michael?

The past is the past. You can't unwrite it. He ought to know that as well as anyone.

Anger stormed through me again as I hopped on the Métro again after finishing up with my client. I stopped at my mother's, then helped her to a doctor's appointment.

"She's doing better," the doctor said. "Her hip is stronger."

My mother nudged me and winked. "See? I'm tough."

"You are," I said, a true smile appearing on my face for the first time today.

"You come from a long line of tough women," my mother said after we left the appointment and headed to a café, my elbow hooked around her arm, our strides slow.

"I do," I said as we found a table on the sidewalk and ordered coffees.

"What's wrong, then? Why do you seem so upset?"

"You're too observant for your own good."

"That's where you get it from." My mom tapped the edge of her eye. "So tell me . . ."

I watched as the crowds click-clacked by on the sidewalk, the cool, crisp air surrounding us and I gave my mother the gist of how Michael seemed unable to deal with my past. The coffee arrived, and we both lifted our cups, lost in thought.

My mother took a drink then set it down on the saucer, her lips curving in a knowing grin. "I knew you loved him."

I knit my brow, shooting my mother a curious look.

"What did he say when you told him you loved him?" my mother asked.

"I didn't say that. I said I was falling."

"Ah," my mother said, nodding sagely. "Therein lies the problem."

"How is that a problem?"

My mother locked her fingers together, forming a bridge. "Falling in love and being in love are bedfellows, but they aren't the same. *Falling* is just a way to float the idea, like testing the waters. If you love him, you should tell him. Reassure him. He loves you so. Michael wears his heart on his sleeve for you, and a man like that needs to know he's special. He knows he's not the only one you've loved, but he wants to feel like he is." She unlaced her fingers and stared at me, her eyes holding me captive, softly demanding. "Does he feel like he is? The only one?"

My gut twisted. He was the only one for me now, but perhaps I hadn't exactly made that clear. "I really don't know."

My mother patted my hand. "Make sure he knows."

That night, I wrote to him. I wasn't entirely convinced I

wanted to say those three words in a letter, but there were other things to say. Things that were as important.

The truth of all my fears.

When I was through, I dropped it at FedEx. He would receive it in two days.

64

MICHAEL

Sometimes when you drive to a familiar place, you're not sure how you got there. You know the route by heart. You've done it so many times it's a part of you.

As I walked across the grass with my sister, my feet guided me in that same fashion along the path we'd traveled many times—on a winding stone walkway, over spongy grass, then through a row of headstones, guarded by oaks and elms. Shannon clutched a bouquet of sunflowers.

She came here often, leaving these flowers on our father's grave each time. Today I accompanied her. It wasn't the anniversary of our father's death, nor was it his birthday. It was just an average day, and that was why we came. To remember those who were gone. Both our father and the baby Shannon had lost ten years ago, only eleven weeks into her pregnancy.

I was grateful to be here with Shannon. I could focus on her, as I'd often done. I didn't need or want to focus on me. I wanted to put the ending of my Paris trip behind me. The way I'd acted. The unfair words I'd said to the woman I loved.

For the umpteenth time, I shoved it out of my head.

"You hanging in there?" I asked, eyeing Shannon's belly.

She nodded. "I wish I could speed up time though. Fast-forward and have the baby in my arms, to know he or she is safe and healthy and alive."

I draped an arm around her shoulder, squeezing. "Yeah, me too," I said, rather than giving her a platitude. *Everything will be all right.* I hoped it would, but both my sister and I had seen enough to know those sorts of statements were meaningless.

The morning sun rose in the sky, and soon we reached our father's resting place. I read the engraved words out loud, as I always did when I came here with Shan. *Thomas Darren Paige. Loving father.*

"He was," my sister said.

"He was." And once again I wished he were here. Wished I could ask him how to unsay what I'd said. How to fix things with Annalise. We'd talked some since I'd returned, but not enough to soothe the shame in me.

Shannon set the flowers at the base of the headstone, then kissed the granite. My throat hitched watching my sister. I kneeled down briefly and wrapped my arms around her, holding her close as tears streamed down her cheeks.

Soon she rose, wiped her hands across her cheeks, and plastered on a smile. "I'm all better now."

I smiled back and tucked her hair behind her ear. "Of course you are, Shannon bean."

"So tell me about Paris . . ."

"Ah . . ." The subject I'd both been avoiding and needed to talk about, and Shan was precisely the person who'd understand best. As we stood by the grave, a cool fall breeze rustling the leaves, I shared the fears that had bubbled to the surface that last night in Paris, culminating with the fact that I was wrapped in envy still.

"And I think I might be a total asshole who has no perspective, since I'm jealous of a dead guy," I said with a forced laugh as I finished the story.

She rubbed my arm reassuringly. "No, you're not. You're just in love, and it's hard, but I don't know why you're so worried that she's living in the past or can't move on fully with you."

"How is it possible for her to feel the same way about me that I feel about her?" I gripped my chest, as if grabbing at my heart. "I'm so crazy for her I can't imagine ever feeling this way about anyone else. How could she do it? She is the great love of my life. How will I ever be anything to her that comes close?"

Shannon parked her hands on my shoulders. She was tiny, and I towered over her small frame, but in that moment, she was the strong one. "You are my big brother I have always looked up to, leaned on, and relied on. You've been like a watchdog, looking out for all of us. But you've forgotten to take care of yourself."

I rolled my eyes. "Fine," I said, not denying it. "But what does that mean?"

"That you've got it wrong, Michael. Because you understand love on this powerful, intense level. That's your strength, but it's also your weakness. To you, love is an all-or-nothing proposition." She moved her hand back and forth like a pendulum. "You love Dad; you don't love Mom."

I scoffed. "Of course I don't love her. How could I?"

She sighed and squeezed my arm. "All I'm saying is you feel everything in your bones, down to your marrow. And it's not conceivable to you that love can be more than one person, more than one thing. Like how you felt about Brent and how angry you were with him."

I flashed back to my reaction when Shannon told me she was with Brent again. I hadn't been happy, and I'd told Brent as much. But I'd softened eventually. I'd welcomed Brent into the family because of the man's deep love for my sister. "But we're good now. Brent and I get along."

"And I am so, so glad. But my point is this—right now with Annalise, you're stuck in All-or-Nothing Michael Land. And you have to let the past go. I had to let my own mistakes with Brent go. There are so many things I could have done differently ten years ago. But we found each other again. Remember that. You and Annalise found each other again. You're together. *Now.* Alive and in love. You have each other's true hearts. You do."

Something inside me broke at her words. Something dark and consuming. Something like fear. It broke off and fell away.

To the ground.

"I'm an ass," I said.

Shan laughed, shaking her head. "No, you're just a man madly in love. And you're also a man who doesn't always see what's obvious."

My brow furrowed. "Okay, what's obvious?"

"It's possible to love two people deeply, madly, and truly."

"How? How can you say that?"

Her next words came out in a soft breath. "I love two people deeply."

I arched an eyebrow in question. As far as I knew, Brent was it for her—her one and only. Her first love and her last love, and she hadn't fallen for anyone in between. "Who?"

"Brent," she said, raising her chin, saying his name matter-of-factly. "I loved Brent in college for who he was then—a goofball, a funny guy, my hero. He's still the same man, and yet he's also completely different. And I fell in love again with the man he is now. A strong man, the guy who makes me laugh, a great father, my biggest supporter. The one."

"But he's the same man," I said, trying to make sense of my sister's theory.

She nodded. "I know. Of course he's still the same person, but . . . he's also not. He's different now than he was the first time we were together, and I loved him then, and I also fell in love with him all over again now. With the man he is today," she said, stopping for a beat.

In her silence, a bird chirped in a tree, and somewhere on the other side of the cemetery, footsteps crunched over grass, and I spotted others visiting headstones too. These moments surrounding me—of life and death and love and memory—tugged at everything inside me, yanking on all my heartstrings. I loved Annalise in high school. I loved the memory of her. I loved the idea of her. And then I fell in love with her again in the present, with the woman she is now. "I think that's how I feel for her."

"And how *she* feels for you," Shannon added. "But you have to rethink your all-or-nothing view of her. Because she's falling in love with you now too." She poked me in the chest for emphasis. "She loved you then, and she loves you now, and you're fixated on what came in between. You need to let it go, because it's foolish to think there's only one great love."

"There is for me," I protested, but it was fainter this time, and my words seemed to hold less weight than they had before. Was she right? Was I proving my own theory wrong by falling in love with her all over again, but with the woman she was today?

"The girl she was at sixteen and the woman she is today

are the same, but they're different." She ran a hand along her belly. "And look at me. I love both of my babies. I love the baby I lost and the baby inside me," she said in a broken whisper. Then she held my gaze. "We have so much more capacity for love than we let ourselves feel when we're grieving."

I exhaled, then inhaled, letting her words expand and dig roots inside me. I knew she was right. I knew she was onto something. And I knew I needed to get out of my own way and let this love take shape.

Because even though my father wasn't here, I knew what he'd say. I didn't have to wonder. He made plans for me to learn French. He wanted me to be with Annalise. He believed in love.

He'd tell me to live with love.

* * *

Later, I sent her an email inviting her to Ryan and Sophie's wedding.

Dear Annalise,

It goes without saying that I miss you terribly. But I've learned that things that go without saying still need to be said.

I miss you.

And I want to see you again. As soon as we can.

Would you please be my date to my brother's wedding? It would mean the world to me to see him marry the love of his life with you by my side.

With love,

Michael

That was only the start.

But I needed to figure out what to say to her about everything else.

* * *

When I returned home from work the next day, she'd replied with a *yes*.

And an *I'd love to*.

And an *I can't wait*.

That emboldened me, and I planned to write her a proper letter, to say I was sorry, to say I wanted what she had to give.

We'd always communicated well through the written word.

But I had to do more than write. I had to *do*. To act. To show. I had a plan, and I'd research the possibilities as soon as I was home in a few minutes.

But once inside my building, there was a delivery waiting for me—a slim lavender envelope. Gripping it tightly, I rode the elevator up to the twentieth floor. My nerves were tense, tight, in case this was bad news, in case it was the end. If it was, I needed to be alone to read it.

As soon as I entered my house, I leaned back against the door, slid my finger under the seal, and ripped it open.

Dear Michael,

Sometimes phone calls don't suffice, and email becomes insufficient for expressing what's in our hearts. But I worry I've been negligent with yours. That I've assumed too much and said too little, that my fears of losing someone I love—you, I worry about losing you—have held me back. Sometimes the fear is like a fist squeezing my voice, choking it.

I have that fear now with you.

So I turn to the written word. We've always been good with letters, haven't we? I can write down what is too hard to say at times. And that is this. You asked me something on your last night in Paris, and I gave you an answer you didn't like.

But the bigger issue is this—I didn't say enough.

And I want to say it all now.

A part of me never stopped loving you. How could I? You were my first, and I wanted you to be my last. That part became quieter over the years, while we were apart.

But now that part is an active part. And what I feel is so much more than a lingering fondness for a first love. It's an aching, hungry place in me, and a blissful, joyful one too. I want you in my life, Michael. I want new experiences with you. I want pictures of you and of us, of the places we'll go, and the things we'll do. Together.

I'm trying to give you all I can. I said it badly in Paris, so I'll say it again and again.

I'm falling in love with you.

Will you please let me fall in love with you?

xoxo

Annalise

My heart beat furiously, like it had a thousand wings, trying to carry me away to her. When I called, her phone went straight to voicemail. I called a few more times but she didn't answer.

I wrote a letter to her. I'd send it in the morning. And then I got online, researched flights, and booked the next one to Paris. I had to see her. I called my brother, told him I needed a few days off, and he said he understood.

"I'm leaving in the morning," I told him.

"Go get your woman," he said as I tossed some clothes into a carry-on.

"I will."

I checked my phone once more, hoping to hear from her, but she was probably asleep.

At some point, I crashed on my couch, the lights of Vegas flickering brightly through the windows, watching over me.

My phone bleated sometime well after midnight. Blinking, I rubbed my eyes and hunted for it. I must have knocked it off the couch, since it sounded from the floor. I grabbed it, a slow smile spreading across my face when I saw her name.

Sliding my thumb over the screen, I answered, my voice still gravelly from sleep. "Hey you."

"Hi. Is there any chance your bed fits two?"

65

ANNALISE

Anticipation skated across my flesh as I walked down the hallway on the twentieth floor, as I raised my fist, as I rapped on his door. It was nearly one a.m. My flight had been late—I was slated to have landed at nine. And while I'd toyed with emailing him from the plane, I'd opted for the surprise.

There was something both comforting and appealing in knowing the other person would like the surprise . . . of you.

In less than five seconds, he opened the door, looking sleep-rumpled and impossibly sexy. He wore black pants and a striped button-down shirt. The top two buttons were undone, and the shirt was wrinkled. His black hair was a mess, his jawline was thick with stubble, and his blue eyes twinkled.

A slow smile spread across his face as he drank me in, then before either one of us said a word, he tugged me inside, ran his fingers through my hair, and kissed me like crazy. I wanted to melt in his arms and spend the night like that.

When he broke the kiss, I nearly stumbled, woozy and drunk on him. He reached for my arm, steadying me, then he brushed a few loose strands of hair from my face, searching my eyes.

"Forgive me," he said, his eyes vulnerable, his expression contrite.

A lump formed in my throat. "For what?" I asked, needing to hear it from him.

"For the things I said. I handled things poorly in Paris. I'm sorry for being distant and pulling back. I love you so much I lose sight of things. But I need you to know I love the woman you are. I love your heart, your strength, your character. You are so tough, so resilient, so giving. And so true. And I am not letting you get away."

A smile gripped me, deep inside my soul. "I don't want to get away. I want you to have me, and I want to have you." I took a beat, pausing to collect myself even while this wild riot took place in my heart. "And I'm glad you know that *this*—now—is our time. Let's not let it pass us by."

"I won't," he said, cupping my cheek, making a promise I believed thoroughly. A grin curved his lips. "So, what brings you to town?"

I collected my thoughts, shifting away from his kiss. "You."

"Me?"

I nodded. "You." I cast my eyes to my suitcase. "Is it presumptuous for me to not have booked a hotel room for the next few days?"

He shook his head, taking the suitcase and shutting the door behind me. "It would be a travesty for you to stay anywhere else."

I glanced around, taking in his home for the first time ever. His was sparse and neat. A wide gray L-shaped couch looked out on a glittering view of the city. A metal coffee table was littered with magazines, papers, and a silver laptop. In a cabinet was a huge TV screen, with a stereo system perched beneath it. I suspected Michael listened to music more than he watched TV. On the walls were framed photos of his family. His brothers and sister, a black-and-white border collie, and a picture of Michael and his father from many years ago.

But my interest in the setting waned quickly. I had more important matters on my mind, and in my heart.

"Did you get my letter?"

"I did. I loved it," he said with a simple smile. "And I wrote one for you."

My heart thundered. "You did?"

He handed me a sheet of white paper, folded in half. I opened it, my pulse hammering hard with joy before I even read it.

Yes. It is always yes with you. Yes, come fall in love with me. Yes, come see me. Yes, I'll come see you. You have all my yeses. Always.

And that was all it took. I was unleashed. I was free. I'd flown across an ocean to surprise him, I'd come to his home to tell him what was in my heart, and I was no longer going to let my fear of losing rule the day.

And he wanted what I had to give.

I had everything to give. I had my whole, healed, gigantic heart. It was big and full, and it beat madly for him.

"I love you," I blurted out, standing in the quiet entryway of his home.

The corners of his eyes crinkled. "You do?"

I nodded and couldn't stop the grin from bursting across my face. "I love you, Michael. I do."

"You're not just falling in love with me?" he asked, his eyes sparkling with mischief.

"I'm. In. Love. With. You." I took my time enunciating every word, then I held his face in my hands. He sighed happily and closed his eyes. I tilted my chin to kiss him, brushing my lips over his. "I love you."

"Feel free to say that all night long," he said, tugging me closer.

I met his gaze. "I love you, and because of that, now I'm terrified of losing you. Even so, I won't let that stop me from feeling everything with you. Because I do feel everything, and I want to keep on loving you. Just let me love you with all I have."

He swallowed, his Adam's apple bobbing as he nodded. "Yes. It is always yes with you. You're all I want. Now and always."

"The same," I whispered. "It's the same for me with you."

"In fact," he said, his gaze drifting to his couch. A corner of a small suitcase poked out from next to the arm. "I'm booked on the morning flight to Paris to tell you I love you."

A wild grin spread across my face. "You are?"

"I needed to see you. To apologize in person. To love you in person," he said and I didn't think it was possible to be happier, but here it was—it had happened.

"Better cancel your flight."

"I will."

I pressed a kiss to his chest then traveled up his neck,

layering his throat with kisses, his jaw, his ear. I nibbled on his earlobe, and he groaned. Then he scooped me up in his arms, strode across the hardwood floors of his apartment, kicked open the door to his bedroom, and set me down. Whispering sweet, dirty words, he stripped off all my clothes as I took off his shirt.

"I missed you," he said, his voice soft and vulnerable as he pushed my red panties to the floor.

"I missed you too."

He slid a finger between my legs. "And I missed fucking you."

"God, I missed that so much too."

"And making love to you. And hearing you come. It's my favorite thing in the world—making you come," he said, dipping his head to my neck, sucking on my flesh as he rubbed his finger across my hot center. "The sounds you make. How you say my name."

I gasped. "I love it all with you. I want it all with you."

"Now?" he asked in a sexy growl.

"Now, please now," I said, begging as I unzipped his pants and he kicked them off.

"Show me how wild you are for me," he said, rough and commanding as he sank down on the bed, patting his chest. "Here. Ride my face, my love. I need you to come on my lips before I fuck you."

Sparks zipped across my skin as I climbed over him, straddling his face. With strong arms and a ravenous look in his eyes, he pulled me onto his mouth.

"Oh God," I cried out, and in seconds, we found a rhythm. I rocked against his face, and he gripped my hips, his strong fingers digging into the flesh of my ass as he devoured me.

He wasn't teasing. He wasn't playful. He was a hungry man, and he was eating me. With each lick, a savage pleasure tore through my body, twisting and coiling inside me. I thrust against him, moaning and fucking his tongue. With my hands braced against the wall, my hips moved in a frenzy, and he consumed me, sucking, kissing, licking until I was mindless with pleasure and aching to come.

Then a hot flush raced over my skin, and desire curled inside me, shattering in a white-hot neon burst in my body. His name tumbled from my lips as I cried out.

I barely had time to come down from my high when he shifted me off him, tugged me down the bed, and spread my legs wide. He stroked his rock-hard dick, staring between my legs. "So beautiful. You taste so fucking good. I want to have you in every way," he said, then lowered himself between my legs and sank inside.

In one deliciously intense thrust.

My eyes rolled closed, and my back bowed. "God, it's so good."

He pushed in, thrust deep, then lowered his chest to mine. "Do you know why?"

"Because I love you," I answered in a murmur.

"Because I fucking love you too."

And that was it. That was why I was in another world with Michael Sloan, fucking and falling and loving and living and feeling. So much feeling. Every nerve snapped, every cell blazed, everything else faded as he fucked me with so much passion, so much need, and so much love that I nearly burst. I wanted him now, I wanted him always, and I wanted him to know that he was mine, and I was his, and I would give him everything. As the pleasure built inside me again, nearing another crest, I tugged him even closer, whispering in his ear. Nothing complicated. Nothing artful. Just the three simple words that I knew he'd longed to hear. I'd never known anyone to love so deeply, so intensely, and I wanted him to have everything he wanted.

Me.

I could finally give him myself.

"I love you," I gasped, as another orgasm crashed into me, and he fucked me through it, chasing his own release.

66

MICHAEL

"Well, that was a helluva surprise," I said minutes later, flopping on my back next to her in bed.

She laughed. "Glad you liked it."

"My favorite surprise ever," I said, then rolled to my side, resting my head in my hand. I traced a line down to her waist. "So, how long are you here for?"

"Four days."

"Let's make the most of it," I said, and that started with grabbing my phone and cancelling my flight.

"We always make the most of our time together."

"That we do," I said, setting down my phone, and traveling across her stomach with my fingers, letting her know which terrain I meant. "I want to do everything with you," I whispered, squeezing her rear, letting my meaning register.

She met my gaze with wide, earnest eyes. "Anything. You can do anything with me," she said in her sexy, vulnerable voice. "I'm yours and I want it all with you."

But before I got wrapped up in her, again, I remembered Ryan. "I should tell Ryan I'll still be in town. I asked him to cover for me while I went to see you."

Annalise gave me a wry grin. "Tell him to cover for you while I'm here."

I dropped a kiss to her lips. "You're brilliant."

I sent a quick note to Ryan, then turned off my phone. "I bet he'll have no problem with that."

"He likes you. He wants you to be happy," she said, and then straddled me, pinning my wrists in her hands, the ends of her red hair tickling my chest.

"I'm a likable guy. And look at you. You like me too," I said playfully.

"I do like you. I'm in love with you. Just like I was all those years ago. Just like I wanted to be again when there was no forwarding address. Do you want to know what I said in that letter?"

"Sure," I said, because of course I did.

She stared at the ceiling, concentration in her features. "Dear Michael, I have never stopped thinking of you. I've finished school now and I'm free. Free to see you again, if you'll have me."

My heart thundered, and I played out a thousand what-ifs. What if I hadn't graduated early. What if I'd received it then? What-if, what-if, what-if.

But I was done with what-ifs.

I wanted the present and all the wonder of *it*.

"We have each other now," I said.

"Yes, we do Michael Sloan." Before I could respond, she tilted her head, as if considering what she'd just said. "Michael Sloan," she repeated, like my name was new to her. "Funny. The first boy I fell in love with was named Michael Paige-Prince. Now I'm in love with this Michael Sloan guy."

"Same guy?" I asked, arching an eyebrow.

"Same. But different too," she said, and with a sharp burst of clarity, I understood completely what my sister had meant—understood it because I felt it deep within my bones, all the way through my blood, and right into my heart.

67

JOHN

With the Thomas Paige investigation closed, and both TJ Nelson and Luke Carlton in jail awaiting trial, I'd taken on a few new cases, digging into another complicated homicide that demanded my attention.

With a crack-of-dawn run behind me, I headed into the office before seven, ready to tackle the workload.

But as I studied the evidence folder at my desk and downed my first cup of coffee, something nagged at the back of my mind about the Paige case. The limo company.

We'd studied it from stem to stern.

No red flags.

No issues.

It was almost too neat. Too clean. But if TJ Nelson had worked there, if he shook down another employee, was it truly neat and clean? And there were the extra work trips, the suspicious logbooks. The missing rides.

That didn't spell easy.

That spelled complicated.

And that's why something didn't entirely add up.

Because something about West Limos was a little too easy. There was one more thing . . .

As I hunted for the case file, my phone rang.

"Detective John Winston here," I answered.

"Hey, Winston. This is Special Agent Laura K. Reiss with the FBI, Las Vegas division. We've got a case we're working that might have hooks into one of yours."

I returned to my chair, spun around, and said, "Tell me more."

68

MICHAEL

"I'm betting this place has amazing breakfast potatoes because the fries I had a few weeks ago were out of this world," I said as I held open the door to the diner where Mindy and I had met Morris recently. It seemed almost like a lifetime ago.

"Can't wait. I'm famished," Annalise said, after she told the hostess we needed a table for two. The woman in the pink dress showed us to a booth, and Annalise ordered a coffee.

After the waitress vanished, Annalise flashed me a smile. She was radiant this morning—freshly showered, barely any makeup on, and her hair swept into a clip on her head. Then she yawned. "Jet lag."

I nodded. "I think we'll both be dealing with that a lot these days."

"We definitely will."

Even though I wished it were possible to see her more, I would take what I could get. I would live off the time we were able to carve out together until hopefully someday we could find a way to be in the same city more regularly.

For now, I at least had faith in the two of us, and that was a beautiful thing.

"So what brought you here a few weeks ago?" she asked, after we ordered eggs and the waitress brought coffee. "This diner isn't exactly down the block from your house."

"The private detective I hired wanted to meet here to share some leads. The info about the piano shop that helped break the case open."

"Ah," she said with a nod, reaching for her mug.

I picked up the tea I'd ordered. "And you were incredible in helping us put the final pieces together."

She shook her head, as if what she'd remembered was no big deal. "It was nothing. Just a tiny memory. But I want to hear more about how it all went down. We didn't talk much about it in Paris. I sensed you didn't want to get into the details then, but you know me. I'm always curious."

I smiled. "I do know that about you."

And so I started to tell the story.

69

ANNALISE

As Michael spoke about the night of the last arrest, a memory tugged at the back of my mind. It was of my last conversation with his father.

The morning before I left Las Vegas, I'd gone out to breakfast with Michael and his dad. We'd ordered eggs and toast—standard diner fare. We'd discussed plans for how the two of us could see each other again. I'd always loved that about his father. He was so supportive of our young love.

It was so odd that a little more than twenty-four hours later, he was gone.

I shook my head briefly, chasing away the memory. Being here with Michael now, at another diner, took me back.

"And one of the gang members they'd already nabbed had tipped off the cops about where TJ could be," Michael said, when a faint buzz sounded from his side of the booth.

"Is that your phone?"

He glanced down, patting his back pocket. "Yeah. I'll get back to whoever it is," he said, then continued the tale, and

I tried my best to focus on what he was saying, but my mind kept tripping back to that day in the past.

Conversation with Thomas had been easy, even when Michael went out to the car to grab an umbrella. Rain had started to fall, and he said he didn't want me to get soaked when we left the restaurant after breakfast.

"He's so chivalrous," I said to his father. "He takes after you."

Thomas smiled. "He's a gentleman. Makes me proud."

"How is everything going at work? Were you ever able to sort out the missing details you were looking into?"

He scratched his chin and shifted his hand like a seesaw. "Sort of. It seemed like I was getting closer, and I was really hoping it would help me get the job, especially since the company was worried about being audited."

"What happened then?" I asked, catching sight of Michael yanking open the car door in the parking lot.

Now, though, Michael's phone buzzed again at the table.

Grabbing it from his back pocket, he silenced it without looking at the screen. Worry prickled at the back of my neck. "What if it's important?"

He inhaled deeply and shot me a small smile. "I'm sure whatever it is can wait for us to finish eating," he said as the waitress returned with our plates.

"Eggs and our famous breakfast potatoes," she said, depositing our meals, as a bearded man in a black windbreaker passed behind her.

When the waitress left, Michael finished his story. "So, they set up a trap, basically, at the club. The gentlemen's club we do security for."

I nodded, recalling this part of the tale.

I picked up my fork and dug into my eggs, taking a bite.

"And as soon as TJ was there in the cigar lounge at White Box—"

I choked. Grabbing a napkin, I brought it to my mouth, coughing.

Those words.

Those two words.

Chills raced across my flesh.

"Are you okay?" he asked, knitting his brow and thrusting a glass of water in my direction. I waved him off. My blood had gone cold, and all my senses warned of danger. This was the same feeling I'd had as a photojournalist when situations in war zones became too dicey.

"What did you just say?" I whispered. The hair on my arms stood on end.

"About the cigar lounge?"

I nodded, fear racing over my skin. "The cigar lounge. Where was it?"

"White Box," he said slowly, his brow furrowed. "Why are you asking?"

My palms turned clammy. "That name," I whispered, my voice sounding haunted even to my own ears. "Your father said something the last day I saw him, something about White Box."

Michael blinked, confusion in his blue eyes. "What did he say?"

Like a diver rising up from the sea, the memory broke through to the surface. "We were talking about work. His company. The missing rides. When you'd gone to the car to get an umbrella, I asked him how everything was going, and if he'd found out anything."

"And what did he say?" Michael asked, gripping the table, his jaw tight, his eyes wide with concern.

Something so simple. So offhand. So *nothing*. It had never seemed like more. Until now.

Until it was.

I hurtled back in time to that last conversation.

Thomas Paige shook his head. "I didn't get the job. But there will be others, I'm sure. I'm thinking of maybe switching to another limo company. Once I tried to move up at this place, it became a white box of information."

I arched an eyebrow, my mind catching on the expression he'd used. I'd never heard that before. Perhaps it was an American saying I wasn't familiar with. "What does that mean?"

"That's what I heard some of the guys there calling it. Stuff was just erased. Rides disappeared. They called it a white box, and then one of them said it was the white box of information. I guess the guy who ran the place used that term. I was going to ask Sanders about it, since he drove him around, but I decided it doesn't matter in the end. I'm just going to let it go."

"What a funny little saying," I said with a small laugh.

The check arrived, and so did Michael. "Got the umbrella," he declared, joining us as the conversation shifted back to the future, to our plans.

With a crystal-clear recollection, I told the entire story to Michael.

70

MICHAEL

The ground began to sway. The whole diner seemed unsteady. "Did he say who ran the company? I always thought it was a guy named Paul, but someone else owned it. West was his name," I said in a barren voice, while my world seemed to spin off its axis.

Annalise shook her head.

I wanted to believe it was a coincidence. I wanted to reassure her that they were just two words. *White box.* But when my phone buzzed again in my pocket, and the name flashing across the screen registered, all I could think was that it wasn't over.

I answered the call from Morris in a split second. "What's going on?"

"Hey, Michael. Need to give you a heads-up. I've been hacked, and some of the online research I did into Luke Carlton was accessed. Someone put two and two together and figured out I was working for you. I got an anonymous call early this morning to keep my nose out of the case. Which is weird, since the case is over."

My blood chilled to subzero temperatures, and instinct kicked in. *Get the hell out of here.*

"Any idea who it was?" I asked as I fished in my wallet, tossed a twenty on the table, and reached for Annalise's hand. I pulled her up and walked out as I talked to Morris, scanning the diner from the booths to the foyer to the exit as we left.

"No clue," Morris said, as I raced with Annalise to my car. "But I think I was followed as I looked into the piano shop. I think that tipped someone off. I'm sorry."

"I have to go," I said, ending the call as I made sure Annalise was safely in the car. I ran to the driver's side, slid inside, locked the doors, and reversed out of the parking spot. In my rearview mirror, I spotted a bearded man in a silver sedan pulling out too.

"Michael, what's going on?" Annalise asked, her voice quaking as I drove.

"Nothing good."

I placed my phone in the holder, clicked on missed calls, and my heart sank when I saw John Winston had rung me twice.

As I turned onto the highway, I returned the call, but Winston didn't answer.

"Shit, shit, shit."

I gripped the steering wheel, trying to drive and connect the dots, but I couldn't fucking figure out how they were all joined. The thing that kept nagging at me was why Sanders had been so goddamn evasive, and what, if anything, that man had to do with White Box.

Whether White Box was the club or something else entirely.

As I neared the exit for my place, my phone buzzed, and I wanted to thank all the stars above that Winston was calling back. I answered on speaker.

"What the hell is going on with the case?" I bit out.

"We've got some new information. I got a call from a federal agent this morning about some RICO charges that might be connected to your father's case."

My head swam with this news. "RICO? As in racketeering?" I glanced at Annalise, whose eyes were wide with shock and fear.

"Where are you?" John asked. "I'm leaving my colleague's office. I'll meet you."

"Heading home," I said, then rattled off the address.

"I'm heading down the elevator right now, so I should be there in twenty minutes."

"Wait," I said, as tension gripped me. "Who's behind it? Who's involved? I need to know. Does it have to do with White Box? Is White Box a part of this?"

John started to answer as I reached my street, but the words came out choppy. My phone was cutting out. Fucking hell.

"What did you just say?"

John kept talking, but only words like *informant*, *protection*, *guns*, and *drugs* were clear enough to make out. The rest was garbled. Finally, the line died, and a minute later, I pulled into the parking garage at my building.

My pulse pounded dangerously fast. As I cut the engine, I met the gaze of the woman I loved, and saw so much fear in her eyes, but a toughness too.

"Let's get inside and wait for John," I said, and she nodded.

I slammed my door, walked around to the passenger side, scanned the lot, and when I was confident it was all clear, I opened her door. She stepped out and I tugged her close, wrapping an arm around my Annalise and scanning once more.

My breath fled my chest.

All the alarm bells in my head sounded. By the door to my building stood a man I was far too familiar with—waiting for me.

"It seems we have business to settle."

71

CHARLIE

Normally, I liked to delegate—have my men handle petty tasks like shaking people down. But sometimes you had to clean up your own mess. Like Michael Sloan. He was a tough one. He was too close, he knew too much, and he had figured out more than he should.

He'd connected the dots, according to what my man eavesdropping at the diner this morning had told me. That was something no one else had ever done. Not since years ago, when Michael's father had come way too close for comfort.

Since then I'd operated cleaner. Neater, under the radar. But with the case blasted open, I'd had to dart and dodge.

Now it was time to do my own dirty work. And I *hated* doing my own dirty work.

"Your mother was easy to manipulate into doing what I needed her to do. I fear you might not be so pliable," I said, stepping away from the wall of the parking garage and walking closer to the blue-eyed son of the man I'd convinced Dora Prince to have killed nearly two decades ago.

"You're right on that count," Michael said crisply. "This won't be easy. There are people who know you're involved."

I waved that concern away, stopping at a green Lexus as Sloan grabbed the auburn-haired beauty with him and pushed her behind him. Fucking redheads. They were nothing but trouble.

I nodded and clucked my tongue. "You're right. There are people who know enough to be dangerous, like you and her. But that's going to end soon, isn't it? Unless you want to come work for me? Your mother did, for all intents and purposes."

Michael's eyes narrowed, burning at me, his jaw set hard. He was like a fuse waiting to blow, and I was going to enjoy every second of setting him off. The man was too good, too pure. Watching men like him turn into animals was such a high.

"This isn't about her. This is about my father," he spat out, seething.

But I wasn't scared of Michael. I wasn't scared of a thing. I'd let go of fear many years ago. After my brother was killed at age nine in a robbery back in my home country, I'd vowed to never let anyone fuck with my family again. Not Thomas Paige, sniffing around my limo company all those years ago, asking far too many questions.

And not Dora Prince.

Damn shame she went to prison. She would have made an excellent lieutenant in my organization. A bit too emotional and unpredictable, but she was willing to act, especially when I'd threatened her children that one time she tried to back out.

Oh, that woman was willing to protect them. I really should visit her one day and thank her. But I'd deal with that another time.

Right now, I had her pesky oldest son to shut up.

I extended a hand in Michael's direction, even though I was twenty feet away. The nerve of him saying it was about his father—the boy didn't realize he still had so much left to lose. "Or perhaps it's about you, and the only chance you have before you," I said, scratching my chin. "As I see it, your only way out is to come work for me."

Michael shook his head. "Never."

"You can do it. Everyone is corruptible if you threaten their family. It worked for your mother," I said, as Michael shifted his eyes to the woman behind him.

"I'm not working for you, Charlie," he bit out as the redhead cowered.

"But you do work for me. I hired you. I knew who you were, and look what happened." I flashed my winning smile. My plan had worked like a charm—ingratiating myself with the security brothers, making them think I cared deeply about doing the right thing. Donating to the community center. Playing the concerned citizen. "You wound up liking me. We got along so well, Michael. Cleaning up the city together. Ridding Vegas of those nasty Royal Sinners I wanted to eradicate. You helped me get rid of the bad apples from my street crew—like TJ. He was a good one at one time, but he was giving me a headache by the end, so turning him in was a win-win, and you made it so easy for me to be helpful."

Michael clenched his fists, holding in all his rage. Ah, what an absolute delight to watch the carefully controlled Michael start to boil over. "What do you want?"

I stared at him like he was insane. "What do I want?" I repeated. "Isn't it obvious?"

I took a step closer. Michael moved back, the woman now sandwiched between him and the back of his car. "Use your brain, Sloan. I want you to stop asking questions. If you can't do that, you can go ahead and join your father." I reached behind my jacket and took my gun from my holster, my eyes on Sloan.

Who moved like a goddamn cheetah. Before I even raised my weapon, Michael's gun was pointed at my face.

I didn't flinch. I'd stared down more frightening men. I'd stared down death. Besides, Michael wasn't tough enough. "You're not your mother's son," I hissed. "You're your father's son. You don't have it in you to fire that thing. You're too good, like he was. So we have two options. You either work for me, or we say goodbye."

"I'll take option three," Michael said, his finger closing in on the trigger.

72

MICHAEL

The devil moved quickly, hissed even faster, waving his gun in the direction of Annalise. When I'd moved closer to Charlie, she was no longer completely shielded behind me, and when he darted to his right to aim for her head, my only thought was to protect her. In both slow motion and terrible fast-forward, I moved back, shoving her farther behind me with my free hand as I pulled the trigger.

The bullet barreled through the air, on track for Charlie's head. But keeping Annalise out of harm's way had the twin effect of shifting the target by inches.

The last thing I saw was the bullet ripping through the devil's arm.

Then a feral yell tore from the man's throat.

My world warped as my own gun clattered to the ground. Like thunder after a bolt of lightning, the pain came a few seconds later, cutting through every cell in my body.

73

ANNALISE

With a bone-shattering *thunk*, Michael crashed to the concrete, his skull whacking the floor of the parking garage. Blood poured from him, leaking all over his shirt, turning it crimson.

Everywhere.

His chest bled absolutely everywhere. Terror dug roots into every corner of my body. My throat burned with tears, and my lungs tried to escape from me as I cried.

My head roared in protest, my mind shouting *no*, trying to deny the horror. I dropped to the ground next to Michael, grasping, desperately trying to do something, anything, as I fumbled for my phone.

Panic welled up inside me, spilling over, suffocating me as I grabbed it from my pocket.

Not again. This couldn't happen twice. I couldn't lose someone I loved again. But the blood . . . it was on my hands, my face, all over him. My hand pressed against his chest. Oh, thank God, his heart was beating still. But there was so much red. I couldn't see a thing through my tears, wasn't even sure I could hear past my own cries. Somehow

I stabbed the numbers 911 on the keypad with blood-covered fingers before I screamed out a sob, the phone clattering to the ground.

Then a long, low moan fell on my ears.

It didn't come from Michael.

The hair on the back of my neck stood up, and I jerked my head toward the sound.

Ten, perhaps fifteen feet away, the man who'd shot Michael had dragged himself upright. He clutched his left arm as it bled through his jacket sleeve. With his right hand, he groped around for his gun on the ground.

In the distance, shouts burst through the late-morning air—maybe from inside the building, maybe from somewhere else in the parking garage.

I didn't know where they were coming from, or who was on the way.

I knew one thing and one thing only.

The man had found his weapon, and he was reaching for it.

74

DORA

Eighteen years ago

I'd decided. I was backing out. I told Luke at the fabric shop where we'd agreed to meet that morning. There in the last row, amid buttons and ribbons, I wrapped my arms around his neck and said, "I can't do it. I can't go through with it. But I can't be without you either. I'll leave him, and we can be together. I don't need money. I have you."

He smiled warmly, that smile I loved. "Of course, Dora. Just talk to Jerry Stefano and call it off."

I drew in a sharp breath. The man I'd hired to kill my husband terrified me, with his cold eyes and his even colder heart. He wouldn't be happy. His eyes had glittered when I'd told him the price for the hit, and I was sure he wanted the money. "Can't you tell him?"

Luke shot me a sad smile and shook his head. "Oh, honey, I want to. But you know how this works. I need to keep my distance. The only way I can run the street operations for Charlie is by keeping myself clean. The less people suspect me, the more I can do his bidding and the better I can do. The more I earn in the next year, the better the chance we can get away. I promise, baby. Give me one more year to close out my deals, and then we'll find a way to get out of town with all the kids." He pressed his hands to my belly. "Including ours. I wish I could feel the baby kicking," he whispered.

I smiled. "Soon. Another month or so."

But Stefano didn't take the news well when I tried to cancel the hit, nor did Charlie. The man in charge of the city's burgeoning drug operation summoned me, picking me up for a drive one day while my kids were in school.

I got into Charlie's car, and he talked as he drove out of my neighborhood. "Good to see you again," he said. We'd met once before.

"Yes, you too," I said, even as nerves prickled down my backbone.

"I hear you want to back out."

I nodded. "I do. I can't go through with it."

He flipped on the blinker to turn right. "Ah, but therein lies the issue, Dora. You can, and you will."

I shook my head, holding my ground. "I thought I could, but I need to move on from all this."

He glanced at me, knitting his brow. "From what? You're my top dealer. You run a magnificent route. I have plans, Dora. Big plans. You can work with me."

I swallowed, sucking in all my fears. "I can't do it."

He slammed on the brakes and pulled over to the side of the road, then stared at me. "It's too late for you to make that choice," he said in a snake-like hiss.

"Why?" I asked, my voice quaking.

"You're in too deep. Your husband has gone too far. His questions threaten my business, and when my business is threatened, my family is too. I don't like having my family threatened. You understand that, right?"

I nodded, bile rising up in my throat. I reached for the door handle. Maybe I could escape. Run. Call the police. But what would I tell them? That I was a drug-dealing, cheating woman who'd ordered a hit that was going sideways?

Oh, the sheer, bitter irony that I'd met the man of my dreams at a simple work party and had tumbled into this dark underworld of money, drugs, and power. A world my husband barely understood. A world I wanted to escape.

75

CHARLIE

Eighteen years ago

Oh, Dora.

This woman.

She made me laugh. With her naïveté.

With her utter, imbecilic, childish naïveté.

She didn't know me if she thought she could get out of this. With a chuckle, I pressed the lock button. Then my laughter ceased to nothing.

I stared at her, unflinching, unblinking. My voice was low, because I didn't need to raise it. That's what I had learned from years at the top: He who yells controls nothing. He who controls everything speaks softly, and his words are a force. "You are not leaving my car. And you're not backing out. Your husband is figuring things out, and I can't have him knowing what I do."

"But—"

I shook my head, shutting her up. "Think about it. How would it look, after all, if a mere employee had discovered I laundered money through West Limos? Money from guns and drugs that were sold on the streets by my Royal Sinners, who managed their gang business from the back of a piano shop? How would that look? Think about it, Dora."

"It would look bad," she said, her poor little voice all wobbly. Silly little woman. Silly little emotional creature.

But she had the heart of a killer in her. I simply had to remind her of the stakes.

Stakes she ought to understand. Especially since her lover, my right-hand man in the Sinners, had set up that end of the operation to run so smoothly that no one could link Luke, the Sinners, the piano shop, the limo company, and me. No one.

Except . . . for that little matter of Dora's husband playing a deadly game of connect the dots. Thomas didn't yet know that I was involved.

And I intended to keep it that way.

Because my job was to provide for all my brothers and sisters. My businesses made money that had put them through school. Years ago I'd moved them, along with my mother and father, to America to keep them safe from the dangers in our home country. My parents had since passed on, but I still took care of all my siblings, thanks to my businesses and the way they turned money into more money.

So when someone tried to mess with my business, they might as well be screwing with my family.

And no one went after my family and got away with it.

Not a single soul.

Thomas Paige was trying to, sniffing around my limo company, asking far too many questions. Thankfully, Curtis Paul Wollinsky, my cousin and comrade in arms and the manager of West Limos, had alerted me to Paige's queries. We'd tried to shut him up through TJ, our chief intimidator with the Royal Sinners, only that hadn't worked.

But fate had a way of stepping in. Once I'd learned that Dora Prince was already making moves of her own to order a hit on her husband, I had an ironclad solution—provide the means, and the pressure, for Dora to go through with it.

I simply had to impress upon her what she might lose if she stepped out of line.

People were so easy to manipulate once you understood what they'd be willing to lose, and willing to protect.

To protect at all costs.

"Do you see what I'm getting at, Dora?" I asked.

Her lip quivered. "What if I leave? What if I leave town with my family?" she asked, casting out desperate ideas.

I scoffed. "What if? What if? What if?" I mimicked her like a parrot, then grabbed her chin, leveling her with a cold stare. "I'll give you the only *what if* that matters," I said sharply. "What if you do as you planned?"

Because . . . I knew Dora's stakes.

I knew what she was willing to protect.

"And then I won't hurt your children." My eyes roamed to her belly, my message clear. A fresh wave of fear flickered in her eyes. Ah. Yes. She was getting my point. But just to make sure everything was completely transparent, I added, "*All your children*. Michael, Ryan, Shannon, Colin, and the one in your belly. Are we clear? You don't cancel the hit, and you come out on the other side with a neat, clean robbery-gone-wrong, executed by one of the finest hitmen in the Royal Sinners, and then you are free. That is your last debt to me in our business dealings. And then you don't say a word."

She trembled. "Why do you need me to order the hit? If

you want him dead, you can call Stefano yourself," she said, grasping at straws.

She had a point.

But so did I.

So I made it.

I narrowed my eyes at her and spoke once more, low and menacing. "I don't order hits. I don't have to. I don't need a hit connected to me, because I haven't made the mistakes you have." I shrugged, scratched my jaw, and fixed on a smile, my tone shifting to an easy one as I dangled the thing she wanted most—freedom from her mistakes. All she had to do to be free was this. One simple job. "But if you pull this off, and you don't say a word, I will let you go. You can leave town and be free."

76

DORA

Eighteen years ago

Later that night, as I lay awake in bed next to my husband, I imagined calling the police. Asking for help. Turning in Charlie. But how could I say anything and be believed? I was a drug dealer. A former drug user. A woman who was conspiring to commit murder for hire. An adulteress. They wouldn't believe me—they'd lock me up, and my children would be in real danger then.

Thomas was better off dead than with Charlie hunting all of us.

I tiptoed out of bed, grabbed the cordless phone from the kitchen, opened the screen door, and closed it behind me. In my nightgown, I walked far into the yard and called Stefano. "It's back on."

I hung up, closing my eyes, the ground swaying as I made my horrible choice. My only choice. This was the only way I could protect Michael, Colin, Ryan, Shannon, and the baby in my belly.

And I did protect them. Even when it all unraveled. Even when I got caught and the police locked me up. Even when Stefano went to prison. Even when the court sentenced me to life too. I never gave up the names of the others.

I took Charlie's warning to heart. It became seared on my very soul. It was what I clung to. *Don't say a word. Don't say a word. Don't say a word.*

I wasn't innocent. Not by a long stretch. But my silence made sure no one else ever knew who was involved.

It was my last chance to do the right thing when I'd done so much wrong.

For the next eighteen years from my six-by-eight prison cell, I'd pulled it off, my silence driving me mad. But at least my children were safe from men who killed without mercy.

77

SPECIAL AGENT LAURA K. REISS

Four months ago

Huh.

What do you know?

Sometimes a speeding ticket wasn't just a speeding ticket.

Sometimes it led to more.

As I hung up with the trooper, I rubbed my thumb and forefinger together, feeling the possibility. The hope that maybe, just maybe, what the trooper had found in this scofflaw's car might lead to something a whole lot bigger.

So big that perhaps we were veering toward my passion project.

To something I'd been trying to tackle for years.

I stared out the window of the federal building, as that possibility started to grow, to expand.

I returned to my files, poring over the ones I'd amassed over the years, reading and rereading details that might now be made clear.

Tension rolled through me, but it was chased by hope. Hope that I might be able to embark on a path I'd longed to tread for years.

When Sanders Doyle entered my office later that day, I was eager, so damn eager to hear what the man had to say.

If I could get him to talk, this could be the start of something big.

78

SANDERS

Four months ago

My future hung in the balance, and I needed a touchstone so I wouldn't lose it. When I entered the cluttered office of Special Agent Laura K. Reiss, I looked around, cataloging it, just to have something to keep my mind occupied. Her desk towered with papers, mugs, and picture frames. The bulletin board behind her was stuffed with notices. A busy woman. Perhaps all she did was work.

Her eyes were kind, her focus was intense, even behind the cheery smile.

She handed me a mug of coffee and sighed sympathetically as she took a seat across from me.

"How's it going, Mr. Doyle?"

"I've been better."

"I bet you have. But maybe that can change."

"How? How can it change?" My question came out desperate. I was desperate.

"I need your help," she said, and her voice was deceptively sweet. She was petite and had blonde hair that bounced in a ponytail. A Reese Witherspoon look-alike.

"How so?" I asked, forcing my voice to stay steady even as my gut twisted with worry.

"Here's the thing," she said in that soprano voice. "Some of those guns you were transporting were illegally obtained. Which makes *you* a trafficker of illegally obtained guns." She spelled it out like I was five, then lowered her voice to a stage whisper. "That's kind of a no-no."

"I didn't know what I was transporting," I protested, because that was the God's honest truth. I'd worn blinders for years. Don't ask, don't tell. "I swear to God. I've never known. They give me the packages, and I take them from point A to point B." That was the truth, the full truth, and nothing but the truth. I'd never asked questions.

Laura nodded sympathetically. "Oddly enough, that's not really a good enough answer," she said with a frown. Then she turned it upside down, her cheery demeanor returning. "But I believe you. I believe you're telling the truth."

I sighed with relief. "Good. Then can I get out of here?"

She laughed, then shook her head. "Not so fast."

"What do you need?" I asked, worry pitching in me again.

"You have a few options. I can work up some charges against you for your role in transporting firearms as part of the illegal gun trade in Las Vegas, and you'd face time behind bars."

That sounded horrid. "What's the other option?"

"Or you can use what's in here," she said, tapping her head, "to help me catch some bigger fish."

She wasn't offering chocolate or cake. But even so, only

one of those options was even remotely appealing. "What sort of fish?" I asked skeptically.

"Let's just say I'm looking into organized crime in Las Vegas. And I would really like to find out if your guns are tied to something a helluva lot bigger."

I startled, surprised. How was my work tied to that? "I don't know, Ms. Reiss. I guess I should think about it," I said, trying to buy some time.

She pointed at me playfully and shot me a knowing grin. "Well, think about it fast, Mr. Doyle. And keep in mind, you'd be doing the city a huge service. Because the more we talk, and the more you share, the better chance I have of putting away the men who are really making Vegas a nasty place. So how about a deal? I keep you out of prison, and you become my informant?"

The only thing I'd ever done was skirt the law. I'd never hurt anyone. Never killed anyone. All I'd wanted was to make a few extra bucks to provide for my family.

I loved my wife, loved my kids, loved my freedom more than anything.

So there was really one choice.

79

JOHN

Present day

Goddamn cell phone towers.

As I peeled out of the garage of the federal building, I tapped my fingers on the steering wheel, stealing glances at my phone as I waited impatiently for the signal to return.

"C'mon, c'mon," I muttered as the wheels met the road, heading toward Michael Sloan's house.

Soon the bars returned, and the second they did, I dialed Michael's number again. I had to warn the guy. Michael's White Box client had set him up. I was sure of it now. I'd had an inkling this morning that something didn't add up about the company, and that something was that it was almost too easy on the night of TJ's arrest. Almost like we'd been led there by the White Box guys.

But there was no way to know the specifics until Reiss called.

As I'd just learned, in return for not going to jail for gun-running, Sanders Doyle had shared everything he knew about the operations of what turned out to be a very shady company.

The same company where Thomas Paige had worked years ago.

A company that had been washed so clean, it raised no flags in relation to the murder, and showed no ties to the present-day White Box either. There was no paper trail at all to link the drugs and guns to the limo service—or the murder, of course—but it turned out Sanders had overheard a few conversations during his runs, and those clues had been enough for Reiss to tie Charlie, Curtis, and White Box back to West Limos.

Charlie knew how to operate like smoke in the wind, hiding his tracks, never leaving a trail. But at least there was evidence now to bring them in.

As I turned a corner, I tried Michael once more. The phone rang and rang and rang.

I kept dialing, but with each non-answer, my senses told me something was gravely wrong.

My suspicions were confirmed when a crackle came over the radio. Paramedics were hauling ass to the same building that I was. Words like *multiple gunshot wounds* and *critical* pierced my ears.

Oh God. I was too late.

When I arrived, an ambulance was racing away, sirens blaring, speeding faster than I'd ever seen one go.

80

COLIN

I burst through the doors of the emergency room, my pulse hammering in my throat as I raced to the information desk, Elle by my side. The past and the present slammed into me in punishing jolts with each footfall—memories of my father's murder mixed cruelly with *this*. My oldest brother, the one who'd looked out for me, helped me stay sober when I first got clean, helped raise me . . . Michael had been shot in the chest and rushed to the hospital. We had no clue what his condition was, or if he was even alive.

I choked back that horrific thought as I stopped short at the desk, words tumbling out in a traffic jam. "Michael Sloan. He was just brought in. I'm his brother. How is he?"

The brunette in pink scrubs and wireframe glasses looked up and nodded. "Give me just a minute."

I turned to Elle, taking deep, sharp breaths, but they barely seemed to fill my mouth, let alone my lungs. "Elle," I said in a whisper. I couldn't say anything else. If I did, I would break.

Her lower lip quivered, and she looked like she was trying to form the words *He'll be okay*, but instead, tears slid down her cheeks and she clasped a hand to her mouth. We'd been in bed asleep when Sophie called fifteen minutes ago, hysterical with the news. Elle's son, Alex, was at a friend's house, and we'd uncharacteristically slept in until nine a.m., when we were awakened by a screeching phone call and sobs on the other end.

The whole family was on the way, but Elle lived the closest, so we'd arrived first. I dragged a hand through my hair, trying to breathe, to ignore the beeping of machines, the clatter of equipment, the hushed conversations between nurses and doctors circling nearby, and the faces of all the other people waiting in the emergency room.

"Elle," I croaked out again.

She wrapped her arms around me. "He's going to be okay."

But she didn't sound like she believed it.

Resting my chin atop her head, because I felt like I might topple over if I let go, I turned back to the woman at the desk. "Do you know where he is? Is he in surgery? What's going on?"

The woman held up a finger as she toggled through her computer screen. "One minute."

"Elle, is your mom working?" I asked, desperation coloring my tone. "Can she find out something?"

Elle shook her head. "She's not an ER nurse, but I can try to find her."

"Wait." I snapped my gaze in the direction of the woman in pink scrubs who'd spoken. "Sloan, you said?"

I let go of Elle and gripped the counter. "Yes. Michael Sloan. What's going on?"

She'd opened her mouth to speak, when I spotted John

Winston rounding the corner. His eyes were downcast, his arm was wrapped around Annalise, and he looked like someone had died.

My ears rang, and I heard nothing but the screaming in my own head.

81

ANNALISE

Thirty minutes ago

Silver gleamed on the concrete—two, maybe three feet away from me, next to the wheel of the car—like a beacon.

A harsh pant came from Charlie, then the dragging sound of unsteady feet across the pavement.

My hands were covered in Michael's blood, my vision was blurred from my own torrential tears, and my pulse thundered in my brain.

But Michael's heart still beat, and in an instant, my options crystallized into just one.

There was nothing else to do but this.

I lunged across Michael for the gun, rose to my feet, and spun around.

"I'm not done," the man seethed, as he pulled himself to his full height, his gun in his uninjured right hand. "You and your 'white box' comment this morning at the diner," he snarled. "You know nothing about my brother. Nothing about how he was buried."

I had no clue what he meant, and I didn't care. I was nothing but nerves. I'd never held a gun, and had certainly never fired one. I didn't know how to hit the side of a barn, let alone the heart of a man. But I didn't have the luxury of practice. I didn't have a second to spare.

My life tunneled to this moment, only this moment.

Nothing else in the world counted.

Nothing that had come before mattered.

All there was, was this—I had a gun, and I had to use it.

One choice. *Life.*

As the man lifted his arm, my focus narrowed, and my mind sharpened.

Adrenaline bathed my brain in pinpoint clarity. I was alive, I was unhurt, and I was going to be faster than the man who wanted to kill me, then finish off Michael.

I hoped to God I'd know how to shoot it. I hoped instinct would take over. I might as well be blindfolded right now.

Except . . .

I wasn't flying blind.

This wasn't unfamiliar.

I realized I knew precisely what to do.

For all intents and purposes, I'd had a lifetime of practice shooting.

It was like taking a picture.

That's all I had to do.

Snap a photo.

Point.

I raised my weapon.

Aim.

Focus on the subject.

Shoot.

The bullet flew.

And I prayed. And hoped. And wished. My heart, my life in my throat.

In a second that felt both as if it lasted for days and took no time at all, the bullet hurtled at rocket speed, hell-bent on the mission I sent it on, and entered the man who'd tried to kill my love.

All at once, Charlie crumpled over, grabbing his belly where I'd hit him.

I couldn't move. I wasn't sure I could breathe. I didn't know if I could speak.

Seconds later, the ambulance screeched to a stop, the medics rushed out, and I was on the way to the hospital with Michael, while my love was losing his hold on life.

82

CHARLIE

It was the nightmare when you can't speak. When you open your mouth and call out.

But nothing comes.

No sound. No noise.

In your head, you hear it crystal clear.

What you're trying to say.

As I lay in red, so much red, I fought desperately to say a single word.

West.

The name that had driven me.

My reason for everything.

More than forty years ago, I found my little brother dead, gunshot to the head. He was only nine.

West.

My throat constricted. Breath barely came.

Pain ripped through my gut.

Pain, and something else too.

Anger.

Because I wasn't done.

I wasn't done at all.

I hadn't finished everything I started the day my brother died.

Revenge.

I had so much more to exact.

I had so much to do to fix all that had gone wrong.

So. Much. More.

A cough wracked my body, a horrible cough, a terrible sound.

Because it told me that all my plans were slipping through my fingers.

That everything I'd wanted was disappearing before its time.

I wasn't finished at all, but it seemed the world was finished with me.

83

JOHN

Now

Dead on arrival.

Annalise had shot him in the stomach, the bullet nicking an artery and tearing through his intestines, the doctors had said. No time to question Charlie Stravinsky—no chance for a deathbed confession, but one was hardly needed.

His confession had been given when he'd arrived at Michael's building, ready to kill.

I had already put most of the pieces together that morning with the federal agent, and I needed to talk to Annalise to learn what had gone down in the parking garage. Her hands were still shaking, and she'd only managed to say the barest of details. There would be time enough for that later. After she'd been checked over and cleaned up, I walked her to the ER waiting room where I was rushed by family members—Colin and Elle first.

"What's going on?" Colin asked, grabbing my arm.

"He's in surgery. That's all I know," I said, wishing I had more news. The doctors didn't know. The nurses hadn't supplied any more details. That was standard practice for this type of trauma. Get the patient in the OR and try to save a life if they could.

"Okay. But how does it look? Can't we get any more information?" Colin implored, his eyes wide with the plea.

I shook my head. "They don't have any other details to give. As soon as he arrived, he was rushed to the OR. They're probably trying to figure out the extent of the damage. If—"

"If they can save him?" Colin cut in.

I nodded. "Yes. That's what they're trying to do."

Then an animalistic cry ripped from the throat of the woman next to me, and Annalise slipped from my arms, crumbling to the floor. In an instant, Elle gripped her, wrapped her arms around her, and ushered her away.

84

THOMAS

Eighteen years ago

I tried.

I tried so hard to hold on.

I drew a shaky breath.

Fighting for air.

Fighting for life.

Or really, wishing I could. Wishing I could try to live.

But that choice was gone.

Taken.

I lay on the driveway, blood pooling beneath me, my eyes fluttering closed, and I knew this was the end.

I could no longer even move my lips to utter the word *help*.

The night seemed to wink on and off, the stars in the sky coming in and out of focus and then blurring. My body felt light, as if it were floating away from me.

But hell.

I wasn't ready.

I wasn't ready at all.

I had plans. I had things to do for my children.

Oh God, my kids.

My beautiful, precious children.

If only I could see them.

One more time. See Shannon, Colin, Ryan, Michael.

But the world . . . it warped away from me. It unwound. My breath barely came. My lungs hardly moved. My eyes could no longer stay open.

If only I could say my last words.

If my children were here, I'd call them to me. They'd gather around, and I'd whisper my final goodbye, rasping out the only word that would ever matter.

Love.

That's what I would tell them all.

To live with love.

That was all that mattered.

That was the *only* thing that mattered.

As I gasped one more breath, one breath closer to the last, I took some solace in knowing—no, in being certain beyond any and all shadows of a doubt—that they knew. That they'd carry that knowledge with them for the rest of their lives—my love, their love, and their love for each other.

I said one last silent prayer. I prayed to God. I prayed so goddamn hard that they would live beautiful lives.

The world narrowed to a pinpoint, thinning, spiraling away. Blinking. Slowly. So slowly now.

The night wrapped its arms around me, lifting me away from my body, letting me know I was going, my time was over.

The agonizing pain had ebbed, and as I left my body,

my last thoughts were of my children. How I would continue to love them for the rest of time . . . here in this world, and forever in the next one.

As the earth turned dark, I hoped I wouldn't see them again for a long, long time . . .

85

ANNALISE

My head was in my hands.

"I killed a man," I whispered barrenly. "And the man I love is dying."

Doubled over in shock and consumed with the sharp, cold sensation of impending grief, I sat on the hard wooden bench in the hospital's chapel.

Elle, who I'd just met today, stroked my hair, trying to comfort me. She must have been the one who'd brought me here from the emergency room an hour ago. Or was it minutes ago? I hardly knew anything anymore, except that all my fears were on the cusp of coming true. The prospect of Michael dying hurt so much—it was an ache in my bones that wouldn't go away.

"You did what you had to do," Elle said, her voice strong as she ran her hand over my hair.

"I did," I choked out, needing the reassurance. I had no regrets about picking up the gun and firing. I'd only hoped it was enough to save Michael. But he'd barely hung on the whole ride to the hospital. I hardly heard the words the paramedics barked as they gave him an IV and fought to keep him alive while he bled and bled and bled. The ambulance had seemed to fly at the speed of light, confirmation of how tenuous his hold on life was.

Oh God.

I couldn't imagine losing him. Couldn't conceive of burying him. My chest heaved, and I coughed, choking on the pain.

Now he was in the operating room, and no one knew if the doctors could save him. There was a bullet in his body. Near his heart.

The door creaked open, and I lifted my gaze as a platinum blonde rushed toward us.

Sophie kneeled by my side and placed a hand on my thigh. "How are you doing, sweetie?"

I shook my head. "I don't know. I killed a man, and Michael is dying," I repeated, because those twin moments of my life felt like *everything*. My before, my after, my now.

"You saved a life," Sophie said, reaching for my hand. "Come now. You need to be strong for Michael."

Strong? What was that? Did I even know what strength was anymore? Did I know anything? My world had been twisted inside out, shaken cruelly by the hand of fate, and now Michael was . . .

I squeezed my eyes shut, blocking out the word *dying*.

"Annalise," Sophie said, her voice gentle but firm. "You're allowed to be sad. You're allowed to be terrified. But don't think negative thoughts right now. Michael is in surgery, and they are fighting to save his life. He needs you. You can do this."

Sophie held one of my hands, and Elle took the other. I was keenly aware that the three women in this chapel were in love with three brothers, and these two were here to help me be strong for the one who needed me. The man I loved.

I took a breath, inhaling hope and letting go of all else.

There was no room for thoughts of that killer. There was no room for hate or vengeance or for cold, heartless enemies.

There was only room for love. I would do everything I could to send my love to Michael, and my strength to the doctors working on him. We left the chapel, Elle and Sophie leading me to join the rest of the family in the OR waiting room.

We waited and waited and waited.

For an hour.

Then another.

Then for nearly one more.

Until at last, a woman in green scrubs pushed open the door and surveyed the scene. She had lines around her blue eyes, and strong cheekbones. "I'm Dr. Brooks. Are you the family of Michael Sloan?"

86

ANNALISE

Everyone stood.

Elle, Sophie, Ryan, Colin, Shannon, and Brent, his arm protectively around his pregnant wife. Their grandparents. Even the detective, Sophie's brother, had stayed, and Michael's friend Mindy had also joined the vigil.

Collectively holding our breaths, crossing our fingers, and praying to whoever listened, we waited for the surgeon to speak again.

"It was touch-and-go there for a while. We didn't know where the bullet hit him until we opened up his chest. And he lost a lot of blood," the doctor said, her tone measured and even. I was poised on the balls of my feet, every muscle strung tight, waiting, wanting, aching for answers. "Turns out he was shot in the spleen. We got lucky."

Lucky.

Oh God, never had a word been more beautiful.

Never had anyone said such a perfect word. *Lucky* was good.

"We were able to remove his spleen, and he'll be able to live a normal life without it."

"Oh my God. He's really alive?" I asked in a breathless rush, desperately needing a second confirmation.

The surgeon smiled and nodded. "Yes. Very much so."

"Can we see him?" The question came from Michael's grandmother.

The doctor shook her head. "He's in recovery now. He hasn't woken up yet."

Two hours later, a nurse said he was asking for me. I brought my hand to my heart, then turned and embraced Elle and Sophie. "Thank God," I whispered, my voice breaking as it had in the chapel with them, but this time for a much happier reason.

87

SPECIAL AGENT LAURA K. REISS

A few hours earlier

Some guys were easy to catch. Some guys were slippery as eels. Either way, one rule applied to both.

Be faster.

That was one of the toughest parts of the job, because it was highly unpredictable as to when you need to put the pedal to the metal.

Timing.

It was everything since there's a whole lot of hurry up and wait when it comes to cracking cases.

But once you've got the goods, you had to get the guy. I'd spent the last few years trying to break up organized crime in Las Vegas.

And the last few months working my butt off on a particular pair of crime lords.

Today, I had the chance to nab the number two man before he learned what had happened to the top guy.

So when my surveillance team told me where Curtis

was, I didn't even take a moment to roll my eyes at the sheer irony of his location. Instead, I went in motion, racing, heading to the place where he went every Saturday.

The thing about guys who'd been skirting the law for more than two decades was this—they get complacent.

They got lazy.

That was just the reality. It was human nature.

It's like going to the gym and using the same piece of equipment every day. Your muscles got bored. You missed a workout.

And you turned cocky too.

The longer you evaded the law, the longer you thought you could slide through life, doing anything you want.

This guy? He had a routine. He followed it regularly. They all did, whether it was the errands they ran, the joints they frequented, the associates they met for drinks the same night of the week.

And for Curtis, it was golf.

That's why I wasn't surprised to learn where he was today.

I reached the golf course in record time. Got out of my car, my partner by my side, and marched across the parking lot. Opened the door to the clubhouse.

There he was. Chatting with his caddy. Golf bag at his side. Just a guy, with lots of dough he didn't earn, ready to hit the links.

Acting like he was a regular joe.

Curtis held a five iron, like he was assessing the weight of it, as he talked to his caddy. "This one. Can't play a game without it."

The young guy grinned. "It's your lucky club, sir. It always makes for a fine day."

"I don't believe in luck." Curtis handed it to the guy, a stern look on his face, like he was about to give a life lesson to his caddy. "Don't you either. You can't rely on luck. You need to show up, do the hard stuff, work your way up. That's what makes for a fine day."

The hard stuff.

My jaw tightened from the grotesqueness of his words of wisdom.

And if it were up to me, this would be the last time he dispensed it on the outside. I closed the distance, flashing my best Southern grin as I said, "Curtis Paul Wollinsky?"

He turned to me, a big man, with a big face, the shape of a square, and a body to match. A man unaccustomed to people questioning him. A man definitely unaccustomed to women being anything but playthings at his clubs.

I'd talked to those women.

Interviewed them.

Protected them.

I knew what had gone down at the clubs, at the piano shop, at that damn limo company.

And God willing, what would stop today.

A slow, lazy, lopsided grin spread on his geometric face as he took me in. The grin he gave told me he thought I'd be the next plaything at his club.

"Depends who's asking, sweetheart. If it's you, I can be anyone you want."

I didn't cringe. I didn't recoil.

This was all par for the course.

And in some ways, it was a blessing in my line of business that I didn't look like an FBI agent. I looked like I stepped off the set of *Sweet Home Alabama*.

And sometimes criminals treated me as such.

He wasn't the first to underestimate the petite blonde in front of him. Wouldn't be the last.

"Allow me to properly introduce myself to you, Mr.

Wollinksy." I reached into my pocket, removed my badge, and showed it to him. "Laura K. Reiss. Federal agent."

He blinked.

"You're under arrest for suspicion of racketeering. You have the right to remain silent. Anything you say can and will be used against you in a court of law. You have the right to an attorney. If you cannot afford an attorney, one will be appointed for you."

The words were so damn satisfying to utter.

Curtis groaned as my partner snapped on the cuffs. "Are you kidding me? Are you fucking kidding me, woman?"

I gave him my best cheerleader grin. "It's Agent Reiss, please. And no, I'm not kidding. I am absolutely not kidding at all."

We escorted him out of the clubhouse, off the golf course, to the back of our car, and took him in.

Yes, today was a fine day indeed.

88

BECKY

I'd been at water aerobics when the call came.

Missed it, of course.

But after I got out of the pool, dried off, and headed into the locker room, my phone blasted a message from Victoria Paige.

Victoria: Give me a call as soon as you can. Michael's in the hospital.

Terror ripped through me. I nearly rushed out of the locker room in my one-piece. Instead, with my heart lodged in my throat and fear eating me up, I called her back right away.

Fought like hell to hold in the tears as she told me what happened.

"I'll be right there," I said to Victoria.

"It's pretty crowded. Why don't I call you when we know more?"

"Okay, but I want to see him. And you," I said, desperation coating my voice.

"He'll be okay. No one is tougher," she said, but there was someone who was—her. She was the toughest. She'd had to be. After everything she'd gone through. And now this.

"Let me know if I can do anything," I said, but the words felt hollow. What could I truly do? All I'd been able to do was support my husband when he became an FBI informant.

And I hoped the information he'd given them over the last few months was enough.

Every day I'd hoped that it would be.

That it would bring justice.

The call ended, and I sent up a prayer, tugged on my clothes, and called my husband. "We'll wait in the coffee shop by the hospital. We can be there if they need us," I told him.

And we waited.

And waited.

Until later, when another call came.

This time, Victoria told me her grandson was okay. And I wept.

"Michael's okay," I said to Sanders, as tears streaked down my cheeks.

His too.

I set down the phone, wrapped my arms around his neck, and kissed his cheek.

"Best news I've ever had," Sanders said, and I heard the gratitude thick in his voice. It matched mine.

We stayed like that, in an embrace, for the longest time.

I'd stood by my husband through the last few months,

just as we'd supported each other over the years, faithful and true, through life's ups and downs.

He took a deep breath, and I felt him relax for the first time in months. He wasn't perfect. He wasn't above reproach. He'd made mistakes. But I hoped Michael and the Sloans would understand, would forgive him.

"I still can't believe the men I worked for had wanted Thomas dead and had used Dora to make that happen." He shuddered. "She was a pawn."

"She was absolutely a pawn," I echoed. "But she made her choices, and she's living with them."

"I can't forgive her for taking my friend from us. From his kids. But at least they've got the others. Finally, Beck. Finally."

I cupped his cheek. "It means we can breathe easier, knowing that all her accomplices at last have been rounded up."

"That's all I've ever wanted. To live out all my days with you."

"Same for me, sweetie. It's always been the same for me."

I stayed there in his embrace for a long time.

Later, we'd go see Michael.

We'd always do our part to look after Thomas's kids. Always. We were his friends. Then and now and always.

That was part of our vow.

89

SPECIAL AGENT LAURA K. REISS

At last.

Months of poring over evidence.

Endless days of interviews.

Countless hours of investigations.

All worth it.

I couldn't even sit. I was so jazzed. We'd taken Curtis Paul Wollinsky into custody this morning, hours after Charlie Stravinsky was declared dead.

Today was a damn fine day in my line of work.

As soon as Detective Winston came to my office, I said, "Let's go for a walk."

We strode along the sidewalks of Las Vegas, this city I loved. A city I wanted to hold up. To elevate. To make better.

"It all started rolling once we had the intel from Doyle. That's how we were able to focus in on West Limos," I said, and rattled off the details.

Energy raced through me, powering my breath, my feet, my mind. "I've been looking into local racketeering activity for some time," I explained, but that barely covered it. Breaking up mob activity was my passion, one that had grown even stronger since I'd gotten married and had kids of my own. My people to protect, to look out for. Busting the mob was in my blood too—my father had been a federal agent before me, and his father had too. The family business, we joked, because that's what we aimed to do. Keep the city safe, not just for our kids and spouses, but for everyone, and we did it by breaking up crime families. The Stravinsky one was mine to bust. I'd been tracking Charlie for years, trying to find a way to topple his empire, to destroy his army on the street. Who knew the opportunity would begin with a speeding ticket?

God bless state troopers for doing their job. When Sanders Doyle was brought in for so much more than speeding, for transporting illegal firearms, he'd become the linchpin in the feds' case against the local crime ring that ran guns and drugs across Nevada.

"He didn't know what he was transporting, Winston," I said, that thrill of the bust zipping through me.

"He just took money and did the jobs with blinders on. Some of them are like that," Winston said as we turned the corner, the sun shining brightly overhead.

"And that was a good thing. Because I could give him immunity. And he gave me details about who he worked for and the runs he'd made over the years, and bit by bit that helped us narrow in on one company."

I stopped in my tracks, meeting Winston face to face, my expression deadly serious as I pictured the criminal mastermind. "Charlie was so good at what he did. His company appeared squeaky clean. It was owned by a supposed West Strauss. But as it turns out, West has been dead a long, long time."

"The guy in Canada?"

I nodded, a satisfied smile on my face. "The guy *not* in

Canada. West Strauss is an alias for West Stravinksy, the brother of Charlie Stravinsky. He was killed by an unknown assailant in a poor neighborhood in his country more than four decades ago. After that, Charlie moved to America and has been laundering his money through companies he set up with a fake identity in his brother's name."

John let out a whistle. "Holy shit."

"Apparently, West Strauss had many assets around the United States—a car wash in Texas, a dry cleaner in San Diego, a limo company in Las Vegas, a gentleman's club in San Francisco. And after some time in California, he came here and established White Box with the guy we brought in this morning on racketeering charges, his cousin and business partner, Curtis Paul Wollinsky."

A knowing grin spread across his face. "I take it that's not always the name he used though? Let me guess. I bet he was once just Paul."

I tapped the air with my finger, punctuating the point. "You guessed right. Years ago, he was simply Paul. The guy who managed the limo company. Seems all the questions Paige had asked about missing rides tipped off Paul, who tipped off Charlie, who decided he wanted Thomas dead."

John scrubbed a hand across his jaw. "And I imagine the task of ordering the hit was made all the easier because Thomas's wife was in love with the man who ran Charlie's army on the streets—the Royal Sinners."

I licked my lips, nearly bouncing on my toes. "I'd always wanted to know why they were so powerful."

"One of the most powerful street gangs in the country," Winston echoed. "Because they had access."

"To criminal masterminds, to men adept at both violent and white-collar crime. Luke was the head, giving orders on behalf of Charlie and paying the Sinners better than average money for selling and dealing."

"Did he offer health insurance too?" he asked with a derisive scoff.

"I wouldn't be surprised," I said. "They were good, Winston. Damn good. But . . ."

"But we got 'em."

He didn't say we were better.

And I was glad. You couldn't get cocky in our line of business. You simply had to be smart, fearless, and ready.

Being suspicious as hell helped too.

And that's why our paths had collided.

When things didn't add up, you kept going and you called others.

You asked for help, and you put your heads together.

That's what truly made today a damn fine day indeed. Working together to get the job done.

And send the bastards where they belonged.

90

JOHN

Funny that our investigations had been on parallel tracks for a few months, never meeting until all of a sudden they merged.

That moment occurred when Annalise remembered the term that Thomas had heard years ago, still a favorite of Charlie's today. *White Box*. While waiting for Michael to wake up, Annalise had told me what happened at the diner, how someone from Charlie's ranks had likely overheard her conversation with Michael as they'd put two and two together courtesy of that term.

"'White box.' What do you make of that?" I asked Reiss. "Supposedly, according to what Annalise said, it meant something related to Charlie's dead brother. Everything Charlie did circled back to his brother."

Reiss's jaw dropped. "Oh . . ."

And I realized it too at that moment. "Do you think...?" "I do."

"Charlie's last words. Annalise told me what he said. 'You know nothing about my brother. Nothing about how he was buried.'" My blood chilled as I realized Charlie's brother, at age nine, must have been buried in a white coffin.

"Because he was a child. Because his brother died an innocent child."

"And so Charlie named his businesses after him, and after the way he left this earth."

It was oddly commemorative and terribly twisted at the same time. Which described the man who'd built, raised up, and run the Royal Sinners. Terribly twisted.

The ways in which people remembered the dead could turn them into killers or into lovers.

I chased away the philosophical thoughts, pushing my sunglasses up the bridge of my nose as I refocused on what we were discussing. "Crazy to think this all started with a speeding ticket," I remarked as we headed the other direction.

"Right? But that's how it goes, like I was telling my husband the other night. Nothing happens for a long time, and then one misstep and all the dominoes fall."

They were falling indeed. In the last few weeks, the most notorious street gang in the city's history had been effectively dismantled. And I would never have been able to do my part without the help of the Sloan family—each one of them had played a role.

That was fitting.

After we finished and said goodbye, I stared briefly up at the sky, the sun poking through clouds.

Today was something like justice, and that was all I could ask for in this line of work.

91

ANNALISE

Gently, I pushed open the door to Michael's room, nerves thrumming through my body. Instantly, his eyes swung to me, the blue irises sparkling as he lay in the hospital bed.

"Hey," he said, his voice scratchy from the anesthesia.

"Hi," I said, unable to contain a crazy grin, or the relief that flooded my heart. I crossed the few feet to his bed and drank in the sight of him. An IV drip snaked out of his arm, and his chest was bandaged. His face was tired, but a gorgeous smile tugged at his lips.

"You look beautiful," I said.

"I'd laugh, but it would hurt too much."

"Are you okay?" I asked, wonder in my voice, still amazed, still overjoyed that he was here.

"Yes, and that's what they tell me too. But I suspect the morphine helps that feeling."

I smiled once more and raised a hand, wanting to touch his face, his arm . . . him.

"You can touch me," he rasped, answering my unspoken question.

I bent forward, touching him first with my lips,

brushing them across his cheek. A quiet sigh escaped him. "I thought you were going to die," I whispered, the words spilling out with a fresh round of tears that fell on his cheek. I'd hoped to be strong. I'd told the other women in Michael's family that I would be. But it was hard, so damn hard, and now all the relief and happiness bubbled up and poured out of me in these salty streaks.

"Evidently, a lot of people did," he said wryly, his sense of humor as robust as ever. "The doctor said she wasn't sure I was going to make it through either. Can't say I'm bummed that I don't remember a thing that happened after I hit the parking garage floor."

"Do you want me to tell you?"

He nodded, and I pulled back. He patted the side of the bed that wasn't tangled up with his IV. "Sit with me, and tell me about the last six hours of my life."

I didn't need to be asked twice. I perched on the side of his bed and held his hand in mine. I cleared my throat, took a breath, and met his gaze.

Then I told him everything that had happened.

92

MICHAEL

My mouth fell open as I took in the enormity of what had happened after Charlie shot me. But that moment when Charlie's gun had aimed at Annalise still played before my eyes. I gripped her hand tighter. "He was aiming at you. My only thought was to protect you."

"I know." She ran her finger across my hand.

"And then you . . . you finished it," I added, wonder in my voice.

She winced, her face squeezing as if in pain.

"Are you okay?"

She nodded. "Yes. Just processing it all still. But I'm more than okay."

I shook my head, trying to make sense of everything. "You killed the man who tried to rip my family apart."

She nodded, tears slipping from her eyes. "You're the first man I loved, and the last man I'll ever love. I wasn't going to let anyone take you away from me."

Even though it hurt, even though I wasn't supposed to move, I lifted my arms, reached for her face, and held it in my palms. "I'd die to save you," I whispered softly, reverently.

With fierce eyes and a strong voice, she answered, "I know you would. And I wouldn't let you. Because I'd kill to protect you, and to protect us. I've got plans. I'm planning on loving you for the rest of my life."

As she pressed her soft lips to mine once more, I felt her love deep in my bones, all the way to my soul.

Love had once been an all-or-nothing thing to me, but with her, love was more than all. It echoed across time, deep and intense, reverberating in the past, soaring to the future, and living vibrant and bright in the here and now.

93

MICHAEL

A month later

I leaned against the bar, drinking a scotch and surveying the scene. The waterfalls at Mandalay Bay hummed, splashing down gently along the rocks, while a man at the black baby grand piano played a Billie Holiday tune. The man was Sophie's ex-husband, who was still one of her closest friends, and I thought it was pretty damn cool that the guy was at her wedding.

What was also fantastic was that the piano player was just a piano player, not a camouflaged front man for crime.

Well, at least I was as sure as I could be that Holden was one of the good guys. Everyone here was, even Sanders, who was grabbing an appetizer from a waiter. He handed it to Becky, and she nibbled on it with a smile as he brushed a kiss to her cheek.

I turned to Colin, who nursed a Diet Coke next to me at the bar. "Think you'll be next down the aisle?" My brother shrugged, but he had a sheepish look in his brown eyes. I stared at him. "That seems like a yes."

Colin laughed and set down his drink. "Maybe," he said evasively.

"C'mon," I teased. "I got myself shot. The least you could do is get married."

Colin frowned. "Wait. What does you getting shot have to do with me getting married?"

It was my turn to laugh. "Nothing whatsoever. I just like milking this for all it's worth," I said, tapping my abdomen where the bullet had gotten acquainted with my body one fine day a month ago.

"Bastard," Colin muttered with a smile, as we scanned the crowd once more. Over in the corner, John snagged what looked like tuna sashimi on a fancy potato chip from a waiter's tray. Nearby, Ryan and Sophie chatted with a group of his hockey buddies from the league he played in. Sophie looked stunning, like a '50s movie star, all Marilyn Monroe and radiant, while Ryan looked like the happiest guy on earth.

Annalise snapped a photo of them. She'd taken the official wedding photos, and was also shooting candids throughout the day, from Sophie getting ready, to her arrival at the hotel, to the reception.

I nudged Colin with my elbow. "Seriously though. Are you thinking about asking Elle?"

"I'd like to know the answer to that question too." Colin's eyes widened when he realized Elle had just appeared by his side. I cracked up—I hadn't seen her coming either.

Colin pulled her into an embrace. "Would you say yes if I asked you?"

Her eyes sparkled. "You'll have to ask and find out."

Colin pressed a kiss to Elle's neck, then turned to me.

"What about you? Want me to go ask Annalise if she'll marry you?"

I gestured in the direction of the woman who'd saved my life, in more ways than one. "Be my guest."

I had no worries in that area. We'd get married on our own terms and timeline. But I didn't need a ring or a piece of paper to know she was my forever. I had the confidence in my heart and the faith in my soul that I'd always find a way to be with her and give her everything she'd want and need. "But hey, maybe our little bro will be next."

I cast my gaze to Marcus, who cleaned up well. The kid wore a gray suit and tie and had brought along a date—a dancer named Cassidy, who worked for Shannon's Shay Productions. Marcus was heading back to Florida where he was going to school, so this date might be a one-time thing, but judging from the way he looked at her, held her hand, and listened when she talked, maybe it would be more.

After all, sometimes long-distance relationships had a way of working out. When Cassidy pointed to the ladies' room and excused herself, Marcus scanned the tables until his eyes locked with mine, then he headed in my direction.

Funny, how he'd only been in our lives for a short while, but he was definitely part of the family.

And that meant he was mine now to look out for.

94

MARCUS

My oldest brother clapped me on the back. "Hey there. Seems like you're having a good time."

"I am. First wedding I've ever been to," I said, still drinking in the opulence of the Mandalay Bay. *This* had never been my life. Opulent wasn't how my father had lived.

More like average, though his bank accounts had been opulent. The trips he'd taken when I was younger were too. He'd used the money he'd claimed was an inheritance from his mother, who'd died years ago. Turned out, he was the one who'd funneled all that money to her from his illegal operations.

I'd seen him a few weeks ago in what was becoming a far too familiar pattern for me—visiting a parent behind bars. He was in custody in a detention center, awaiting trial. I'd gone to see him. Because, well, it was the right thing to do.

Years of practice made it, sadly, a little easier.

Guilt, though, made it harder, since I'd played a part in putting him there.

But that was where he belonged.

Did he forgive me for the role I'd played?

He said as much, but honestly it didn't matter if he did. If I didn't go to the detective, someone else would have, I'm sure. My father had made his choices long ago, and they were going to unravel on him sooner or later. That was inevitable.

I did what I had to do.

I did the right thing.

And now I was moving forward with my life.

Michael nodded toward Colin and Elle, who had moved to the dance floor. "Probably won't be your last wedding."

"I have a feeling there will be lots of Sloans tying the knot," I said.

He laughed. "Count on that, my man. Count on that."

My man.

I loved the sound of that. Loved the feel of it too. The sense of belonging in the right place with the right people.

He dropped a hand on my shoulder, his expression shifting to that of the sheepdog watching his herd. "You doing okay?" Michael asked, concern in his tone.

"As much as I can be okay," I said softly. "You know what it's like."

"That I do. But you have lots of people who love you," he said, squeezing my shoulder and bringing me in for a hug.

Briefly, I choked up, and Michael did too.

But then we separated, cleared our throats, and straightened our shoulders as we regarded the scene. All this happiness. All this love. All this moving on.

Moments like this were part of what made my strange life easier. Things like my new family. Like my stepmom, Angie, who'd had no knowledge of what my father had done those years they were together. I tried to see Angie when I could, to spend time with my little sisters, and to take care of them, knowing how hard their lives were going to be now.

School was another anchor for me.

And maybe Cassidy would be too. We'd gone out a few times, and

her life was the opposite of mine—two happily married parents. And somehow she had an excess of happiness to give.

I was lucky that she gave it to me.

"But everything else in life is good," I said, fixing on a smile, because I wanted Michael to know I was going to be fine. "And I am kicking ass in school."

"You get that from me," he said, deadpan.

I scowled. "I thought Colin was the whiz kid."

He laughed. "Yeah, just pretend it's me though. You gotta humor me. I took a bullet to the chest."

"You're still milking that?"

Michael nodded. "And I will for a long, long time."

I nodded, considering that. "Fair enough. You deserve it, man."

We knocked fists, as Cassidy returned, sliding up next to me, lifting her chin and smiling.

I dropped a kiss to her lips. Yes, everything was going to be all right.

95

MINDY

Ah, weddings.

They were wonderful. And they were . . . complicated. Especially when Ella Fitzgerald crooned "Let's Fall in Love."

I watched as Sophie and Ryan moved to the dance floor, swaying, so happily in love. John inched his chair closer to mine. His bow tie was undone. He looked like a million dollars in his tux—the same one he'd worn the night he apprehended Kenny Nelson. Sophie had purchased it for him right before he'd made the arrest, he'd told me later.

But tonight wasn't about arrests.

It was about black tie and music and relaxing with friends and family.

John was relaxed tonight. So was I. This sort of gathering is what we'd all worked hard to have—celebrations of love, of the future.

"Ten bucks says she's making me an uncle in nine months," he whispered.

My jaw dropped. "Did you actually just bet on your

sister getting pregnant?"

His eyebrows wiggled, and he seemed to noodle on this. Then he nodded. "Indeed, I just did."

Laughing, I scolded him. "You are terrible."

The man who'd become my friend shrugged, then shot me a lazy, charming smile. One I'd seen more and more from him lately, since we'd spent more time together on the investigation.

I had my resources on the street, and just as I'd worked with Michael and Morris to help crack the case, I'd worked with John too, ferrying information, sharing tips, offering leads where I could.

We had the same mission, a similar drive, and every now and then, I'd had the sense that maybe we'd had the same desires.

But nothing had happened.

Perhaps that would change tonight.

After all . . . *weddings*.

"Well, if you are correct in your prediction, I wouldn't be surprised," I said, answering him. "Your sister is immensely happy, and she'll be a terrific mother. And Ryan, well, we all know Ryan is an eager beaver." I'd come to know Ryan well too, since we were in the same field of security. He'd changed since he met Sophie, and the doting new husband seemed primed to become a doting father.

John cast his gaze around the room. "The whole lot of them. It's in the air."

A flush crept across my shoulders at those words. And sparks shimmied down my spine. Did he sense what else was in the air between us, or was it a one-way street?

I'd like to know. I'd absolutely like to know.

He nodded to the dance floor. "Want to take a spin?"

My heart raced. Maybe I'd find out tonight if there really was something brewing between us.

96

MICHAEL

Later, I joined Sanders and Becky, who were chatting with my dad's old friends. "Retirement treating you well, old man?" I asked.

"Best thing I've ever done," Sanders said.

"Glad you got to see your dream come true," I said, and I meant it from the bottom of my heart. The man might have bent the rules, but his sins were small, and thoroughly forgivable, especially since they'd been instrumental in putting an end to so much pain and hurt in the city around us. I had learned in the last several months that the world was sometimes split into good and evil, black and white. But more often than not, people were shades of gray, like Sanders. He was still one of the good guys though. He'd genuinely loved my dad and been a good friend to him, so Sanders was okay in my book.

"How is the cruise planning going?" I asked.

He beamed. "Bought the plane tickets. We're flying to Miami in two weeks, and leaving port from there."

"Got your sunscreen and Tommy Bahama shirts?"

"Of course. Packed 'em all already."

Becky ruffled his hair. "We'll be suntanned and full of daquiris when we return."

"Excellent," I said. "One thing though, Sanders?"

He arched a brow. "Yeah?"

"Obey the speed limit."

"Always." Then he nodded to Annalise. "Your dad would tell you to marry her."

"My dad would be right."

My attention wandered away from the two of them when a redhead in a slinky green dress and black heels winked at me from across the room. Her eyes seemed to sparkle, lighting up with mischief as she raised a finger to beckon me.

I excused myself, weaving through the crowds of friends and family, heeding the call of my woman.

"*Bon soir,*" she said in a sexy, low voice.

"*Bon soir.*"

"I missed you," she said.

"But you've seen me all night."

"True, I guess I like you a little." She tapped her chin.

"Or maybe a lot."

She rolled her eyes. "Fine, I love you madly, Michael Sloan."

I smiled. I would never tire of that. "And I love you."

She ran her hands along my chest and down to my scar. "Did you know this is one of my favorite parts of you?"

"Why is that?" I asked as I bent my head to her neck and kissed her throat, inhaling her scent.

She spread her fingers across the fabric of my shirt. "Because it says you're alive."

I smiled against her skin, kissing her more, soft and tender. "So alive," I said.

She looped her arms tightly around my neck, and I kissed her fiercely.

"Mark me with your words," she said in a breathy whisper. "Like you wanted to that night in New York."

I'd held back then, keeping them inside. I no longer had to. I brought my lips to her throat and kissed her hard, murmuring, "I'm so in love with you."

I traveled along her neck, kissing and nipping, each time giving voice to the words she wanted to hear, and the ones I wanted to say. They were one and the same.

"I'm so in love with you too," she said, and soon we untangled and returned to the wedding.

She would be going back to Paris in a few days, and from there we'd schedule the next visit, because we were making our long-distance love work.

I had faith in us.

Enough faith to keep crossing an ocean for her, over and over again.

Because I believed in our love. Believed in it to the depths of my soul. And I knew, finally knew, that we were meant to be together *now*.

That this was our time.

This was our opportunity.

Not ten years ago.

But now.

Now is what made this great love possible.

And it was great with her. It was neither all nor nothing. It was, quite simply, everything.

EPILOGUE

Michael

A year or so later

With her arm linked around my elbow, I strolled with Annalise's mother along the pathway by the fountains at the Bellagio. We stopped at the thick stone railing that surrounded the man-made lake, gazing at the placid waters and the crowds waiting for the aqua ballet.

"In about five minutes, the water show will begin," I said to her in French.

Marie narrowed her eyes, shooting me a sharp stare. "English, young man."

I laughed deeply, then repeated myself per her request.

"I cannot wait to see the water show," she said slowly, answering me in English too.

"You'll love it. It's spectacular."

Marie had insisted on a crash course in all things

American, since she was now living here six months a year. I had bought her a condo in a nearby building, and I spent time with her a few days a week, helping her around the city and acclimating her to Las Vegas. Marie saw her daughter nearly every day, since that was the point of this arrangement. Marie's health was improving, but she still needed assistance from her family, so I'd devised a solution.

I'd moved her to America six months a year, and Annalise stayed in my home—now ours—during those six months. We'd spend the next six months in Paris, and while there I worked remotely as much as I could, but mostly I enjoyed my days wandering around the city, eating the occasional coffee éclair and apricot tarte, and spending as much time as I could with my beautiful wife.

And in between? Sometimes we traveled together. Sometimes we traveled for work. Occasionally she'd be in Paris and I'd be in Vegas because of our busy schedules and cross-continental families. But we always came back together, and truth be told, the time apart made some things even hotter.

With the new schedule, my workload had lessened, and that was fine with everyone involved. I'd once thought I couldn't give up work, but it turned out nearly dying changed my perspective. Work didn't matter as much as family. I had two families now—my own and my wife's—and I loved them both dearly. Besides, Sloan Protection Resources had Ryan at the helm, and my brother damn well knew what he was doing.

"How was your visit to Hawthorne?" Marie asked.

I didn't answer right away. I inhaled deeply, lingering on the question. Seeing my mother was hard. It was tough. It challenged me like nothing else had. But I'd made the decision a year ago to let go of my all-or-nothing attitude toward her. I didn't call it forgiveness. Though I understood more of why she'd made the choices she did, I could never abide by them.

I didn't have to though. I could choose to be the man my father had raised. A man who lived a life full of love, compassion, and hope.

And that was why I'd decided to visit her, now and then. To honor the lessons my father had taught me—lessons in mercy, lessons in grace.

Today my mother had been chatty, talking about a new book she'd read, a fantasy novel about dragons and shifters. When she was through, I'd updated her on everyone, telling her about how cute Shannon's little boy was and showing her pictures. Then I told her about Marcus. Turned out the kid was a chip off the old block. He'd kept up the long-distance relationship with the dancer, and that devotion had paid off. Cassidy had moved to Tampa recently, having landed a ballet gig there, near his college. He'd graduate with his business degree in a few years, and he was doing well.

On prior visits I had updated my mother on other news of the last year. Luke Carlton had been sentenced to life in prison for conspiracy to commit murder, as well as multiple counts of racketeering. Curtis Paul Wollinsky had received forty years on RICO charges, and TJ Nelson was likely in the big house for life too, joining Kenny, since both had been convicted on multiple counts of conspiracy to commit murder. There had been no rumblings, nor even any whispers, of Royal Sinners gang activity in a long time. And White Box had been shut down. As it should be. I'd eyed the shuttered property the other week, and had an idea for it. Something I'd need to run past my brothers and sister. I'd do that when I saw them tomorrow.

"It was a good visit," I said to Marie, shooting her a

smile as the sun dipped lower and the music began, signaling the start of the show. "It was good to have Annalise with me."

A few minutes later, I felt Annalise's breath on my neck, then a kiss from her lips. "Hi, handsome," she said softly. She was freshly showered after the long drive back.

She gave her mother cheek kisses, and wedged herself between us, an arm around both of us. "My two favorite people," she said, and then we watched the fountains at the Bellagio spray water high into the sunset sky.

"We finally made it to the Bellagio," she leaned over and whispered to me.

"We finally made it."

Later that night, after she showed me the latest pictures in the photographic book of kisses she was working on—one of her dreams she'd told me and it was coming true—we gazed out the floor-to-ceiling windows of our Las Vegas home, watching the lights of the city, one of our favorite pastimes. It was something we also loved to do from our home in Paris. Her flat had become my home as well, and was now full of pictures of the two of us.

She pressed a hand to my torso. "You're still the sexiest guy I know, even if you don't have a spleen."

I laughed. "Amazing that I work without it."

"You have all the parts that matter," she said as she moved closer, cupping the side of my head then dropping her hand to the front of my jeans, squeezing me. She traveled up my chest and stopped at my heart. "But this one works best of all."

"Yes. It works pretty damn well, if I do say so myself." I set a hand on her heart. "So does yours, my love."

And I felt in my heart, in my soul, that we were each other's, now and always.

I felt something else too. Something I hadn't felt for nearly two decades.

But since Annalise came back into my life, I knew peace.

In my family, in my home, in my soul.

Both outside our home and between these walls, there was peace and hope and so much love that I knew it would carry us far into happily ever after, and then some.

As we lived with love.

THE END

This series is dedicated to the memory of the innocent victims, to the children left behind, and to the hope that they find love and peace in their futures.

Want to know what happens next with Mindy and John on the dance floor? Find out in a brand new book in the Sinful Men series! The novella My Sinful Temptation is a new addition to this series. And you'll also see how everyone is doing and learn a little more about Michael's plans alluded to in the epilogue.

Eager for more sexy romance? Brent's brother Clay has a story to tell in Seductive Nights! You might like THE VIRGIN NEXT DOOR and THE GOOD GUY CHALLENGE! Be sure to devour the entire Ballers and

Babes MF football series here! You'll also love my #1 NYT Bestselling Big Rock series! You might also like the Happy Endings series of standalones, the Always Satisfied series of standalones, and The Guys Who Got Away series of standalones!

Sign up for my newsletter to receive an alert when these sexy new books are available!

ALSO BY LAUREN BLAKELY

FULL PACKAGE, the #1 New York Times Bestselling romantic comedy!

BIG ROCK, the hit New York Times Bestselling standalone romantic comedy!

THE SEXY ONE, a New York Times Bestselling standalone romance!

THE KNOCKED UP PLAN, a multi-week USA Today and Amazon Charts Bestselling standalone romance!

MOST VALUABLE PLAYBOY, a sexy multi-week USA Today Bestselling sports romance! And its companion sports romance, MOST LIKELY TO SCORE!

WANDERLUST, a USA Today Bestselling contemporary romance!

COME AS YOU ARE, a Wall Street Journal and multi-week USA Today Bestselling contemporary romance!

PART-TIME LOVER, a multi-week USA Today Bestselling contemporary romance!

UNBREAK MY HEART, an emotional second chance USA Today Bestselling contemporary romance!

BEST LAID PLANS, a sexy friends-to-lovers USA Today Bestselling romance!

The Heartbreakers! The USA Today and WSJ Bestselling rock star series of standalone!

CONTACT

I love hearing from readers! You can find me on Twitter at LaurenBlakely3, Instagram at LaurenBlakelyBooks, Facebook at LaurenBlakelyBooks, or online at LaurenBlakely.com. You can also email me at laurenblakelybooks@gmail.com

Made in the USA
Coppell, TX
28 November 2022